WARHAMMER®

40,000

SPACE MARINE

BY

IAN WATSON

First published in the UK 1993 by
BOXTREE LIMITED
Broadwall House
21 Broadwall
London SE1 9PL

10 9 8 7 6 5 4 3 2 1

Typeset by DP Photosetting, Aylesbury, Bucks.
Printed in Great Britain by Cox & Wyman Ltd, Reading, Berkshire.

ISBN: 1 85283 840 X

Illustration on cover by Jim Burns
Illustration on title page by Stephen Tappin

A TIMELINE FOR THE WARHAMMER 40,000 UNIVERSE

Millennium	Event

15th Humanity begins to colonise nearby solar systems using conventional sub-light spacecraft. At first, progress is painfully slow. Separated from Terra by up to ten generations in travel time, the new colonies have to survive mainly on local resources.

The Dark Age of Technology

20th Discovery of *warp drives* accelerates the colonisation process and the early independent or corporate colonies become federated to Terra. The first alien races (including the ubiquitous Orks) are encountered.

The development of the *Navigator gene* allows human pilots to make longer and faster 'jumps' through warp space than was previously thought possible. The great Navigator families, initially controlled by industrial and trading cartels, become a power base in their own right.

Humanity continues to explore and colonise the galaxy. Contacts are established with the Eldar and other alien races. A golden age of scientific achievement begins. Perfection of the *Standard Template Construct* (STC) system now permits an almost explosive expansion to the stars.

The Age of Strife

25th Humanity reaches the far edges of the galaxy, completing the push to the stars begun over ten thousand years before. Human civilisation is now widely dispersed and divergent - with countless small colonies as well as many large, overpopulated planets. Localised wars and disputes with various alien races (especially the Orks!) continue, but pose no threat to the overall stability of human-colonised space. Then, two things happen almost simultaneously. First, humans with psychic powers begin to appear on almost every colonised world. Second, civilisation starts to disintegrate under the stress of widespread insanity, demonic possession, and internecine strife between these new 'psykers' and the rest of humanity. Countless fanatical cults and organisations spring up to persecute the psykers as witches, and/or degenerate mutants. At this time, the existence of the creatures of the warp (later known and feared as demons), and the dangers they pose to the human mind with newly awakened psychic powers, is far from understood.

Terrible wars tear human civilisation apart. Localised empires and factions fight amongst themselves as well as against fleets of Orks, Tyrannids, and other aliens whose forces are quick to seize the opportunity to sack human space. Many worlds fall prey to the dominance of Warp Creatures whilst others revert to barbarism. Humans survive only on those worlds where psykers are suppressed or controlled. During this time, Terra is cut off from the rest of humanity by terrible warp storms, which isolate the home world for several thousand years, further accelerating the ruin of humanity.

The Horus Heresy

30th Humanity itself teeters on the brink of the abyss of extinction. Civil war erupts throughout the galaxy as the Emperor of human space is betrayed by his most trusted lieutenant, the Warmaster Horus. Possessed by a demon from the warp, Horus seduces whole chapters of humanity's greatest warriors - the Space Marines - into joining his cause. When the final battle seems lost, the Emperor defeats Horus in single combat, but only at the cost of his own humanity.

His physical life maintained by artificial means, and his psyche by human sacrifice, the Emperor begins the long task of reconquering human space. With the creation by the Emperor of the psychic navigational beacon known as the Astronomican, the foundations are laid for the building of the Imperium, as it to be known in the 41st millennium. Fuelled by the dying spirits of those psykers who would otherwise fall prey to the demons of the warp, and directed by the Emperor's indomitable will, the Astronomican soon becomes an invaluable aid to Navigators throughout the galaxy. Interstellar travel becomes even easier and quicker, while the repression and control of psykers and creatures from the warp releases much of humanity from its hellish bondage.

The Age of the Imperium

41st Throughout the portion of the galaxy known as the Imperium, humanity is bound within the organisations and strictures of the Administratum. The Emperor grows ever more detached from the day to day concerns of his mortal subjects, while the Inquisition works ceaselessly to protect humanity from the ever-present dangers posed by renegade psykers and the terrible creatures inhabiting warp space. The armies of the Imperium - the Guard and the almost superhuman Space Marines - maintain a constant vigil against the threat of invading Orks, Tyrannids and other aliens. But still the numbers of psykers increases steadily, and other more sinister groups associated with Warp Creature domination continue to gain ground...

PART ONE

Three Brothers of Trazlor

Chapter One

On Necromunda, so it is said, you grow up at an early age.

Or else you die early.

In the hive cities which stud that deathly world as warts crust the face of a plague corpse, to join a gang is a swift route to maturity—though equally this offers no *guarantee* of survival.

Warts, do we say? Are those hive cities mere pimples? Indeed they are—from the perspective of a food barge approaching that orb from deep space; or from the viewpoint of an incoming transport ship belonging to the Imperial Fists Space Marines, who maintain a fortress-monastery in the Palatine hive on Necromunda...

Approach closer, and those same pimples become huge termite mounds. Closer yet, and the clustered spires of each hive soar from the wastes of ash to pierce the highest clouds. Now many are almost too vast to comprehend as mere cities built by human hands. It seems as though habitable mountains have grown up precipitously and cancerously from out of the ravaged landscape in defiance of gravity the leveller. Unto its myriad inhabitants each of these hives is a separate, vertical world.

Habitable, do we say?

Aye, eminently so for young Lexandro d'Arquebus, who was born into the privileged higher levels of the Oberon spire of Trazior hive.

Meagrely so for his contemporary, Yeremi Valence, son of technicians domiciled on the lower hab level of Trazior.

Not in the least so for Biff Tundrish, a scumnik in the polluted, lawless undercity!

Already, by the untender age of fourteen, the paths of these three individuals had crossed abrasively and violently...

Lexandro's father was Calculator Maximus to Lord Spinoza, whose clan owned lower hab factories that built Mammoth class land-trains to traverse the ash wastes on great cleated tracks, stoutly armoured to resist assault by nomads.

Naturally, d'Arquebus Senior never sullied his own hands—or his eyes—by descending with bodyguards from the Spinoza estate to inspect the actual processes of manufacture by tech clans. Still less did his son care a hoot for such mundane details, except insofar as techs might provide amusement for himself and fellow members of the Lordly Phantasm brat gang...

Often the Phantasms—daemon-masked, each dabbed with different costly scents, and gowned in luminous silk appliquéd with lascivious emblems—would bomb around the broad upper avenues on their jet-trikes, and through almost deserted midnight malls, seeking stylised mayhem with another brat gang or hunting for an odour bar or an elegant brothel which they could take over for a few hours before fleeing just ahead of a Judge patrol.

Whenever the Phantasms rode the dropshafts down from their native upper levels into tech factory territory—or daringly deeper still, into the filthy honeycomb of the undercity—the impact of those brats was far from foppish. Armed with laspistols concealed under their silks, they were intent on "doing a burn," as they put it.

Raphaelo Florienborque, leader of the Phantasms, joked that maybe they should take that phrase literally. In the heart of Trazior, as in every other hive on Necromunda, a vast tube of plasteel plunged all the way down through the crust of the planet. Kilometres wide, with a wall hundreds of metres thick, this conduit for the world's inner heat fed the various power stations that were built within that wall from the factory levels upwards: heat into energy. This enormous hollow thermal spike also served as anchor and root for the hive.

What a jape it would be, declared Raphaelo, to gain access to the heat sink. What a prank to capture some upstart tech gang member, or some undercity riff-raff, and throw him into the heat sink itself—to slide or tumble or simply fall free, down, down, tens of kilometres down into the inferno. Would their victim burn up through friction? Would he be cooked alive? Would his lungs bake, and his eyes poach, and his skin crisp to crackling before he had even fallen or slid a hundred metres? Would any remains of the wretch even reach the bubbling molten magma at the bottom?

"Imagine his *sensations* as we launch him!" Raphaelo had drawled; and the Lordly Phantasms had giggled and flapped their obscenely embroidered, scented silks.

"What a burn that would be!" they agreed.

Gangs of the energy clans jealously guarded those ports which gave access to power stations and thus to the heat sink. Down below the functioning factory levels, however, ancient levels of the hive had long been abandoned to dereliction. Only scavvy and looter gangs roamed the accumulated choking filth of that undercity—where, mostly buried under debris, but sometimes still exposed, antique ports had been welded shut millennia ago. Some of those welds had corroded, so Raphaelo had heard...

Down in the stinking, toxic undercity that night, the Lordly Phantasms stalked a tech gang who were raiding in the direction of the central heat sink. Such tech gangs held the frontier between the tangled civilization above and the bestiality beneath. Yet this self-protective brand of public service was of no account to the Lordly Phantasms. A tech could be their target as easily as a scumnik.

In a dim, foul labyrinthine catacomb braced with baroque plasteel arches bending under the weight of the hive, and choked with refuse, ambush erupted: a surprisingly well-armed scum gang attacked the techs. The scumniks, who had been lying in wait for prey, used stubguns, grenades—then, at close quarters, a chainsword and knives. At first the techs had retaliated with bolt guns and heavy stub weapons. Arches and debris intercepted many explosive bolts and bullets; and ammunition was soon exhausted on both sides. Pressed closer, the techs resorted to their own blades, some of chill steel, others humming with hot power.

The percussion concert of cartridges, bolts, and shrapnel had died away into a hush of gasps and swishes pierced by the occasional piccolo note of a scream. Into this lethal mêlée flew the Lordly Phantasms, flourishing their laspistols and power stilettos, their gowns fluttering as phosphorescently as the wings of radioactive moths, their daemon-masks leering.

Tonight they didn't wish to kill; they intended to capture. So they used their superior laser beams mostly to sting and scorch and put surplus scumniks and techs to flight.

From behind a grotesquely warped arch that was strung with ropes of cobweb like a harp, a scum boy leapt to tear Lexandro's mask from his face as a trophy.

The boy was stocky, his greased black hair knotted with a score and more of decorated beads as though his skull was an abacus, or was sprouting a family of shrunken baby

heads. The pattern of his facial scars—radiating ridges
pigmented with tar or carbon—pictured some many-legged
mutant spider. Its body was the boy's flat nose and its
mandibles were his sharpened teeth. Even in the dismal
gloom, strobed by laser flashes, the boy's green eyes
gleamed with evident intelligence... and with fierce
enmity... and with a kind of fascination, as he weighed
the mask in his hand and stared at its former wearer, now
revealed.

For Lexandro sported no scars whatever on his comely,
olive-complexioned face—only a ruby ring through his
slim right nostril. Initiation into his high-hab brat gang did
not involve mutilation, except perhaps of the emotions.
Lexandro's eyes were dark and lustrous, his teeth pearly,
his dusky hair crimped and curled and pomaded.

The scum kid seemed about to fit the mask to his own
face so as to hide his savage features... or to become, for a
few moments, the reflexion of Lexandro who lived such an
unimaginable, foreign life. As the boy strove to imagine
that life, so his countenance rippled, the tattooed spider
twitching and convulsing.

"*High-hab swine*," came a voice from other shadows;
and Lexandro pivoted—to spy a tech boy as tall as himself,
blond, lightly scarred with some pious runes nicking one
cheek. The tech's azure gaze raked Lexandro contemptuously, yet also somewhat longingly.

"We labour for you. We're your bulwark against the
underscum. Yet you treat us all as playthings." The boy
was putting on a high-hab accent that a rich brat could
understand.

"Join us, then," invited Lexandro loftily. "Claw your
way upward. Serve the lordly ones. Partake of pleasures.
But meanwhile..." He swivelled and fired his laspistol
towards the tattooed boy in case that one thought to exploit
the distraction, burning his target's hand so that the scum
kid dropped his trophy.

''My mask, I believe.''

Lexandro swung and fired the other way, just as the tech boy was in the very act of throwing his knife. Lexandro rolled across rubble, tearing and soiling his silks, yet retrieving the mask. Older Phantasms were hustling a wounded tech towards him. Both of the other boys promptly scarpered.

''We have us some scum for the cooking pot too!'' cried Raphaelo Florienborque, who had never strayed into a kitchen in his life. Attired in his pouting purple daemon's mask, he escorted a bucking, snarling, tattooed warrior bound with electrocuffs and firmly gripped by two Phantasms. The warrior's oaths were quite incomprehensible.

''One of each, one of each!'' Raphaelo exulted. ''And now we'll give them the unique burn of a lifetime. Ah yes, cuffed together—united in their *profound* exploration, their *deep-delving* expedition down the taproot of Trazior. We honour their clans, we grace their gangs. Their names will live in legend. Never before, Lordly chums, never before!'' And so the Phantasms propelled their two prisoners in the direction of the heat sink.

Most of the undercity was clammy and chill, though not in the vicinity of the thermal spike. The air, though foul, had already been clement. Before long, the temperature was positively genial. Between pillars and columns—across a subterranean plain of debris—the expedition was soon catching glimpses of a tarnished wall curving gradually away to right and left. The Lordly Phantasms were well aware of techs and scumniks trailing them furtively on either side, wary of their lasers. Indeed, this hidden audience of mutual foes delighted Raphaelo who described loudly and floridly what was going to happen to the captives. If he had not brayed thus, how would those who skulked alongside in the gloom have fully appreciated the final act of the drama which they must necessarily miss witnessing?

Eventually the brats arrived at the plasteel wall and burned entry through the rusted seal into a sultry, branching passageway. After some searching in the entrails of the massive wall, they located an insulated, though hot, hatch—and undogged it.

Had it not been for their masks, the Phantasms' faces must surely have blistered—a gulf of rising furnace-air yawned beyond that hatch. Hastily, so as not to ruin their own complexions, the Phantasms launched their two shrieking prisoners.

To everyone's surprise, the bodies of the tech and the scum warrior stayed in full view, soaring and bobbing on convection currents of superheated gases as if trying to swim away from the wall; though the bodies were obviously changing in texture as they cooked. They did not fall at all. Raphaelo slammed the hatch in petulant frustration, burning his hand.

And then the Lordly Phantasms returned to the upper heights to party.

Not long after, Lexandro also tumbled—not down the inside of the heat sink, but certainly parallel to it. Lord Spinoza claimed that his Calculator Maximus was indulging in some financial irregularities. Perhaps this was true; perhaps not. D'Arquebus Senior's pedantic excuses made no sense. Thus he—and his wife, and two spoiled daughters, and his son—all *fell*, demoted insultingly and perhaps murderously, to tech territory...

...from which Lexandro knew that he must escape quickly.

Now his father was a mere Tabulator to the Ducas clan, clients of Lord Spinoza—charged with inspecting the activities of even lesser sub-contractors.

Not for Lexandro those narrow, serpentine alleys dissecting a jumbled jigsaw of fumy factories where teeming jealous families festered out their lives, crafting gears or pistons, axles or armour plating. Not for Lexandro those thronged elephantine courtyards and grim vaulted catacombs to which glass cables delivered only a diluted memory of distant sunshine, and where ventilator gargoyles exhaled stale breath which had been refiltered fifty times already. Oh no, not for a brat who had worn the obscene, scented silks. Not for Lexandro the dubious privilege of being surgically altered so that he could operate a lathe more speedily!

Fortuitously, there had of late been a fierce trade war in part of Trazior's larger sister spire, Titania—Trazior, that trio of bleached, leprous giantesses fused from the waist down was popularly known, indeed, as "the Three Sisters". The dispute had escalated into rabid anarchy; and the local garrison of the Planetary Defence Force suffered heavy casualties in suppressing the wilder excesses of this social spasm. Now their commander must dragoon several tech or merchant gangs from the Oberon spire into the ranks.

Which might prove to be no bad fortune for those recruits...

By such a route they might escape from the niches of their birth, and gain access to something better—to better weapons, possibly to some real food different from synthcake and synthgruel. A gang *leader* could hope to rise up the hierarchy of a hive. A lucky stalwart might gain the patronage of some powerful upper-hab clan or even of a noble. Yet the Defence Force offered a chance—admittedly small—of subsequently entering the Imperial Guard and leaving the claustrophobic hives of Necromunda entirely for other worlds. Other worlds, and wars...

Swallowing his pride, Lexandro inveigled, connived, and bribed his way as a junior shrimp into the very Ducas clan gang which his father had heard would soon be pressed into service—an action that grieved his parents. For his sisters

needed brotherly protection if they were to remain worthy
to marry into the Ducas clan, and so in turn protect the
future of the fallen d'Arquebus family. An absent Lexandro
could ruin this chance.

Lexandro did not care. "*You* failed us, old man," he told
his father.

"I am not old yet," his father demurred pathetically.

"You soon will be, down here!" was his son's retort. . .

And so the day came when, stripped of their weapons,
the Ducas gang were herded to the garrison block nestling
in the shell of the hive hard by the gateway fortress which
guarded access and egress for the land trains.

Members of several gangs, from earliest teens to
twenties, crowded the cracked plastic benches in the
reception vestibule or squatted on the floor, awaiting
processing, a slow operation. Wary troopers directed stun
guns at the medley of bodies in case of disorder, for there
were tensions and animosities. Except for the matter of who
held the weapons, there seemed little distinction between
gang members and the scarred, tattooed troopers clad in
olive-drab hive tunics hung with amulets. The recruits'
lexicon of facial scars and tattoos spelled out clan and gang
allegiances; similar scarifications signalled the troopers'
own kindred origin.

On the plasteel-panelled walls hung blurred holographic
posters showing the exuberant, ostentatious architecture
within the Palatine hive where the lord of Necromunda held
court—and a view of a balloon-wheeled land-train
traversing crimson and orange dunes of chemical residue
in one of the ash deserts. A recorded voice crackled from a
wall speaker. "*Lord Helmawr's peace prevails here. The
Emperor's peace prevails. Abuse Lord Helmawr's peace,
and you die. Violate the Emperor's peace, and you are
damned*—" A different voice interrupted the loudspeaker's
soothing threats. "Next: Zen Sharpik, known as Nostrils."

A burly, pug-faced adolescent with a violet coxcomb and

a bone through his nose slouched towards the door that led to further processing, or rejection. Such a brute as Nostrils would obviously be welcomed unless he tested out as dangerously insane. Such sharks caught up in the net of pressganging were generally ideal raw material for the Guard. Yet numerous younger sprats swam with a gang too. Some might need to be tossed out; indeed it was these younger fry who mostly glared at one another.

"Why don't the kids all phoo off?" a scrawny, shaven-skulled youth who was lacking a little finger, remarked at the ceiling.

One of the boys in question leaned forward and drawled in an upper-hive accent, "*Shame*, having to hack off one's pinkie to say sorry to one's boss for a blunder. Or maybe the pinkie was skragged as a trophy? What a trooper that one'll make."

The razorhead leapt up, but the troopers leveled their guns, so the youth sank back swearing vengeance. A few of the Dorcas gang chortled appreciatively. However, the reckless, well-bred show of bravado did not exactly endear the utterer to two other boys of like age. All three had glanced somewhat poisonously at one another during the hours of waiting.

Nostrils had only been gone for ten minutes before the speaker announced:

"Next: Lexandro d'Arquebus."

At this revelation of the boy's upper-hab name, many of those in the room who weren't of the Dorcas persuasion whistled scoffingly or spat resentfully. Ignoring this show of dislike from possible future comrades, he who had mocked sauntered nonchalantly towards the door.

A Sergeant with a crudely reconstructed pink blob of a nose—obviously bitten off at some stage in his professional or previous career—sat at a damascened bronze data-desk stained green with cupreous patina. At his side a fussy

11

grey-faced scribe was penning details about Zen Sharpik into a leatherbound ledger. A high-backed iron chair caged with copper filigree and equipped with adjustable iron helmet, as if for crushing the occupant's skull, stood vacant. A tech murmured incantations as he stroked the wires running from this to a bone-framed screen where runes and formulae flickered; the man's left hand had been replaced by a baroque prosthetic voltmeter with electrode claws. Much of the room was reflected in a silvered one-way window behind which a vague shape loomed.

The Sergeant seemed distinctly unimpressed by Lexandro.

"What kinda cadet would you make, pretty boy?" he jeered in a coarse accent. "Can you polish boots with your tongue?"

"I'm fourteen, *Sir*." The honorific stuck in Lexandro's craw but he managed to utter the word.

"Upper-spire brat, eh? Fallen low, is it?"

"My father's enemies conspired, Sir. I despise him."

"Can hardly understand your fancy words, boy. And now you *aspire* to climb back somehow... Too many enemies of your own down in the lower levels of our hive, eh? From your happy days of tech-skragging and scum-hunting?"

Aye, thought Lexandro, they're sitting in the very next room. He nodded, hoping that this would be evidence of his character.

"Bit young for that, weren't you, even so, pretty fellow? Brat gang mascot, eh?"

Lexandro felt cut to the quick, and wished he could kill this impertinent—if perceptive—Sergeant.

"Why we give you sanctuary, eh? Probably soft, from all that luxury and real food. What's real food taste like, eh?"

"I'm *not* soft, Sir. You could ask a couple of other kids out there." Immediately Lexandro regretted boasting. The Sergeant leered at him.

"Well, pretty boy, Trazior's a little hive, as hives go. Three million, four. The pop of all Necromunda's hives is uncountable. We don't need any spare high-hab boys, not even as bait for nomads in the wastes."

Just then, the shape behind the window moved. A door opened; and into the assessment room stepped a giant of a man. A red lens in ormolu casing was clamped over his left eye, and perhaps had replaced the original jelly organ. His other cheek was tattooed with a winged fist in the act of crushing a moon, from which tattooed orange lava dripped like alien blood over his chin, down his neck. His grizzled hair was cropped tight, a pad of wire upon a rock-like skull, and implanted in his brow were two shiny steel studs.

Lexandro's heart lurched, and a certain awe invaded him. From devotional vids broadcast by the Ecclesiarchy, and memory of a stained-glass window in a chapel where his mother had taken him when much younger to drone prayers, he recognized a *Space Marine*...

A fur-trimmed dark blue cloak embroidered with unfamiliar icons and sunbursts hung to lap the Marine's heavy jackboots, partly concealing a pus-yellow uniform chevroned in azure—a uniform bulging with slabs of muscle. Fanged skulls within potent crosses adorned his knees. The giant was wearing an engraved power sword and a similarly enchased bolt gun in a holster of brass lined with slithery lizard hide.

How could any man be so huge and powerful in the flesh? How could he radiate such ruthless adamantine presence? Lexandro's wilful, wayward, snook-cocking soul was seared for several seconds.

In Necromunda pidgin, with a guttural accent, the giant growled, "Test him for me. Fully."

As Lexandro sat caged and almost stupefied in the humming iron chair, his naked body suffering intermittent shocks and needle pricks while spinning flashing lights disoriented his vision, he distantly heard the reports of the tech.

"Musculature potential, point eight seven...

"Drug use readings. Nil blitz or stimm or frenzy. Nil spook. Nil dream-bat addiction. Routine traces of halcyon, hedonic acid, and joyspike...

"Psychosis level, point four two...

"Psychic profile, point zero one...

"Ocular reflex...

"Intelligence...

"Ballistic skill...

"Pain tolerance..." Agony flooded through Lexandro momentarily as if molten iron from a smelter had been diverted through his veins and his intestines. Perhaps he shrieked aloud—but the terrible instant was already past.

Eventually the grille swung away from the iron chair, and the helmet from his head, releasing Lexandro. Yet he did not rise. The giant loomed over him.

"Lexandro d'Arquebus," demanded the possessor of that extraordinary physique, *"what is the name of the Emperor?"*

"I d-don't know, Sir," Lexandro stuttered; and for once the title of *Sir* came sincerely to his lips. He gritted his teeth, angry at his tongue for having tripped him. He had never stuttered before, neither during his humiliating initiation into the Lordly Phantasms, nor on any subsequent hazardous escapade with them. Nor even when the d'Arquebus family was demoted. However, this was different. Goose bumps pocked his bare flesh. He felt genuine awe at this superhuman man, at once so puissant, so self-possessed, so monomaniac in his demeanour.

How could he answer? Surely no one knew the *name* of the distant, immortal Lord of Mankind—in whom Lexandro had only ever felt the most casual interest since his early catechisms.

"Awesome is His name, Sir," he suggested; and the

giant almost smiled.

"So *I* am your Emperor here, it seems. True enough. In His name I can crush you—or increase you. Think carefully: *would you become a Space Marine in His service?*"

Lexandro quailed, surveying the physique before him.

"How could I possibly match you, Sir?"

"Oh, that is no problem. You are not yet too old. Your body still grows. We shall assist it to grow. And assist *you* to grow, as a human being."

Lexandro didn't understand. He imagined bone-wrenching exercises and an accelerated real-food diet, such as had been distinctly lacking since his father's shaming. Whenever he had happened to notice devotional vids, he had presumed that the Space Marines recruited exceptional adult fighters, not... he swallowed his pride... not *boys*.

"Is this a cruel joke?" he asked.

All hint of smile vanishing, the giant cuffed him across the side of the head—only lightly so, yet Lexandro's teeth rattled and the iron chair rocked.

"I guess not," he gasped. "But *how*, Sir?"

"Strangers are listening," was the giant's only answer to that. And Lexandro's spirit swelled, as he conceived hazily of an initiation rite far beyond that of any Necromundan gang, and infinitely more potent.

"I think you understand," said the giant. "Would you forsake your family and your hive and your world? To be sent wherever the Imperium wishes; to be done with as the Imperium chooses?"

"Yes—" Did Lexandro's voice quiver?

"Immediately, with no turning back? No doubts?"

"I came here... hoping... I bribed my way into a gang that I heard would be—"

"Recruited into the Guards. Aye, I believe you have shown a peculiarly passionate intensity. Yet this is a very different proposition—sacredly so. The time for your vow is now; though I may add that your family will be notified. They will learn of your choice with pride; and the reflection of that pride may help protect them. In twenty years, thirty, you may return; with tales to tell. Though this I cannot guarantee. For your heart will change wondrously.''

The giant was addressing Lexandro now as man to... potential man, potential equal.

''I vow,'' Lexandro whispered.

Chapter Two

As Yeremi Valence sat in the iron chair an hour later, he heard distantly:

"Psychosis level, point three nine...

"Psychic profile, point zero two...

"Dexterity, point nine four..."

On and on.

How had that fancily-named high-hab brat come to be here at the garrison block? Mingling, what's more, with Dorcas gang members, or so it seemed? He remembered that one *bitterly*. Yeremi's amazement at being tested in the presence of none other than a Space Marine was spiked with bile at the recollection of how that brat and his fellow high-life hooligans, who stood so contemptuously above any law, had hustled injured cousin Yakobi away to a vile death, crowing and bragging. Aye, coupled to a scum gangster, as though there was no difference between Yakobi and some undercity vermin—whereas Yakobi had been helping hold the line against such vicious filth, on behalf, yes ultimately on behalf, of those selfsame upper-spire revellers!

And how come there had been a scumnik kid present too in the crowd of possible recruits? One whose spider-tattooed face Yeremi recalled clearly from that fateful night!

As stabs of current stimulated Yeremi's nerves and sinews, the runes on his cheek itched fiercely. He prayed silently to the Emperor, for his was a pious family. In the land-train carburettor factory where they lived along with some ninety tech kin, an electrocandle flickered before a precious polychrome ikon in every dwelling cubicle along the gallery that overhung the greasy, acrid furniture of lathes and drills and grinders and the carpeting of swarf like dirty silver snow. Yeremi knew the catechism of the Imperial Cult by heart; and that was the rock of his faith—a faith to the effect that far beyond Trazior hive, and far beyond Necromunda and its bilious sun, was one who watched divinely from afar, one who had already rescued the galaxy from terrible strife, and whose incomprehensible mind surveyed and sifted, ever vigilant, the terrible redemptory Godfather of All.

In their factory, so essential to the prosperity of Trazior—to its trade and supply routes forever preyed on by vicious nomads—the Valences lived their whole lives, many of them adapted by surgery to their specialised tasks. There they laboured and ate and prayed and slept and raised their kids, and treasured their stockpile of bolt guns and heavy stub weapons with which they must defend their domicile and livelihood against families not allied to them nor owing fealty to Lord Spinoza. Aye, and against the scavenging scum of the undercity, from which the Valence factory was not so very far removed.

Oh, to remove oneself further away from the savages beneath! The Valences had held their carburettor factory for fifteen generations, and showed no signs of ever being able to seize a higher niche in Trazior. Yeremi's father had said, "It is *His* will that we cleave to our station, where we are safe, and thus secure the safety of our hive.''

His will.

The *He* in question was an amorphous blend of the remote Godfather of All—and of Lord Helmawr, the dynastic Imperial Commander ensconced in his palace in the central spire of the Palatine like some great spider plucking at the strands of Necromunda, harkening to how those twanged—and of Lord Spinoza of Oberon too.

His will, their will. Their will, his will.

Oh why, then, did that Will allow the armed anarchy of industrial life in lower-hab territory? Why did it allow nomads to raid land-trains, and scumniks to raid techs, and upper-hab brats to descend wreaking wanton mischief?

The triple, bleached spires of Trazior arose from deep drifts of dessicated industrial excrement to pierce foul clouds on the far southerly fringe of the Palatine mega-cluster. Nevertheless, no Valence would ever be likely to travel to the central Palatine hive. No more would they rise above their place within Trazior.

So Yeremi would hardly even be likely to climb a spire within Trazior itself to ask humbly of Lord Spinoza, ''Why are we thus?'' A question which might be callow, yet which was far from childish. For children accept their circumstances, by and large. Being born into such circumstances, how can they conceive of any other conditions?

Unlike Trazior, some of the mountainous stalagmitic hives of Necromunda were wholly disconnected from any neighbour, isolated across immense metallic dunes of glittering despair, across seas of eerie chemical sludge. Trazior did overlook such a desert, as southerly sentinel of the Palatine cluster. However, Trazior also formed part of a mega-complex of hives densely crowding a poisoned terrain, interlinked by transport tubes supported on pylons or suspended from cables. Whoever looked out northward from the massive protective shell of Trazior might suspect that some giant world-spider, nourished on venom, had swung from hive to hive spinning ropes, and depositing multi-millions of hatchlings in each domain.

The spider and its web were potent symbols of Necromundan life. In the secret sign language of the Valence family gang, a hand imitating a spider signified many meanings. Which was why that scum kid's tattooed face had angered Yeremi, as a mockery.

What infuriated Yeremi even *more* was that upper-hab boy's insolently unblemished features...

It was the incident of the heat sink which made Yeremi pray that he should no longer stay in his place, but might somehow enforce... a different sort of order, however paltry his contribution might turn out to be. What could he do but pray—to the utterly remote, barely imaginable Emperor? To the God on Earth. Great Godfather of All.

And his prayer seemed to have been amply answered when the Planetary Guard came for the Valence gang; though, as is the way with prayers which are answered, there was cause for woe too—for the Valences were to be stripped of their best young fighters.

Could it now transpire, wondrously, that his private entreaty to the Godfather of All had only *begun* to be granted?

"Somatic resilience quotient, point eight five," recited the operator of the iron chair finally.

The grille swung away; the helmet lifted. The huge Marine—so much more *distinguished* in his uniform than any motley planetary trooper—planted himself before Yeremi like some human pillar that ten such troopers would be hard put to tumble, should they be so suicidally inclined.

Until now, to Yeremi, Space Marines had been virtually legendary figures. Though utterly distant from his own life, he was nevertheless aware from the confusing gossip of his elders that Marines did maintain a fortress-monastery in a spire of the Palatine. Some centuries earlier, piratical alien space nomads—called Orks—had landed on Necromunda. Allied to the native nomads, those brutish aliens had seized a remote hive cluster. A dozen Valences of those days were among the host of drafted hive gangs and planetary troopers who fought their way across the ash wastes, spearheaded by a company of Space Marines, to relieve and purge those ravaged hives, which ever since had loomed abandoned like smashed skulls.

Only one Valence had returned, to die slowly of poisons he had absorbed during the long march. The episode had become part of family lore, as well as suggesting that the best place to be was Trazior itself.

Despatched to Necromunda at the request of an ancestor of the present Lord Helmawr, those Space Marines had maintained a fortified base in the Palatine ever since.

"Yeremi Valence," said the Marine, "what is the name of the Emperor?"

"Of the Godfather of All?" whispered Yeremi, haunted by the memory of Yakobi being forced towards the heat sink. "*Will-power*: the Godfather's name is that. *Will-power supreme.*"

"A good answer to a question that has no simple answer. A reverent answer. A forceful answer."

"Why, then, Sir, is it His will that we in our hive are beset by so many enemies within? Above, and below. Why does Will not breed stronger Law?"

The Marine regarded Yeremi with increasing interest.

"For thus, Yeremi Valence, is the condition of the galaxy itself. As above, so below! Enemies fester everywhere. Foes and traitors. The miracle is that His will prevails generally across a million worlds. And it *shall* prevail, indomitably! Through death, through blood. *That* is the only universal law."

Yeremi thought of the remote Lord Helmawr plucking the strands of the web of Necromunda. The Imperial

Governor could only ever heed truly weighty wasps that sought to tear that web apart—not the myriad mites that bit one another.

In the Godly mind of the Emperor whole worlds might well be mere mites... A yawning, awesome, black perspective opened within Yeremi's soul.

"Would you yield yourself to Him utterly, Yeremi Valence, to help impose His will?" asked the Marine.

"Psychosis level, point four nine...

"Hubbard-Nietzsche intelligence quotient, point eight eight..."

Biff Tundrish heard the mystic swank-words without fear. The incomprehensible incantations would cast no spell over him, any more than the tattoo of the spider had glued him forever to his gang.

How long was *forever* in the undercity? Twenty years, thirty at most. Then came death from a wasting disease such as took his scavvy parents, if not death in a rumble with some other undercity gang or with habbers from above, better armed though not wise in the ways of the drekzone...

No one else seemed really to *thunk* but Biff.

F'r instance, he hadn't attacked that smooth-faced kid in the other big room, the kid whose mask he once snatched, the kid who lasered Biff's hand, the kid whose cronies dragged Crackpot away to a fiery torment. Noodle or Blueboobs would have flown at the kid to avenge Crackpot. But Biff had sat, and thunk.

Mind, neither Noodle nor Blueboobs would have been sittin' in that room amongst troopies and other enemies, jus' twiddlin' their thumbs, in the first place...

'Cos they didn't thunk too much beyond rumbles and scavvying and the scarring ceremonies and maybe a squirm together when they got high. Oh, the Spidergobs weren't dumb at rumbling, look how they lay in wait for those technerds who got one almighty surprise as to who was hunting who.

But they never thunk *far*. They never thunk *tall*.

Biff's thunks were a bit different. Sometimes his Spidergob mates gave him a bit of a skragging on account of it; not like what you'd skrag a Mad Dog or a Scarface, if you ever got the chance, 'course. Maybe Biff was really a mutie, 'cos his thunks were weirdo. Recently he'd said to his fellow Spidergobs, "We ain't *scavvies* at all, even if others call us so. We're an undercity gang, gor'it? We're on the up and up."

In time—a few years' time—he'd inevitably be boss of the Spidergobs 'cos of his thunks. *They* didn't know it—he was just the Kid to them—but *he* knew.

The Spidergobs would expand and rise, like froth on a pool of filth.

Biff couldn't wait out those years, case he died first.

Not that death was anything.

But *doing* was.

So he'd thunk and thunk. About everything he knew, which wasn't much. But he already knew it wasn't much.

The Spidergobs had once caught a technerd to have fun with, a technerd who could savvy scumlingo, and who'd screamed about how all his gang cousins had been taken into the Troopies up at some gateway fortress where the land-trains left, whatever those were. His cousins would hunt the Spidergob bastards if they hurt the technerd too much; they'd root them out.

Oh no they wouldn't. For one thing they'd never know. And no troopie in his right noddle would come near the undercity unless forced.

But it seemed as how you could *become* a troopie. Troopies didn't just sprout of their own accord. They weren't a separate species, as were muties.

It was almost as though Biff had understood Lexandro's sardonic advice to Yeremi. *Claw your way upwards.*

He'd skived off. He'd climbed on his own, level after level, way up through clanking, pounding, smoking factoryland; which hadn't been easy. He'd ridden up a shaft, clinging to the outside of a vertical rail-car, overhanging an abyss. He'd crept through Twists and skulked along vaulted Straights, jealously admiring the feeble radiance diffusing from the ends of glass cables, the memory of a ghost of daylight.

He hadn't known where to go, but he had a good instinct for *direct*, and he'd reckoned as how a gateway had to be in the shell, far away from the heat sink as could be. Then he'd spied troopies and had trailed 'em, but they'd sussed that. He'd been so lucky, so figging lucky. What was a lone scumnik doing up in the habs, acting like some spy? Maybe scum gangs were uniting for some big upward raid, eh? That's what the troopies musta reckoned. 'Cos they didn't smear Biff right away, and when he didn't fight back they took him in for terrorgation...

"Biff Tundrish," said the huge man in yellow and blue. However, he continued by using swank-words that Biff couldn't comprend at all. Biff shook his head, rattling his beads, and answered in scumlingo, slowly, to show that he couldn't savvy.

The giant nodded. Presently a trooper appeared and translated, after a fashion, glaring hostilely at Biff.

"Bigman says: you give him namenz of the Emp."

Biff puzzled his brains. He thunk fast. The Emp was the Emp, natch. Techs worshipped the Emp. Even scum swore by the Emp. On occasion; mostly they jus' swore. The Emp was megabossgod. Yet who was the Emp? Where was the Emp?

Everywhere. Nowhere.

Somewhere.

Not here.

Not in Trazior.

So maybe *nowhere* near.

Maybe the Emp was further away than Biff could imagine. And even more mega.

What was the most mega thing Biff knew?

He stared the giant in the eye, and said boldly:

"Emp's namenz is Bigger-Than-You. Emp's namenz is Death."

The giant seemed to understand even before the trooper turned Biff's utterance into swankwords. He smiled faintly.

The three boys sat under heavy guard in a glowglobe-lit room hung with a tapestry depicting the march across the wastes three centuries earlier. The translating trooper was there, too, for Biff's benefit as though temporarily that man had been transformed into the scumnik's servant. Yeremi and Biff eyed one another and Lexandro, remembering their previous savage encounter; while Lexandro himself assumed an air of disdain at the presence of two such... companions.

Then the Space Marine entered, and Lexandro felt far less superior.

The Marine Sergeant, Huzzi Rork, felt satisfied with the day's work. To take advantage of the pressgang levy had brought dividends in this instance.

The Imperial Fists recruited principally from two hive worlds, the ice planet of Inwit where cave-cities honeycombed the top ten kilometres of crust world-wide below the armour of three klicks of ice—and Necromunda, the poisoned desert. Not *many* recruits were usually needed; at full strength a Marine chapter numbered a thousand able warriors, who might well live for three hundred years and more, and the loss of any one of whom was a tragedy. And, of course, also a triumph; for what was more blessed than efficacious death in battle in the holy Emperor's cause? Yet such triumphant tragedies must needs occur.

So the Imperial Fists scrutinised transcripts of trials and

criminal records involving youngsters, hunting for a special blend of ingenuity, daring, will power—quite often suitable candidates had already been executed by the time the Fists learned of their existence, now cut short by poison gas or explosive bullet. Such lads of calibre must be sought out early in another respect as well; for bodily modifications must commence as soon after the onset of adolescence as could be. A recruit of eighteen years old was unthinkable; he would become a puissant man but only a runt among his superhuman peers.

And of course many candidates of seeming calibre failed one or another of the diagnostic tests...

But not these three promising lads. Not these.

Who must now be disciplined; who must now be deterred from killing each other, as might otherwise be their natural inclination.

"Lexandro d'Arquebus," said Huzzi Rork, "Yeremi Valence, Biff Tundrish: the name of your hive, *Trazior*, means *Three Sisters*, on account of the triple spires. Whatever you were before, you will now become as *three brothers*. Amongst a band of new brothers. If any of you attacks your brother from now on, if not ordered to do so by a superior, that attacker will be enslaved and used for chirurgical experiments in our laboratories for as long as he lives. Do you clearly understand this?"

Lexandro and Yeremi nodded, but Biff frowned at the trooper's translation. His brow furrowed with the effort to understand the concept of a laboratory and the arcane art of surgery.

So, murmuring a quick litany, Huzzi Rork brought a little screen to life, and fed the mouth beneath the flickering blank white face with a data medallion.

A pastel picture exploded into view, of a pink-skinned adolescent immobilised in a steel framework, with only his hands fully exposed. The pupils of the youth's eyes were fully dilated to azure marbles. Before him was a bowl of clear liquid, in which lay a complicated puzzle of interlocking rings. The twin arms of that mechanical gibbet forced his hands down into the liquid, which sizzled and steamed. The picture focused upon the questing, flexing fingers. There was no sound track.

"The liquid is acid," explained Huzzi Rork. "The rings are of uncorrosible adamantium. The disobedient youth has been injected with an experimental drug, though of course his tactile sensations aren't blunted. For he must uncouple the rings before he can withdraw his hands."

They watched a while, till the Space Marine asked, "Can *mind* and *will* move the bare bones now that the muscles are gone? This is the subject's third attempt. He has already undergone two restorations with a new prototype pseudflesh." Rork pushed a massive finger at an intaglio button, incised with a skull, on the viewing machine. Its screenface went blank; its mouth spat out the data medallion into his hand.

"I comprend," said Biff. "I savvy."

"You will proceed from here in my charge," Rork told them, "by deep military transport tunnel to the Palatine hive, to our fortress monastery there. A carrier will transfer you and other recruits into orbit. A jumpship will convey you to the home-base of the Imperial Fists." The Marine clenched his own fist which seemed almost as large as any boy's head, though this was not actually the case.

"How *do* we become like you, Sir?" Lexandro asked hesitantly.

"That is all you need to know, d'Arquebus. Henceforth the neophyte cadet will not address *any* Imperial Fist unless said Marine first addresses the cadet. Punishment for first infringement will be one minute in a nerve-glove. *Translate somehow, Trooper!* What is a nerve-glove, d'Arquebus?"

"Sir, the cadet postulant does not know."

"Correctly answered, Cadet." The Marine paused, as if to allow time for any of the three to speak out of turn.

None did.

Lexandro, Yeremi, and Biff stared at one another silently. The three brothers of Trazior.

Chapter Three

Lexandro had expected that the Imperial Fists' home-base would be on a world. Perhaps fiery hot so as to test their mettle; perhaps crusted with glaciers. Or maybe the planet might be a savage jungle...

Alternatively, home-base could be a vast artificial satellite, a moon of plasteel in orbit around any of those. Devotional vids had hinted at such possibilities.

Yet not at the reality.

Or at least, the reality for the Imperial Fists...

As Lexandro looked through a quatrefoil window in the observatorium of the corvette, what he saw ahead, moving seemingly slowly across the void-gulf far from any suns, more isolated than loneliness itself, was a great glittering leviathan that seemed carved intricately of ice, with fins and ribbed wings and soaring towers whose pinnacles were linked by flying buttresses.

A long courtyard deck jutted forth like a notched broadsword. Black armoured shrimps nuzzling there were cruisers and troopships which might well dwarf the corvette that Lexandro and the other recruits were sailing in.

Straining his eyes, trying to grasp the sheer scale, he noticed larvae that were also ships.

"Try a lens," said a voice, mock-ingratiatingly.

Valence's voice.

A score of Necromundans from various hives were staring out through the traceried ports; and by now Lexandro could talk to any of them, whatever their original hive and their hab-level lingo. All of the cadets had been force-taught correct Imperial Gothic under hypno-casques. Even the ex-scumnik, Tundrish, spoke with reasonable fluency, though in his case concepts sometimes seemed to be lacking to accompany the words which burbled from his mouth, as if as yet he possessed more words than meanings. Yet how that former scumkid aspired to grasp those meanings and ideas.

"A lens magnifies things, d'Arquebus." The ex-tech couldn't quite achieve a patronising tone. Valence sidled up to Lexandro, offering a rune-chased oculus.

"I know that. Thank you... brother." Lexandro allowed a gentle hint of sarcasm to flavour that last word.

Through the oculus Lexandro could now see crenellated parapets overhanging space, stained-glass galleries, battle banners springing from the tips of spires stiffly in the void, and the bristling snouts of defence lasers. He realized how huge was that flying fortress-monastery of the Imperial Fists where he would remain for at least several years.

"Sizes in space are deceptive," remarked Valence.

"You don't say?" drawled Lexandro. An impish perversity made him add, "Why, I warrant that fortress is huger than the entire heat sink of good old Trazior."

The tech boy flushed, then smiled tightly.

"No, you shan't provoke me, brother. I shan't assault you, if that's what you hope. But I'd make a request that you don't try to offend brother Tundrish similarly. He might behave more impulsively—though I could be mistaken. His native intelligence surprises me, for a scumnik. *Should* you goad him into attacking you, you might find the aftermath disappointing. Odium and opprobrium may well attach to a brother who ruins another brother by such guile.''

Lexandro yawned. "What exactly was your psychosis level in the test?''

"And of course,'' Valence continued airily, "you may merely be masking your own inner poverty by such posturing.''

"If I want moral advice, Valence, I'll ask the Chaplain.''

"And he'll tell you that each of us would-be Marines is one in a million—one in a billion—except for he who sets himself above the rest of his brothers; and *that* one is *less*.''

"Did you perhaps belong to some heretical revolutionary *cult*?''

Just then, the prayer klaxon sounded. The recruits hurried below to pack into the on-ship chapel, where incense burned before a lambent golden icon of the Emperor and an alabaster idol of Rogal Dorn, the founding Primarch of the Imperial Fists. Aye, sculpted in whitest alabaster to emphasize his purity.

The Chaplain had been so injured in combat that his best continuing contribution to his chapter was to act as escort and religious awakener to young new recruits. His body was entirely missing below the waist, the stump of his torso being plugged in to a cybercart of softly gurgling tubes, which he controlled with his one remaining flesh-and-bone hand. His other arm had been replaced by a damascened prosthetic of plasteel and servomotors. Ormolu-cased sapphire lenses had replaced both eyes. How those lenses pierced the hearts of those he spoke to, seeming to flay the skin and flense any fat to lay a person bare.

During the journey, the Chaplain had already inducted the Necromundan boys into proper worship, with a strong emphasis on adoration of Rogal Dorn, whose own gene-seed—bred on from generation to generation of Imperial

Fists within their implanted progenoid glands—would kindle the neophyte cadets into *Marines*, true Marines of the chapter.

A chapter of the First Founding. The chapter which had loyally defended the Imperial Palace on Earth against the berserk, corrupted fury of the Horus Rebellion. The chaplain had displayed a holorama of the Column of Glory, that tower of rainbow metal half a kilometre high close by the Emperor's own throne room, which was embedded with the armour of Imperial Fists who had died there and during the teleport assault on Horus's Chaos-oozing battle-barge nine thousand years earlier. Within those broken suits, their bones; and inside the open faceplates, their grinning skulls. What finer sepulchre of honour could any Marine ever aspire to?

This was their tradition, one that spanned ten millennia.

Now that the corvette was in direct radio contact with home-base, the ship's Astropath was free to join this final service of thanksgiving. The Necromundans glanced curiously at that blind, fey figure of a man who was as alabastine as the idol of the primarch—his flesh almost translucent—yet who could speak with his mind from star to star, and could even report directly to the Emperor, should a sufficiently momentuous situation arise.

"Rejoice," growled the Chaplain. "The Emperor's Voice is with us today. Rejoice that we return to our holy fortress. Yet wherever we may be in this universe, a Marine's transformed body is his temple, containing the eucharist of Rogal Dorn; as yours will soon be also."

Aye, thought Lexandro, before he was fully inducted his body would house many new wondrous organs. As the Chaplain had explained, that was how a promising human being became a giant invincible Marine. Indeed, a Marine must needs become gigantic to contain within himself—how did the litany run?—the Secondary Heart, Ossmodula, Biscopea; the Haemostamen, Larramen's Organ, and

Lyman's Ear... No, he was forgetting the correct order of implantation...

And that was why only boys, yet a-growing, could be recruited and not adult men.

The hormones dripping from the Ossmodula alone would considerably swell the span of the skeleton, would strengthen his bones ceramically, would fuse his ribs into a solid breastplate...

The Chaplain thumped his pus-yellow, azure-chevroned cuirass with his one remaining organic fist. A purity seal of eye-aching purple was offset by a bilious personal heraldic badge, of a nail transfixing a splayed hand, which almost melted visually into his breastplate as though the ghost of one of his hearts showed through the metal at that spot, the fingers being the pulmonary tubes and the palm the iron-pierced heart itself.

"This is my temple! As yours will also be!"

"A shattered temple..." Without moving his lips, Lexandro threw his voice ever so softly towards Valence, imitating the ex-tech's accent.

"Cadet d'Arquebus!" screamed the Chaplain, suffused with a righteous rage which he may or may not have been simulating. "What is the function of Lyman's Ear, which will replace your own lug, should you survive so long?"

"Sir, it prevents the Marine from ever experiencing nausea or vertigo due to disorientation, however extreme."

"*And?*"

"Sir, the cadet does not know, Sir."

"Lyman's Ear also enables the Marine to enhance and filter background noise. My *shattered temple*—which remains a sacred and anointed shrine to Rogal Dorn—is not lacking its Lyman's Ear...

"The nerve-glove for you, Cadet d'Arquebus! Crime: blasphemy. Sentence: five minutes, pain-level tertius. Punishment to proceed immediately in front of present witnesses. Thus we purify this chapel and all of us, in our hearts." The Chaplain seemed to relent just slightly. "Cadet: be advised to beware *which* obscenities you scream during punishment, lest you rate further chastisement."

The Chaplain touched buttons on his cart. A hatch in the floor-plates before him irised open, revealing a shaft; up from which rose a steel framework suspending within it a transparent clingtight one-piece tunic elegantly embroidered with fine silvery wires so that an exposed human nervous system seemed to be hanging there, a semi-collapsed anatomy of nerves.

The tunic only lacked a head and the tops of the shoulders. The framework slowly stretched the fabric apart.

This was the nerve-glove? Back in Trazior, Lexandro had imagined a gauntlet which would slip on to a hand...

Not a *body-glove*. A glove that would cover the whole body up to the neck.

The Chaplain chanted almost rapturously: "The glove will cleave to your whole body, save for your head. Elastic fabric will cling to your legs, to your loins, your trunk, your arms. That mesh of electrofibres will stimulate excruciating pain signals in all the nerves in your flesh without any physical harm being caused to that flesh. Though you shall feel all the agony, and more, of being roasted and incinerated alive, no actual damage will result—thus those agonies may continue unabated."

The amputee's tongue flickered silently, stumpily, as though tasting the molecules of Lexandro's sweat which escaped into the air, before he resumed his discourse: "The longest that anyone has endured a nerve-glove at level tertius until irreversible insanity, is fifty-two minutes—by which time the pain signals were so burned into the nerves that they could never cease thereafter."

The religious officer's artificial sapphire eyes glowed with an inner light as he gazed at Lexandro. Was he relishing this moment, deliberately prolonging it in anticipation out of bile at the cadet's blasphemy? No, not so! There was something sacred, mysterious in his scrutiny, as though Pain itself was a god, and he was its pontifex.

He touched a button on the control pad of his cybercart, and the steel gibbet descended back into the cylindrical pit with glove distended, ready to be worn, the gaping shoulder-mouth sinking level with the rivetted plates of the floor.

"Discard all clothing, Cadet."

Momentarily, Lexandro hesitated.

"Be advised that refusal of orders is a capital offence."

Lexandro stripped off his mustardy cadet's tunic, and boots, and loincloth quickly and stood naked. Goosebumps coarsened his sleek skin, and he tried to still a trembling in his limbs.

"Drop yourself down into the glove, d'Arquebus. *It* will not rip apart."

Lexandro jumped forward and plummeted down. The glove caught him, encompassed him. It clung around him as a second, intimate skin. Only his bare head remained clear, level with the deck.

The framework reared up once again, to display him: a body webbed with argent tracery clutched within a thin unyielding skeleton of steel.

"Pain is... a lesson that the universe teaches us," intoned the Chaplain. "Pain is the preserver from injury. Pain perpetuates our lives. It is the healing, purifying scalpel of our souls. Pain is the wine of communion with heroes. It is the quicksilver panacea for weakness—the quintessence of a dedicated existence. Pain is the philosophic vitriol which transmutes mere mortal into immortal. It is the Sublime, the golden astral fire! I am in pain always, in blessed pain. Recommend that you fix your attention on the countenance of Rogal Dorn, Cadet."

A moment later it seemed that boiling water scalded Lexandro's whole body below the neck. Simultaneously furnace-fire incinerated him. He knew what those two victims must have felt when tossed into the heat sink.

Except that they had died quickly. Or so he supposed.

He could not die.

For his convulsing limbs, gripped within the slender yet firm framework, were not being consumed—even in his agony he understood that his substance remained unblemished.

His legs were not simply dipped in molten lead; they were *made* of molten lead. His belly was a crucible, his ribs were a gridiron, and his fingers were tongs. A shrivelled stub of white-hot poker jutted from his groin. Lava coursed through his arteries.

Nor could he lose consciousness...

Then the boiling water became superheated. The furnace-fire was incandescent plasma.

Screeching, he exhausted all air. Could he shriek himself unconscious through asphyxiation?

No, for his lungs dragged in air to make more screams. The bellows bellowed.

But not curses directed at the Chaplain. Nor cries for mercy, either. Even in this excruciating extremity a part of Lexandro acknowledged that the former would be folly, the latter would be futile.

Somehow the glove was keeping him aware and conscious, blocking any opiates of the brain, preventing any saving reflex of a swoon. It played his body thunderously like a piano of pain.

The alabaster face of Rogal Dorn branded his retinas: a crag of a face, with lush tough lips. Those lips seemed to phrase words intended for himself alone, kissing these words into the soft matter of his brain: "*Though you are cast into the ultimate heat sink, you hover indestructibly. In torment you fly, invincible, superior to mere victims of the fire.*"

Those words stroked a node of madness within him

which somehow detached him from his excruciation so that he flew above it fleetingly before sinking back into molten anguish. Even though his mouth still screamed throughout.

At last the ordeal ceased—so abruptly that Lexandro imagined that his body had evaporated, vanished, and that he had become pure spirit.

The framework sank down until his lips were level with the floor. A cool hand gripped him under each armpit. Oh cool, so cool. Those two seemingly soothing hands hauled him up from out of the glove.

One hand belonged to Yeremi Valence, the other to Biff Tundrish. Were they assisting Lexandro—or participating in his punishment?

Naked, Lexandro knelt before the idol of Rogal Dorn and adored it...

The Chaplain watched intently. After a while he directed his cybercart to Lexandro's side and reached out his true arm to touch the cadet.

"Even before the gene-seed of the Primarch is implanted in you...," he murmured reverentially. "Even before... As if the blessed Dorn has marked you out in advance."

Lexandro had no rational idea what the Chaplain meant. Yet in some zone of his mind where reason played no part, bizzarely he rejoiced.

"You must not deliberately offend so as to *invite* such punishment," whispered the puissant amputee hoarsely. "You must obey and revere and *obey*! Dress yourself now and stand in rank."

And so while the corvette glided on towards its illuminated dock, as a minnow might swim into the mouth of a vast phosphorescent deep-sea predator, the interrupted service of thanksgiving continued.

The elevation of the nerve-glove had been sacramental too, in its way.

The Necromundans were to be in the fortress-monastery for

six imperial months before suffering their initiatory hazing at the hands of older cadets. Earlier, and none of them might have survived the ritual of the tunnel of terror...

Chapter Four

Under the guidance of educated slaves whose forebears had served the Chapter loyally for many aeons, knowing no other world than the massive fortress-monastery, the Necromundans became well acquainted with its topography: its galleries and halls and gymnasia and oratoria, its foundries and chapels and firing ranges, its surgeries and its various scattered scriptories where librarium data could be accessed.

Given the sensitive functions of the librarium which doubled as the communications centre, naturally entry to that chamber was restricted. Astropaths and defence officers were forever on duty in the librarium; and within too were stored the original codices of the chapter's ten thousand year heritage. Hence, those separate scriptories where one could study the electronic ghosts of unrestricted documents.

Techs who were expert in the Machine Mysteries, autonomous-minded slaves, administrators, ship crews— all the host of support staff for the Marine chapter—slept in modestly comfortable dormitories... assuming that they needed, or could avail themselves of modest comfort during sleep-time. The task-adapted Technomats, whose original personalities had been erased and replaced with electrografted data and blithe, benign personae, did, and could. So did the Servitors who remained fully human. Others of those supplied to the chapter by the Adeptus Mechanicus on Mars were automata—programmed drones. Still others were specialised cyborgs, part-machine, who could never lie down on a bunk.

Marines and Marine Scouts and cadets spent the artificial nights in barren cells. In their own refectories they ate a ceramic-reinforced, drug-laden booster diet in silence, ending with a prayer recited by an older initiate.

D'Arquebus, Valence, Tundrish and companions soon received their first two sets of implants from devout Chirurgeons in the Apothacarion wing. First, came the Secondary Heart which would sustain them should their original heart be destroyed in combat. At the same time, the skeleton-boosting Ossmodula—and the Biscopea gland to stimulate muscle growth.

Later, came the Haemastamen, and Larraman's Organ: the former to monitor the Ossmodula and Biscopea and to enrich the blood, the latter to alter the blood's clotting properties so that scar tissue would almost instantly close up any wound.

The Necromundan neophytes became very familiar with the operating altars and biomonitoring and chemical assay machines of the Apothacarion—with the mantis-like laser scalpels, the stasis tureens cradling the precious new organs, the examinator device towering like a brass-banded armadillo, its tapering snout scanning the innards of the body, and with the soporificator instrument resembling some giant spider that stung metacurare into the nerves; to which the drone of surgical incantations from the adepts, whose robes were embroidered with arabesque prophylactic hexes and purity emblems, was a macabre lullaby.

The cadets would become ever more familiar with those chambers of the Apothacarion during the next few years. Here was the shrine to the holy art of Surgery, which could transform men into demi-machines—or into paragons of transhumanity.

One unfortunate boy from the Palatine hive died early. His Haemastamen failed to synchronize his Ossmodula. Spurs of bone grew from his spine, bursting through his skin, and his fingers began to fuse into shovel blades. Unthinkable that this anomaly might be due to a misspeaking of the orthodox surgical liturgy! Yet despite remedial chemotherapy and amputation the syndrome continued. So the boy was honourably mind-wiped and his zombie anatomy retained for study in a nutrient tank in a laboratory of the Apothacarion.

One day, during a recreation period, Lexandro betook himself to a scriptory to study– only to discover that both of his ''brothers'' were already ensconsed there, although at data consoles some distance apart. The eagerness with which Biff Tundrish would make a bee-line for the nearest scriptory to soak himself in Imperial Fist history stirred amusement and a certain irritation in Lexandro's breast.

''Of course,'' he remarked loftily, loitering beside Valence, ''our Biff does start from a low base-line of knowledge...''

''And you, from a high vantage point?'' asked Valence witheringly.

''Ah,'' replied Lexandro, ''yet what is knowledge of *facts* worth compared with religious *experience*?''

Experience such as Lexandro had gained, or thought he had gained, in the nerve-glove... He himself spent hours in the chapel reserved for cadets, praying to the image of Rogal Dorn, and to the Emperor, attempting to recapture the moment when he had *flown through fire*, sure that this would stand him in good stead in battle. As he smelled the smouldering frankincense, he would imagine his own body inflamed and his soul soaring from it like smoke.

Tundrish paid no apparent attention, seemingly lost in the scrolling details of a campaign four thousand years in the past. But Yeremi eyed Lexandro calculatingly.

"It's much too soon to provoke an affair of honour," he remarked.

And this was true—for only mature Battle Brothers were permitted to duel. Permitted? Nay, almost encouraged, so it seemed—yet apparently within the strictest of chivalric constraints...

Valence's sly voice insinuated itself again. "I hear that he who is *scarred* is he who is honoured, being graced by a Brother's nick upon his cheek—a nick like a dainty bite, like a loving kiss. Would you desire the honour of your own cheek being blemished by Biff? Or would you honour *him* in that style... one day?" Idly, Valence rubbed one of the runes on his own cheek, as though the ex-tech had already been similarly honoured, or anticipated honour.

Lexandro shrugged. "How do you come by this wisdom about duels?"

"Through observation and study, Brother, rather than through ecstatic intuition. Imperial Fists are dedicated to fastidious and meticulous *detail*, by the grace of Dorn— detail in military tactics, and in personal conduct too. That is why we adopted—"

"*We?*" sneered Lexandro.

"—why we adopted the *Junker model of behaviour.*"

Lexander did not know the word *Junker*.

"Yes, the ancient Prussic code." Valence was only too happy to explain. "Named after Prusse, on old Earth. There's a subtle poison in the germ plasm we receive, d'Arquebus. A heady, intoxicating venom—which you seem almost to be drunken on already."

"This is blasphemy I'm hearing!"

"Would I be so foolish as to blaspheme? Consult the codex of our heritage a little more, d'Arquebus. Religious afflatus alone, and agony, may not win a battle. Any Marine casualty is a tragedy as well as a triumph.''

"You're a blasphemer, who doesn't believe in prayer! Or a prissy tech pedant, who should have been one of my father's scribes.'' So saying, disdainfully Lexandro left the scriptory and returned to his small cell to recite in private one of the liturgies they had all been taught.

"Oh Dorn, the dawn of our being,
Let your sun shine on us, your sons;
Oh Primarch, precursor, asperge us..."

In one of the firing ranges attached to the foundries, Brother Artisans—who had once been hive-dwellers, too, before their transfiguration—introduced the new Necromundans to military bolters, flamers, plasma guns, melta guns, laser weapons. The Brothers demonstrated power axes as well as heavier weapons which the neophytes as yet lacked the physique to wield unaided unless those weapons were equipped with suspensors. Nor could the cadets yet don the power armour necessary to heft such bulk. The neophytes were still growing, and only a good while after they had received their final implant of all—the carapace—would they be able to jack into an armoured suit.

Yet they *were* growing—apace. Swelling, toughening, expanding.

The cadets did not as yet, of course, visit the vast locked guarded complex of the Armoury, with its racks of weapons and magazines of ammunition both pristine and ancient, protected within stasis fields inside chambers of adamantium.

Nor as yet, to Lexandro's regret, the holy Reclusiam, home of the chapter's most sacred relics and trophies; only initiates might step in there.

Nor yet the immense Catacombs down at the base of the fortress-monastery, where heroes ancient and modern lay in ranks of caskets. Too sacred a place, for neophytes.

Nevertheless, minor relics abounded in the home-base.

The mature Battle Brothers—the giant knights of the Imperium, whose attention a cadet must not disturb—were bound on a crusade, the details of which were hardly for cadets to enquire about. When not exercising, training, or praying, the Imperial Fists often carved scrimshaws meditatively in their cells. Their work, accumulated over millennia, could be seen everywhere. Examples were mounted in tooled silver reliquaries in niches, or displayed in rococo gilt cases which cyborged Servitors dusted. Officers wore scrimshaws as jewellery along with the most noble, holy decorations incorporating tiny slivers of the Emperor's own armour from aeons ago, prior to the time when that Divine Immortal was prisoned in his prosthetic golden throne.

Some of the polished, engraved scrimshaws, so mellow in lustre, depicted weapons; others, armour, or miniature cameos of battle. The raw materials which the Marines used for their scrimshandering were none other than the mighty, ceramically strengthened finger bones—the meta-carpals and phalanges—of Imperial Fists who had died in battle or, surviving to old age, been permitted honourable euthanasia. Few of those skeletons resting in caskets in the Catacombs sported hands. Most had been amputated. Even a dead Imperial Fist, as the saying went, kept his hand in.

In the rune-friezed, banner-hung oratorium reserved for cadets the Necromundans hung on the words of crippled veteran lecturers; and on one such occasion Lexandro learned that Valence had been correct in his seemingly blasphemous comments uttered in the scriptory...

The paraplegic Brother Rhetoricus was strapped into the saddle of a powered chair designed in the image of a crouching subhuman. He wore round his neck a scrimshaw on a silver chain. Other scrimshaws hung from the chair itself on thongs. An imperial eagle lectern carved in jet supported upon its open black wings a huge, chained copy of the Codex Astartes. This rulebook of Space Marine organization was bound in many layers of flayed, cured, alien skin, its letters illuminated ornately with the colour-fixed green and orange blood from two alien races. The Brother spoke from memory, and indeed his theme today was *not* the structure of the Legiones Astartes.

He commenced in a rasping voice which scratched his words into his listeners' minds as a claw might groove butter.

"You have already received some of the precious germ-plasm of our blessed Patriarch to kindle you as a true Imperial Fist..." Seated along a wide curve of plasteel stalls, their canopies embossed with battle scenes, the cadets hardly moved.

"Your new organs and glands have only one ultimate source—namely the gene-seed of the godly Rogal Dorn enshrined from generation to generation within the temples of our bodies. From those seeds we culture the superhuman glands and organs that shall make you Marines. Before you receive your carapace, the Adepts of the Apothacarion will implant the two Progenoid glands which will, during the next half-decade and decade, soak up the pattern of your Imperial Fist metabolism. Harvested from you, these glands will enable our Adepts to culture further organs to kindle further Brothers in future.

"Woe betide if you die before at least those first five years of service! For you will thus deny us the possibility of an additional Brother. This is why you will first join a Scout company with a hardened survival-conscious veteran as your Sergeant."

Currently, no Scouts at all were aboard the fortress-monastery. Those who had already received the carapace and graduated to the status of probationer-superhumanity were elsewhere in the galaxy fighting as terror troops. The carapace required almost a year to become fully symbiotic with the body—and its owner required purification, distillation in the alembic of combat before his augmented natural body could be judged to be fully transmuted in spirit as well as in flesh and bone, and thus worthy of donning complete Marine armour...

"We are not, we are never berserkers," stressed the Brother Rhetoricus. "Be not chary of sacrificing your life, should necessity demand! *In extremis* we can obtain new progenoids slowly through test-slaves. Yet be not rash. An Imperial Fist thinks and plans his every deed meticulously, even in the crucible of combat when our spilt blood hardens like cinnabar, thanks be to Larraman's Organ. Indeed, let *that* be your precept: the hot blood gushes forth, yet instantly the Marine is firm as stone in his intellectus—aye, and spry as quicksilver which can flood through a maze of branching routes in a trice, illuminating all possibilities!"

The power chair hummed back and forth as if the mechanical subhuman was advancing towards its argument, then retreating; and the scrimshaws hanging from it rattled like a sorcerer's skirt of juju bones.

"Be it known," declared the paraplegic, who had been paralysed irreparably in some nerve-eating attack by aliens, "Õbe it known that some precious organs of the Venerable Dorn have been lost to us utterly during the vast lapse of time. We no longer possess the Sus-an Membrane that would allow a Marine to enter a state of suspended animation. Nor do we have Betcher's Gland, which would let a Marine secrete corrosive poison to spit at a foe.

"Do we bemoan such losses? No! We are the Fists! We do not need to hibernate or spit venom. We *crush* our enemies.

"Be it also known that mutation can twist the rune-signs written in gene-seed. Of this, you have already witnessed one severe example: your former companion whose spine branched uncontrollably and whose fingers fasciated.

"He was unfortunate. He was an exception. His mutation was a freak event. I hasten to add that no curse caused it— no hex or bewitchment, so far as the Adepts can determine;

nor even any lapse in liturgy. The phenomenon merely occurred.

"Yet we *all without exception* share a subtler and ambivalent genetic flaw, which expresses itself not in branching bones but in our very behaviour. Can any cadet say what this flaw might be?" The imperious cripple's gaze raked the ranks of cadets.

Valence stood to attention, tipping up his misericord seat with a *klack*. For a fraction of a second Valence's look darted in Lexandro's direction.

"*Speak*," prompted the paraplegic.

"Sir, our attitude to pain, Sir."

"Ah, you have studied to some effect... Expound, Cadet Valence."

"Sir, an Imperial Fist may become obsessed with conquering pain by force of will. This is a good quality in that we will fight on despite terrible injuries, Sir. Yet if subconsciously we invite such injuries—"

"Aye, such heedlessness—such invitation to injury, as if to a friendly playmate—can imperil our battle planning, risking loss of personnel and material. We must beware of this tendency, even when we exploit it. For we are not berserkers! On the contrary, we Fists are exemplary *planners*, fascinated by the minutest detail. You may sit, Cadet."

As Valence obeyed, the paraplegic's fingers clawed at the air, as though inscribing some complex, arcane pattern.

"We believe in meticulous, scrupulous conduct and tactics. Hence, the renowned *courtesy* and the *artistry* of our chapter. As you mature, the fingers of your fists, when idle, may well itch to scribe wondrous designs upon the finger-bones of your dead Brethren, honouring and adorning their now fleshless fists. This is how we love to express our dextrous craftsmanship. Within the mighty power glove which can crush an alien skull like a puffball, there resides such microscopic discipline!

"Aye, after a battle once you have recited your thanksgivings, or prior to a campaign, while you are girding your soul for a crusade—as now, as blessedly now—many of you may yearn to kneel in your cell with saw and magnilens, with rasp and buffing wheel and carbide graver, with brush and inkhorn. And with the handbones of a slaughtered or euthanased comrade in front of you..."

The lecturer's own hands twitched, and his pallid cheeks flushed red as he recited:

"Fists of beauty,
Fingers of death;
Emperor's fists –
With death is our tryst."

The import of the art of scrimshandering as a meditative pastime for the Imperial Fist chapter became more evident to Lexandro when, on a later occasion, he happened to pause near two Battle Brothers who were disputing courteously though passionately not far from the Librarium.

A Servitor with a tracked, snail-like body and padded hands that secreted fragrant antiseptic polish was buffing the floor of the rib-vaulted passageway where electro-candles flickered on sconces in front of scrimshaw-framed ikons; and Lexandro must halt, so as not to incommode the two Marines.

He had been thinking, as he frequently did, of pain, and of how it almost seemed as though Rogal Dorn had singled him out for special benediction even *before* the Primarch's germ-plasm had been introduced into his body...

The two Marines paid no attention whatever to him as he stood waiting to pass. What he overheard provided his first insight into the intimate sentiments of mature Fists who had been warriors for over seventy years—as the seven long-service studs on the craggy, crewcut forehead of each star-knight signified.

"But, Brother," said one, "suppose you soak a finger-bone in hot paraffin after the fine-sanding stage—once the surface has attained a frosted finish, as you say—you are introducing a foreign substance into the relic of a comrade.''

''Bone possesses a certain porosity compared with horn,'' argued the other, ''even though a Brother's bones are strengthened ceramically.''

''But—''

''That porosity is perceptible to me! Perhaps my Occulobe organ grants me keener micro-eyesight than yours? Immersion of the bone in melted paraffin wax fills any pores and so stops the ink of the design from bleeding.''

''But those pores are already occupied with ceramic, Brother!''

''*All* the myriad pores? Always?''

''Perhaps your Occulobe is overstimulating your vision so that you see details that do not quite exist. In battle that might prove perilous.''

''Brother, one must study a bone *intently*, not merely scrawl upon it. Shall we duel over this?''

Each man bore several nicks and scars upon his cheeks.

''I believe we must,'' said the other. ''Shall we resort to the Solitorium first to fast and search our souls in silence about your accusation?''

Stiffly, arm in arm, the Brothers walked off towards that place of deprivation which was in a dark gondola jutting below the fortress-monastery into the lonely void.

The gastropodic semi-automaton moved over reverentially to polish the section of ancient riveted floor where the two Marines had stood for a while.

Yes, this was the closest that Lexandro had yet come to communion with elder Brethren.

The older *cadets* were another matter...

For the first six months, those who were further advanced

towards full Marinehood had simply treated the latest Necromundan intake as juveniles, as sprats who might or might not grow into sharks. There was no question of the younger cadets acting as Servitors to the older ones by, say, scrubbing out their cells, however.

Yet now, as Lexandro began to wax burly, he detected a tension mounting between those even burlier youths and the freshmen neophytes. It was as if those brawnier possessors of more organs were impatiently awaiting a signal, a pheromone in the air...

One evening two hulking boys delivered a summons. The new Necromundans must accompany them immediately.

Without further explanation, their escorts led the puzzled party away from their quarters. Soon they were passing through a domed concourse, ruddily lit and scented with smouldering camphor—then through another. Techs who were squatting outside their rune-daubed dormitories quailed as the boys passed by.

A gloomy, whale-ribbed corridor led after half a kilometre to a moist cloacal side-passage aglow with lichen where ventilator gargoyles exhaled dazing smouldery fumes. Now they were passing by the foundries, the guides choosing neglected routes to disorient the younger cadets, so it seemed. Occasional mute mind-wiped drones trudged by on some robotic task, perhaps simply ordered to exercise their zombie limbs prior to cleaning out a toxic sump; and cyborged Servitors trundled here and there.

Finally, in a remote zone of the fortress-monastery, the guides ushered Lexandro and company into a scarcely-lit, groin-vaulted chamber—and promptly skipped back out, slamming the plasteel door that was wrought with the face of a carnivorous lizard.

Glowglobes brightened. The chamber proved to be very long. A score of older cadets were waiting at the far end behind what was evidently a transparent plascrystal wall.

Another wall of the same crystal—unbreakable by any unaided human body—stretched across the chamber close by. Linking the two walls was a transparent tunnel perhaps six hundred metres long, and of considerable girth, sufficient to accommodate at least five people side by side, and banded periodically with control hoops.

"Despicable neophytes," jeered a loudspeaker, "welcome to the Tunnel of Terror. This is an amusing variation on the nerve-glove. You will enter naked. An energy membrane denies access to anyone wearing any protective garments. Along the tunnel there exist a few modest zones of safety. Between these are zones where you will experience mischievous phenomena such as incandescent heat, absolute cold, airless vacuum, induced agony, and such. Oh yes, and gravity increases the further you proceed. It will be interesting to see which safe pockets you end up cowering in. Should any puny neophyte reach our end, which seems unlikely, you will be rewarded with a brand of honour on your buttock. You will of course all *enter* the Tunnel of Terror because, commencing now, the air is to be exhausted from your end of this chamber. Proceed, and entertain us!"

Ventilator gargoyles started to hiss, sucking in instead of breathing out. Hastily, the reluctant guests began to shed their tunics, loincloths, and boots.

"For Quinspirus hive!" shouted one lad, and charged into the tunnel, followed by two others.

They stumbled, shrieking, till they reached the nearest safe zone, and stopped.

"Come on, before it crowds up," Biff Tundrish said, with something of a sneer, to Valence.

"For Trazior!" cried Valence. Both raced into the tunnel.

"For Rogal Dorn!" shouted Lexandro, hot on their heels.

Incandescently hot...

Lexandro looked back. His Secondary Heart pounded, as well as his first. His nerves screamed at the shocking transitions his body had endured. Somehow he had traversed the latest scorching zone, feeling that he was being utterly consumed. Those zones were the worst, but Rogal Dorn was with him then. As well as in the agony zones; though not in vacuum or in utter chill.

Tundrish and Valence had reached the previous safe zone, and appeared done for. The other Necromundans were further behind. The kink in the Primarch's gene-seed might indeed confer will power in regard to enduring pain, even a fascination with torment—how else could any of the cadets have progressed any distance at all, let alone as far as they had proceeded?—yet plainly there were limits, which this tunnel—so bland in its appearance, so hideous in its effect—seemed designed to test to snapping point. Aye, by varying the nature of the stimuli so contradictorily, unpredictably, and totally—so confusingly that the mind could not concentrate upon one species of ordeal, but was assaulted instead by a menagerie of martyrdoms, a zoo of torments.

Gravity dragged terribly, increasing Lexandro's apparent weight threefold or more. Would he be able to stagger onward? He already knew, from collision with it, that the very next zone was of a frigidity so intense that it too would burn like fire.

Sucking air into his lungs, he called back along the tube: "Can't take the heat?"

"No, damn you," shouted Tundrish.

Lexandro prayed passionately.

And it seemed to him that he heard a voice answer him from within.

"*In torment you fly, Lexandro. But do not fly alone.*" The voice appeared to issue from the extra Primarch heart inside himself.

He considered. If he did reach the end of the tunnel, did

he wish to be seized naked, and branded? The brand might be no mark of honour at all—but a culminating cruel humiliating jape.

Rage consumed him. How he yearned to attack and injure those burlier youths who stood watching, grinning. What if he were to be punished for his vengeance by a plunge into the nerve-glove? That might yield a perverse bliss compared with his present adversity. Would those older cadets actually report him for such an infringement, on Lexandro's part, of cousinly courtesy? When *they themselves* were responsible for inflicting such an assault upon fellow cadets?

Yet could he mount such an assault on his own?

"*The one hand: a Fist,*" said the voice within. "*The other hand: held out to your Brother.*"

He had once been an upper-habber, with the upper hand... If he extended that hand graciously, he would still keep the upper hand. He imagined himself as an officer, in command of Valence and Tundrish.

"I'm coming back for you," he called. "I'll drag you through the heat."

"*I shall make you superhuman,*" vowed the voice.

Lexandro returned.

First, he hauled Valence. Returning once more, he dragged Tundrish with him. The spirit of Rogal Dorn must indeed have granted him supraphysical strength to wrestle with such weight as well as with his own.

Together, the three hunched in the safe zone.

"Would you be branded?" gasped Lexandro. "Or would you brand *them* with your fists—and your feet and your foreheads? For Trazior *now*, Brothers, eh?"

They staggered together from the tunnel, whimpering with agony...

Abruptly the source of pain vanished. Gravity lightened

so much that the trio almost felt afloat. They prepared to launch themselves at the waiting cordon of brawnier, no longer jeering, senior cadets.

And then they noticed the Marine Sergeant standing in an alcove, out of sight of the tunnel, with a viewscreen aglow beside him. The Sergeant was a meaty slab of a man, of fifty years' service, ruddy-faced as though surfeited with a Marine's haemoglobin-plus blood; and through one Lyman's earlobe he wore an alien foetus pendant.

Rage and vengeance warred with respect.

Biff Tundrish was the first to stiffen to attention, clasp his fist across his bare chest, elevate his arm outward and upward, then crash his arm back again over his twin hearts. Lexandro immediately followed suit; as, a moment later, did Valence.

"You have endured ordeal, Cadets," rumbled the Sergeant. "And I see you have mastered your inner mania. You have also helped purge the hormonal tensions of older cadets in whose bodies the new glands strive to balance. You have achieved the respect of your elders."

Unbelievably, the Sergeant saluted the naked trio.

Yet still, there was to be a branding upon the leather-tough buttocks: an imprint of a clenched fist, no larger than a fingernail. Only, this was indeed to be an honour—for the Sergeant himself personally wielded the electro-iron when Lexandro, Yeremi, and Biff bent over to flex the great gluteal muscles of their rumps.

Did he himself bear such a brand, hidden beneath his uniform?

Had he too once conquered the Tunnel of Terror? He must. He must have. Surely. This was one of the arcane rites of passage of the Chapter.

Only after this rite was completed did one of the elder cadets de-activate the control hoops of the tunnel, liberating the other Necromundans who had gazed wonderingly from their sanctuaries within.

The Sergeant could not but have noted how Lexandro had taken the lead...

From this time onward, a kind of oscillating magnetism seemed ever more to bind the *three brothers* of Trazior, attracting each to one, and one to each, yet also—as well—repelling each in a bizzare negative of friendship.

Chapter Five

Soon, the cadets had Catalepsean Nodes implanted in their brains. No foe should ever sneak up on an exhausted Marine slumbering during prolonged combat. The Node allowed one side of the brain to sleep while the other side stayed aware of the environment.

At the same time a stringent course of hypnotherapy commenced in the Apothacarion. Without this, the Node would remain inert. The enchantments of the Mesmer Adepts, accomplished by incantation and hypno-helmet, served another vital purpose too. As ever more exotic organs and glands entered into a cadet's body, dripping and squeezing their juices and secretions into his system, so the cadet became liable to wild emotional fluctuations. Homicidal rage at abhumans. Pain-freaking algolagnia. Crazy bliss. Umweltschmertz. Void mania. Hypnotherapy helped steer him through these squalls towards the final harmony that he should achieve before the final crowning implant of the Black Carapace.

Hypnotherapy... and drugs, and prayer to Rogal Dorn.

Still, the tensions a-building within a maturing cadet

begged for venting at times. Hence, the type of teasing that the older youths had been permitted to inflict on their juniors in the Tunnel of Terror.

By now, a number of younger recruits had arrived from the savage and melancholy ice-world of Inwit. Within six months, *they* in turn would be ripe for constructive torment by Lexandro's peers.

Next came the grafting in of the Preomnor, the second stomach seated within the chest that would let a Marine eat poisonous victuals, if need be, and nourish himself upon mere roughage.

To celebrate the success of this implant, a feast of foul unfood was held in the banner-decked Assimularum Hall, presided over by Commander Vladimir Pugh himself and the Masters of the Chapter. The cadets, who had fasted for five days, now gorged themselves on toxic fungi from a death world specially grown in the hydro-culture vats, slurped up glutinous soup made from decomposing venom-gland fish, devoured foul cadavers heaped with stenchful excremental sauce, and chewed their way through discarded parchment and leather, while officers, Battle Brothers, and older cadets dined more modestly on fresh fruit and vegetables. After half an hour, if each junior cadet was able to fill a three-litre vessel with vomit, the celebrants cleansed their palates with avocado and mango, eggplants and gloryberries.

Implant of the Omophagea followed, so that a Marine could learn from what he ate, absorbing some memories from the molecules in his meal of beast or sapient enemy. During a further feast, each cadet had to announce some details of the inner nature of his disguised nourishment.

On this occasion, Biff Tundrish arose and shut his eyes tight to concentrate. Those eyes, like two green beetles which a squirming tattooed spider had now digested...

"I have four nimble legs," he announced, an eerie whinny in his voice—and Lexandro almost sniggered. Four nimble legs on either side, perhaps? Had they stewed up a supper of some giant arachnid for Tundrish? But no, for the ex-scumnik continued: "I yearn to run across wide grasslands with a rider on my back, my tail pluming in the wind. Yet I am so little and I live behind hard iron bars, eating synthoats..."

"That creature is known as a *horse*," confirmed the Chef Adept, consulting his annotated menu codex. "In this case it is a dwarf specimen, cage-bred for succulence. It dreams its genetic past."

Yeremi Valence reported that his meal had swum in foetid swamps beneath a blue sun. Its many teeth were sharp; so was its appetite. Its tail was long and armoured. Its thoughts were red with blood.

Lexandro rose and shut his eyes.

"I run..." Mist swirled in his mind, a wraith taking shape within the viscous haze, reflecting and congealing his image of that other self within himself. "On two legs I run. My belly is swollen and my... breasts are full." *Could he be wrong? Could he be mistaken?* "My loins are... featureless. My skin is a tattooed map of the secrets known to serpents concerning the invisible world... The serpent god came to me in sleep and filled my belly." Lexandro strained to grasp the memories. "The priestess must be caught and cut, to remove the godling for sacrifice... Yet faceless demons whose hands spit fire have killed my holy hunters..."

"Enough," said the Gastronomus. "You have eaten the liver of a feral tribeswoman from a death world." He clicked his heels and bowed to Lexandro briefly, though ceremoniously. "Always, there is one savage human included in this feast. One day you may need to eat an organ of your enemy in order to interrogate him or her, especially if that enemy is alien."

Next, came the implant of the Multi-lung. Then the

Occulobe, to sharpen eyesight and give night vision. Then Lyman's Ears replaced the cadets' ordinary lugs, which were sliced away and quarried out...

And all the while, as it had for aeons and always would, the giant battle-monastery flew onward through the lonely void, towards nowhere at all.

When the signal for launching crusade finally did come to the Fists' astropaths, Battle Brothers would depart in warships from the jutting sword-deck—to return, perhaps years later in realspace time, as heroes... and some as cripples needing reconstruction by the experts in the Apothacarion... and others as honoured corpses, or perhaps only in the form of retrieved progenoid glands from which new Marines would be kindled.

Meantime, the Brothers exercised, recited litanies, incanted the familiar battle-prayers, meditated, now and then duelled, tested themselves upon algometric pain-meters... and in spare time they scrimshandered the bones of the dead.

Those Brothers who honed their souls aboard the fortress-monastery were by no means the only Imperial Fists. Lesser expeditions departed by warship; and returned. Periodically the Fists would assist a planetary governor to put down a troublesome insurrection. Or a great space hulk might be reported drifting in the void or in the warp, harbouring suspected pirates or, worse, those fierce cunning invasive Genestealers which could infest a human world just as termites infest a house—so that it seems to remain firm timber until it crumbles apart. Several squads or whole companies of the Chapter would quest for lost worlds and for planets posing a potential menace to the Imperium, as well as for any alien redoubts within imperial spheres of influence, so as to sterilise those.

Came the day when the cadets were all summoned to witness the disembarking of one such home-bound expedition, returning victorious, though somewhat mauled.

Warriors in full armour paraded in the colossal hangar, its walls plated with slabs of heat-resistant mica. Several other cruisers squatted dourly like giant hibernating tortoises. Fluted green columns of synthetic electro-generative tourmaline supported a black groined vault from which servicing machines hung down like great roosting mutant bats. Floodlighting reflected from the silvery burnt umber cladding of the walls as though ice-ghosts danced there, and set the green columns aglow.

Those returning Marines crashed their arms across their spreadeagle-painted chest plastrons, saluting Lord Pugh who stood up on a high balcony of traceried wrought tungsten.

Such armour theirs was! Pus-hued, and azure-chevroned. Fanged skulls with potent crosses adorned the knee joints of these warriors' armour. Yet aside from squad markings there were many individualistic touches too. Campaign badges and honour markings, yes, those of course, on the greaves protecting their right shanks—in many cases quartered and augmented with extra honours. Yes, those. But in some instances Artificers of genius had left their mark upon the armour—ten years earlier, or a hundred, or a thousand. Repairs to the thigh-cuisses and groin-hauberks had been plated with damascened silver and gold engravings of the deeds of Rogal Dorn.

Bareheaded, kitted in their lighter padded armour, three squads of Marine Scouts also hailed the elevated figure of Commander Pugh—who would be no distant eminence once the crusade was launched, but would lead from the vanguard...

Nevertheless, not everyone's armour was pristine. Parts had been seared by blistering heat, or buckled by terrible impact. And even in the midst of ceremony, orderlies were already evacuating some severe casualties under the direction of a Frater Medicus. A few caskets were carried from the docked ship, each bearing upon it a stasis box wrapped in a yellow banner embroidered with fanged skulls, protecting the precious Progenoid organs. Were the corpses' hands honourably amputated *during* the funeral rites—or later, after the flesh had decayed? Lexandro had no idea.

And a moment later any extraneous thoughts were driven from his mind—for he saw his first alien prisoner: a mottled green froglike biped of lustrous hue, being frogmarched in chains.

An itch of fascination at this utterly different, aberrant creature twisted within Lexandro, into rage—at the sly, inhuman intelligence which must have been responsible for the loss of those brave champions of Humanity who now lay lifeless in caskets.

"That one's a Slann mage chief," mused a nearby Brother.

An armoured Marine began to hustle the unclad fettered alien away—no doubt to the diamantine dungeons deep beneath the Apothacarion, domain of the surgeon interrogators. "Once puissant—but no longer," the Brother added thoughtfully.

Lexandro could feel no such composure. His pulse quickened. Both of his hearts raced. He flushed hotly. He ground his teeth together, lusting to tear the alien apart and eat of its lurid vitals, so as to comprehend something of its strange nature. A hormonal seizure was upon him, triggered by sight of the bare green flesh of that alien foe of Humankind, whom he was most unlikely ever to see again. He prayed to Rogal Dorn to restore his equilibrium.

Biff Tundrish seemed similarly affected. Tundrish clenched and unclenched his fists, causing the bones to crackle. He reached up to his skull as if to seize the beads which had once adorned his scalp, though those had long since been shorn off along with his excess of black greasy hair; as if to tug those and release an inner pressure.

And Yeremi Valence? The runes on his cheeks had

whitened.

Lexandro sensed homicidal—*xenocidal*—pheromones upon the air.

Another cadet—freckled Hake Bjortson—totally lost his composure. Howling a fervent execrating battlecry, Bjortson broke from the pack of cadets and sprinted towards the alien prisoner. His fingers clawed at the air, his eyes bulged, spittle sprayed from his lips. No command could halt him. Several of the other cadets moved forward inadvertently, as if sucked in Bjortson's wake.

A Medic plucked out a needle-pistol and fired with splendid accuracy at Bjortson's muscle-corded neck. A moment later the frenzied cadet pitched forward and skidded prostrate for many metres, his strengthened fingernails scratching sparks from the plates of the deck before he came to rest. His musculature still spasmed for a while. Briefly the Slann mage chief goggled in Bjortson's direction with a bitter doomed melancholy.

"Cadets!" bellowed the Medic. "Double out of here to your cells, and pray!"

At the end of the first hour of prayer the Sergeant who had branded Lexandro—Sergeant Zed Juron—summoned him and Valence and Tundrish and another cadet, Omar Akbar, the number that would make a squad of Scouts, in fact. They proceeded at the double along plasteel-ribbed corridors in the direction of the Foundries; and after descending several levels by drop-shaft arrived presently at a fan-vaulted vestibule where power swords, power axes, and other weapons hung.

A stained-glass gallery overhung a cavernous environment-chamber where vine-tangled trees surrounded a meadow of viridian herbage under a sun-globe. Smoke snaked up from a campfire amidst crudely plastered and thatched huts. A dozen men and women clad in furs were polishing axes and broadswords monotonously, mindlessly.

Obscene daemonic tattoos decorated the features of these corrupted primitives.

"You will enter," ordered Sergeant Juron, "and cleanse this chamber." He gestured to lockers where rudimentary padded armour hung—not quite a Scout's attire.

As Lexandro donned a cuirass and strapped greaves to his shanks, he wondered whether their soon-to-be opponents were genuinely members of some feral tribe transported here for purposes such as this? Or were they mind-slaved prisoners captured during the suppression of some planetary revolt, and sentenced to serve the Imperium usefully by their deaths? Or were they zombie bodies, specially bred and conditioned, and thus essentially unhuman?

No doubt his fellow cadets were wondering similarly.

The Sergeant did not say; nor would anyone presume to ask, uninvited.

The tribespeople, if such they were, fought savagely, automatically, instinctively, screaming incomprehensible blasphemies. They outnumbered the cadets by three to one. However, an ordinary axe was no match for a humming power axe which could slice bronze like flesh; nor was a broadsword remotely the equal of a power sword. Nor indeed were many unmodified humans nearly as robust as the cadets had long since become.

Presently the four cadets stood surveying severed limbs, cloven torsos, decapitated heads, guts, and blood.

The hormonal tensions had flowed out of Lexandro, earthed through his power sword into the bodies. Calm balmed him: a sense of peace which he knew would encompass him on a return from a devout, loyal, and sensible killing in the future.

With their armour somewhat stained, they returned to discard it and restore their weapons. In the gallery Sergeant Juron stood by with a neuro-disruptor till they had cleaned and cradled those blades. Then he spoke to the four.

"You have been foxes in a chicken coop." They stared at his red face blankly. "You have been feral dogs in a cage of rats." They nodded now. "You are no doubt successfully purged—as will your fellows soon be. But are you not ashamed of your lack of control and grace? You, Cadet d'Arquebus, what do you say?"

"Sir, this cadet believes he has indeed experienced the grace of the Venerable Dorn, Sir."

The Sergeant scrutinised him.

"During your first combat mission, Cadet, you will learn the ineffable difference; as I learned it during mine. Which was on your own world, in the action against the Ork pirates."

Never before had a Brother confided such a personal detail. Lexandro flushed again, this time with a peculiar joy, and amazement. "But Sir, that was three hundred years ago!" This slab of a man still looked to be in his full prime.

The Sergeant smiled. "And a Marine can live longer than most ordinary men, as you should know. Indeed it is his duty on the one hand to die—yet on the other hand to live as long as he can, compatible with Chapter honour. For we are not rabid dogs, of which the galaxy is full enough, but sacred knights whose deeds the Emperor overwatches...

"Besides, our journeys through warpspace stretch time like an unpredictable elastic. So yes, I was there throughout the desert march and at the storming of the hive now called the Skull."

The reminiscent smile vanished.

"Unfortunately, the Cadet spoke to the Sergeant without being invited. Two minutes in the nerve-glove, d'Arquebus. All cadets to witness punishment. Thou shalt learn self-control."

Lexandro stiffened to full attention. Rogal Dorn's grace *would* be with him. The "feral dog" would be redeemed for its lack of inner discipline. Drugs and hypnosis were all very well as tools for coping with the hormonal storms caused by the superhuman organs his body housed; but what he must attain swiftly was a superhuman mind which could command the body to fight on irrespective of injury. Then he would be a real Marine, and one day—he assured himself—an officer of Marines, maybe even (could he dream so sublimely?) a Commander.

So he welcomed his punishment.

How far he had come from the silks and blissful hedonic acid and joyspike of the upper habs of Trazior.

And so, some hours later in the Punitor Chapel, Lexandro was immersed in the ocean of pain once more—as were two other cadets, who had offended subsequent to their own detoxification through bloodshed. Those two screamed— but they were well able to walk to the refectory afterwards, and eat. Lexandro did not scream, though—not outwardly. He endured, moltenly striving to remake himself.

Neither of those two others had been Hake Bjortson. Indeed his fellows were not to see that cadet again. Bjortson's instability had proved too extreme, so the group was informed before Servitors distributed their victuals. He had been honourably mindwiped; his body would be dedicated to research.

After the prayer that ended their silent repast that evening, the cadets were filing out of the refectory to return to their barren cells.

"Beware," Biff Tundrish said to a glowing Lexandro. "You're in danger of becoming a flagellant."

"And what might that be?" Lexandro asked loftily.

"Someone who scourges himself excessively."

"Ah! So you've been educating yourself again."

Tundrish ignored this jibe. "Such a person is psychotic. He would not become an officer of our Chapter. I've seen how you dote on officers."

"You're trying to befuddle me. Undermine me."
Lexandro laughed lightly. "Is not much of the universe
psychotic, so we hear?"

"And so we must be sane. You came from luxury,
d'Arquebus. I came from the very opposite. I do not
romanticise agony as a virtue, nor imagine that it makes me
superior. Be warned."

"How kind of you to concern yourself."

"*I* wouldn't want a flagellant on my flank in combat."

Lexandro stared at the spider-tattoo which was leering at
him, and experienced a flash of *déjà vu*—a piercing
memory of Tundrish in the undercity, unmasking him.

"Rogal Dorn has blessed you with wisdom," Lexandro
said airily, knowing full well that Tundrish spent much
more time in the scriptories than praying in cell or chapel.

"He has been with me too, Brother," Tundrish replied
simply.

"He isn't your private patron saint. He manifests himself
to each of us uniquely."

"To me too," said Yeremi Valence, sidling close as they
proceeded along the grey, gargoyle-ventilated corridor past
rows of sconces bearing scrimshaws mounted in silver
reliquaries. "Why, he was with me when I brought *order* to
that chamber of savages." Was there a tremor in Valence's
voice?

"In the same way that you hoped to impose order on the
undercity?" asked Tundrish sarcastically.

"No," replied Valence. "The savages were doing
nothing to disturb us. If they were truly savages. That I
should simply destroy them arbitrarily... and, yes,
willingly, enthralled by slaughter..." Again, his voice
faltered. "His Will is strange."

"Look, Valence," said Tundrish, apparently sympathet-
ic now. "Death is the Boss—of this galaxy, of a million
human-settled worlds. You obey the Boss. That way,
Humanity survives as a whole against terrible odds. Far

worse than death is disorder, the tool of Chaos.''

Valence shuddered at the mention of Chaos. In his sermons the Chaplain of Cadets had only hinted at the existence of terrible ultimate anti-Gods which stalked the warp, seeking to spill through into the cosmos to corrupt precious reality—the antithesis of all that the Emperor stood for; forces which Marines should pray that they never encountered. *Never. Ever.*

The Chaplain had only delivered veiled hints as to the nature of this "Chaos", which special psychic personnel were equipped to expunge: the Inquisition... Librarians... the legendary Grey Knights... Sufficient unto the hour was the ordinary evil thereof.

Lexandro was instantly alert.

"Have you by any chance stumbled upon *classified* data during your delvings in the Scriptory?" he drawled. "That surely verges on the crime of heresy."

Did Tundrish seem discomfited? Did he seek to change the subject?

"A Marine is worth ten ordinary soldiers, Valence," Tundrish quickly continued. "He is worth a hundred workaday mortals. That was the meaning of our lesson today. Let us be worthy of that lesson, and not flinch at deaths which are needful to protect a thousand billion other mortals. For we may seem to be many here, but we are few. There are a million human worlds, untold millions of alien planets—and only a million Marines amongst all our Chapters. As I have learned in the Scriptory, studying the Index Astartes, as a Marine should."

What did such numbers mean? They were meaningless. Lexandro chuckled. Marines as a mass were invincible. "I still suspect you of deviancy, Tundrish."

"And I suspect you of perversity," Tundrish replied.

"You're both so *alien* to what we seek to protect," protested Valence.

"I think *superhuman* is the word you're seeking," said

Tundrish. "Yet ah, without Him on Earth, and without the heritage of our Primarch, what would we be?"

"We'd be murderers," whispered Valence. "Sanctified murderers."

"Now that *is* high heresy," said Lexandro.

"No, it's squeamishness," sneered Tundrish.

"There must," said Valence, "be an ultimate justice—beyond this savage galaxy. *Wherein*, I assure you, I shall be as steadfast as any, in quest of that truth. And as ruthless, and as clever. There must be justice."

The three sons of Trazior went their separate ways to their cells, each thinking their separate thoughts.

Chapter Six

The cadets received their melachromic organ, which henceforth would monitor radiations bombarding their skin and darken it protectively.

Then, during a single operation, the surgeons of the Apothacarion implanted the Oolitic Kidney and the Neuroglottis. In concert with their second heart, this kidney could perform high-speed detoxification, while the Neuroglottis honed the sense of taste, specifically with regard to poisons—a fitting partner for the Preomnor and the Omophagea. Progressively the cadets were approaching the transhuman condition of Rogal Dorn, though they would never equal their Primarch.

"And *after* the Venerable Dorn had rescued the mutilated, charred living corpse of the Emperor in the wake of that direst of victories against the renegade Horus," declaimed moon-faced combat-Chaplain Lo Chang in chapel; "and after he had overseen the construction of the Golden Throne, guided by the Emperor's mighty spirit as He lay in life-support; and after Rogal Dorn had witnessed the transfer of that unquenchable divine husk into the Great Psychoprosthetic Throne, lo, *afterwards* our Primarch lived for another four hundred and thirteen years..."

The Chaplain's face was as round as a moon. A sweat of devout ecstasy beaded it, the moist sheen reflecting the light of the many electrocandles—moonlike and radiantly, so it seemed to his congregation. Like a moon, too, his cheeks were cratered where his helmet had been riven during some fierce engagement, and those craters were scarred by subsequent duelling nicks.

"And the Deeds of Rogal Dorn thereafter compose an entire hagiography, which we will now start to consider in detail—commencing with our Primarch's role in the expulsion of the renegade Iron Warriors from the Human Imperium into the forbidden zone known as the Eye of Terror, a region about which we speak softly if at all..."

Such history...

History layered upon history in almost geological strata, within the levels of which were preserved corpse upon corpse upon corpse—so that the upheaving rockface of history seemed a veritable conglomerate of compressed cadavers, human, abhuman, and alien, a cosmos-spanning coral reef composed of innumerable crushed skeletons...

Presently came the implant of the Mucranoid, which would—if suitably drug-triggered—secrete oily protective sweat that could resist searing heat and bitter cold.

Eventually, during a sacred ceremony in the Apothacarion, the cadets received the Progenoid glands in their necks and deep in their chests. Henceforth they were true custodians of the Imperial Fists' greatest treasure. From now on, their bodies were temples indeed.

Almost five years had passed since their arrival at the home-base. Necromunda seemed almost as remote as childhood. How long ago it seemed since Sergeant Huzzi Rork had told Lexandro that he *might* return home again in twenty years, in thirty years, if the Fists so wished. *Home? Home? What did that mean?* Whilst Necromunda could not conceivably have changed, it would nevertheless seem as alien as any of the worlds that they might visit in the interim.

The Crusade was still awaiting the Emperor's will. The Imperium thought in terms of decades, even centuries. Yet by now Battle Brothers were as mastiffs straining on the leash; and it began to seem that the cadets might become Scouts in time to participate in the great endeavour, should they be so fortunate.

The ultimate implant remained; and one day Lexandro was opened up surgically—superficially and for the final time—to insert the sheets of black tissue beneath his skin.

Within hours, while he itched and writhed, the tissue was beginning to expand within him, hardening externally, invading his nervous system with internal tendrils.

It would be many more months till the carapace matured into full symbiotic harmony with his body—and of course his spirit must be tested and tempered in combat before sockets would be cut into the carapace, whereby he could plug himself into power armour in a full fusion of man and equipment. Yet already he was cadet no more. Now he could be initiated one vital stage further into the cult of Dorn.

Within days—after a feast of raw, bloody meat, still warm from slaughter—the Brother Reclusiarch, custodian of the cult, led the ex-cadets in solemn procession into the looming vaulted trophy-hung hall of the Assimularum. Skulls of aliens adorned the banner-hung, tapestried walls, their eyeless sockets forever blinded to the mysteries of those who had mastered them, their hollow craniums empty of even the ghost of a twisted, unhuman thought.

The great ancient enamelled screen emblazoned with the Fists' defence of the Imperial Palace against armoured Rebel Titans had been moved aside, to reveal the

Ian Watson

Reclusiam itself. Many Brothers stood within in meditative attendance beneath pieces of the actual glorious armour of the Primarch, guarded there for millennia.

For the first time the new initiates beheld the inner chapel, of cloudy veined marble, to the Emperor Deified— vermilion threads in the milky crystalline limestone were like His agonised psychic sendings that pierced the veils of luminous nebulae.

Directly opposite was the inner chapel to Rogal Dorn, crafted of blocks of compressed sulphurous amber divided by striations of lapis lazuli—and housing the Fists' holiest relic: the mighty skeleton, embedded in clear amber contoured to body-form, of the Primarch himself.

The initiates all kneeled, staring at those great bones within that jaundiced false-fossil resinous flesh. At a signal from the Reclusiarch the lights dimmed, all but one bright narrow shaft descending aslant from a hole in the centre of the stellar vault as though it were liquid starlight. The beam illuminated an altar carved from a block of solid jade, where a knife and a whisk and a chalice were laid upon cloth of gold. From behind that altar the Reclusiarch lifted an oval convex mirror, framed by the spinal column of some alien bent into a hoop around it, the knobbly vertebrae enchased with potent runes. Intoning a liturgy, he tilted that silvered glass so that reflected light sprang at the skeleton, bathing it. The amber promptly fluoresced—a bilious olive hue, so that the mock-flesh appeared alive again, though gangrenous. The Primarch's dead limbs were momentarily restored, all be it clad in a semblance of translucent rotting tissue. Complete, except in one respect...

"*Mani manent cum nostris semper in aeternum, Primarche!*" the Reclusiarch chanted in the hieratic religious tongue, which his listeners only comprehended to be a blend of sacred plainsong and occult invocation. "*Interficere est orare, Primarche!*"

Then he turned and translated into Imperial Gothic:

"Thy hands remain with us always, Primarch. To slay is to pray."

The Primarch's hands were missing...

As soon as the Reclusiarch moved to restore the mirror to its hook, the fluorescence of the amber faded. Now he lifted the whisk and moved to flick the stiff little brush with swift, sure gestures over the casing of the demi-divine dead paladin, commencing at his massive shoulders, descending reverently to his feet, almost as if dusting him—yet with quite a different consequence. For the shorn hairs on the head of every initiate, and on any other hirsute parts of their bodies, prickled and stood on end, as though an electrifying ghost briefly shared their body-space with them.

Restoring the brush to the altar, the Reclusiarch lifted the sharp little knife and the chalice. He knelt before Dorn and held up the knife.

The Primarch's hands were both missing...

Genuflecting, the Reclusiarch carved generous parings of amber from one toe, then another, dropping these into the chalice. Rising, he turned to the initiates and raised that cup, now glowing. Effervescence was occuring within. Aromatic white fumes arose from bubbling oil of amber.

"*Respire corpus memoria!* Breathe the memory of my flesh!"

As he bore the hot chalice along the row of initiates, so each in turn inhaled a heady, strangely fragrant whiff. Fresh molten amber *must* be added subsequently to the shaved toes to replenish what was taken—unless, unless the amber grew of its own accord like veritable flesh due to the miraculous proximity of those bones.

When the Reclusiarch passed back again, each initiate must hold out his middle finger, pointing stiffly forward from his fist. That little knife slashed sharply, circumcising the very tip of the digit, and even before the Larramen cells could clot—or perhaps because the blade was treated with some special anti-coagulant—a sprinkling of bright blood fell like rubies from each fingertip to mingle in the chalice.

Lifting the chalice to his lips, the Reclusiarch drank the potion of hot amber oil blent with blood.

"*Ego vos initio in Pugnorum Imperialorum fraternitate, in secundo grado,*" he sang out. "And after you return from your first expedition as Scouts," he promised, "other secretions from your body will be blent in this same chalice of the Primarch—which was once His very drinking cup!—during your induction into the third degree of Brotherhood; though that in itself will only be the *superficies* of the third degree ceremony..."

The lights brightened.

Where were the Primarch's hands...?

Upon the marble wall to each side of the altar were mounted two sizable ormolu shrines, the double doors of which depicted ancient, angular types of Marine armour.

The Reclusiarch threw one set of doors open, then the other.

In transparent stasis-cases within, with magnilenses inset, hung Rogal Dorn's fleshless fists, entire, scrimshandered with intricately wrought tiny miniatures of heraldic honours.

"It is the privilege of the Commander of our chapter alone to inscribe his heraldry as *minutely* as he can upon these sacred bones," declared the Reclusiarch.

Even so, much of the available surface area of each bone was etched.

Thousands of years of commanders, thousands of years of tradition...

What a chasm of time—and duty.

Space yet remained on Dorn's hands for a future Lord Commander Lexandro d'Arquebus to add his own future heraldry...

The Reclusiarch anointed each initiate with chrism, the sacred ointment, on the brow. Then he began to recite a litany of the individual bones and of the past Commanders who had held this fortress-monastery for the Emperor.

"Whenever you flex your fingers, think of these! Whenever you ball your fist around your weapon, these names are all wrapped in your fist to add the strength of adamantium to your blow, the power of all the Sons of Dorn! Hand Sinister, first metacarpal: the Lords Bronwin Abermort, Maximus Thane, Kalman Flodensbog. Proximal phalanx of thumb: Ambrosian Spactor..."

The litany droned on hypnotically.

Perhaps the strangest talisman—and one (or should one say *many*...?) which made those initiates feel themselves intimately a part of the Fists—was kept in a long crypt below the Reclusiam, reached by a dropshaft which would incinerate anyone who did not sport a Black Carapace beneath their skin.

The adamantium floor down there was inscribed with a maze of tiny coloured channels that bootsteps would never be able to wear away—in a pattern suggestive of a cosmic map—and along all of those channels were spaced little indentations the depth of a Fist's thumbprint, each recess named with a rune. At one end of this seemingly arcane map or game-board an enormous plascrystal bowl held thousands of what at first sight appeared to be bloodshot ochreous eyeballs.

Each ball commemorated the initiation of a group of ex-cadets, throughout the aeons—each being a nugget of the liquid amber and blood drunk from Rogal Dorn's own chalice by the Reclusiarch of whichever epoch, and defecated by him subsequently in this shape.

At the opposite end of the graven floor, a second mighty bowl held darker balls, composed no doubt of the bodily secretions of the third degree likewise embalmed in amber.

What sacred game was played out on this floor? What arcane divinations were performed here? What horoscopy or even psychic sorcery *in extremis* might be enacted in this crypt? The initiates already realized that here were secrets unutterable outside the confines of the Reclusiam—innermost secrets which they themselves might wish never to know.

In the most organic, visceral way possible they now felt bonded with utter intimacy to their Chapter, digested by it.

As a pleasant coda to that solemn and eerie initiation, they were invited to witness a duel...

Two Battle Brothers, who had previously fasted in the Solitorium, confronted one another in the Arena Restricta, a barrel-vaulted hall painted a rich deep Prussian blue chevroned with stylized blood-red lightning flashes. The floor was a metal chequerboard of those two hues. On a red square, and on a blue, still some distance apart, stood two pairs of black leather knee-boots mounted in gleaming steel blocks. Around the walls on hooks hung antique épées, foils, sabres, and daggers, as well as stone drinking steins decorated with double-headed eagles, fylfots, and tusked boars' heads.

A score of Brother witnesses sat on elevated thrones quaffing from other such steins, brought by Servitors. The soon-to-be Scouts sat on high benches, and were likewise served a bitter foaming brew, the potency of which their Preomnor stomach should swiftly detoxify. A cloaked umpire, helmeted for impartial anonymity, sat by a notator machine in the design of a giant vampire bat's head with glowing red eyes; its ear-aerials wove an ultrasonic web recording every movement within the central arena.

Lexandro toasted Valence and Tundrish, sitting to his left.

"Do you remember the zestfulness of Chartreuse Julep, iced and minted?" The intoxicant had stirred a memory.

"Of course not," retorted Valence. "How should I? Does this remind you of some long-lost *luxury*?"

Tundrish said slyly, "Maybe he imagines that if he becomes an officer, he will regain his old privileges. Yet Lord Pugh despises sensual gratification so much, I hear, he had his taste buds excised. His every feast is also a fast for his senses."

Valence nodded, as if in conspiracy with Tundrish. "That was a private penance—because a hundred and seventy Marines were lost in one terrible action, and because the Emperor cannot taste or smell or touch."

"I do rather wonder about that," drawled Lexandro. "If it's private, how do people know? Legends have a habit of springing up." Was he light-headed, despite his second stomach, after several years of abstinence? Was the old sardonic Lexandro reasserting himself during this lull of relaxation? Was a perverse sense of jovial community with his two Trazior cousins affecting him? Was he perhaps viewing them hallucinatorily as fellow Lordly Phantasms about to behold a fight between mind-slaves, between living puppets operated by the spectators?

"Beware of *blasphemy*," Valence advised barbedly— exactly as Lexandro had once advised him.

Of a sudden Lexandro's free hand gripped Valence's wrist with a power which would have crushed any ordinary bones. *Had Lexandro realized his error? How had he misidentified Tundrish and Valence for a moment?* The light of Dorn shone in his eyes.

"*Never accuse me of blasphemy, even as a jest!* A Fist must be accurate. Scrupulously accurate. That was the reason for my remark. And as to my previous remark, I was merely attempting *familiarity*. As a courtesy. Alas, what a waste of time."

"A waste of time, of course," said Valence. "Since clearly you are inherently superior. But now, would you kindly remove your hand from mine?"

Lexandro snatched his hand away—as though he had not even known that he had gripped his neighbour.

"Or else," chipped in Tundrish, "you're liable to provoke duels for the wrong reasons."

Lexandro stared intensely, almost blindly, at Tundrish. This was the gaze of someone staring past any human being whatever, at some imaginary blazing sun beyond. "I am with Dorn," he murmured. Two hearts were in his body now. Were there also two separate *minds* within him? An old upper-hab mind, lurking in hiding behind the new Fist mind? As though hypnotised, paralysed—for the most part—yet still impishly unregenerate... and nostalgic, even?

"So will you too become a legend?" Tilting his stein dismissively, Tundrish tipped out some brew as a derisive libation. A Servitor hastily scuttled to wipe up the spillage.

Lexandro said nothing. He gazed at an ineffable, agonizing radiance which only he could perceive, banishing whatever throwback emotions the brew had triggered. Then he switched his attention to the impending duel.

Two Brothers had mounted those duelling blocks, stepping into those boots encased in heavy steel. Stripped to the waist, the contours of their musculature were faintly graven with decades-old surgical scars. Ever so faintly. Indeed, only Occulobe-enhanced eyesight could perceive such traces of the medical sculpting which had once made them Marines, as if the thinnest of pink veins wended across their bulging rock-hard melanchromic flesh, like a tracery in some golden marble which could become ochre-brown, which could become jet-black. Protective monocles were squeezed into the orbits of the combatants' eyes.

They saluted the cloaked umpire with their thin tungsten épées; then one another. The umpire invoked and activated some instruments attached to the notator machine, then the steel blocks glided forward to within two squares of one another—épée range—and locked magnetically to the floor. One square's separation would have been dagger range.

Superficially it might have appeared as though two brawny giants, immobilised but for the sway of their torsos, were about to jab and slash at one another, piercing and flaying till the vampire bat device decided that sufficient flesh had been sliced, that sufficient blood had coagulated in slim cinnabar threads.

Not so. Sublime grace and accuracy, a ballet of two blades almost dancing together in an aerial *pas de deux* was the aesthetic of the duel—for a minute, two minutes, three, till a single quicksilver cheek wound decided the contest.

The Brothers saluted each other.

"I apologise for my opinion," announced the loser formally. "You grace me with your mark of honour. I thank you. I'm in your debt."

"Nay," said the victor courteously, "but I am in yours."

Released, they stepped from the duelling blocks. Servitors hurried to them bearing great foaming stone steins—one red, one black—to drink in one draught, then smash together into shards.

The umpire stepped forward to scrutinise the pattern of the fallen pieces, to divine how well these two Brothers had knitted their relationship.

Some weeks later, the tocsin bell rang out throughout the fortress-monastery. With joy in their hearts, all Brothers paused wherever they were to recite an angelus of annihilation aimed at the Emperor's enemies. Lexandro almost wept.

For yes, oh yes: the first mission of the new Marine Scouts would indeed now inevitably be in support of a major campaign of full Crusade status...

Part Two

The Karkason Crusade

Chapter Seven

In the ruddily-lit belly of the drop-ship, Yeremi clung to one of the serpentine wall grips as the vessel vibrated. Its hull wailed and its engine whined as the upper atmosphere of Karkason roughly and frustratedly caressed this plasteel intruder which was penetrating it. The world's airy hands were burning with friction. Within that frigate were seeds of destruction that would soon burst forth.

Yeremi's fellow Scouts held tight, yelling loud prayers to Rogal Dorn, to the approval of their Sergeants. The howl of atmospheric entry almost drowned their voices.

"Primarch, Progenitor, oil our coming upon this planet of peril –

"Then let that oil blaze –

"That we may swiftly pierce all defences, as our commanders have conceived we shall –

"That we may abort all evil –

"To Your Glory, and the Glory of Him on Earth..."

"And for the sake of the greater justice," Yeremi murmured to himself as a personal amen.

"Yazoooo!" one of the Scouts from Quinspirus cried in

84

his hive patois, courteous and reverend speech forgotten in the heat of the moment, and Imperial Gothic neglected. His head was shaven but for a topknot. Baring black-stained teeth, he ululated, *"Zooyaaaa-yaa-yaa!"* The rising screech from cleaving gases outside almost drowned this battlecry.

"Yaa-yaa-yaa," chorused some other Quinspirites.

Two squads of Fists in full battle armour crowded the fore of the compartment, standing rigidly, gripping their boltguns and chainswords, the magnetics of their boots locking them to the cleated deck. They would exit under cover of darkness at one of numerous drop-zones fifty kilometres from the vast sprawl of Sagramaso City. Then the ship would jink even closer in to a prosperous hilly suburb, if possible, to offload the terror Scouts.

The Sergeants who would supervise the Scouts were wearing hybrid body armour of eagle plastrons, flexible leggings, and great shoulder plates embossed with jewelled axes, but no helmets—for the more lightly armoured Scouts wore no covering to their heads, either.

Still muttering the word *justice*, Yeremi gazed at the quatrefoil viewscreen. One segment showed a whale-like troop carrier descending towards the world below, carrying one of the regiments of Imperial Guards which had been ordered to attend this conflict, years since in realtime.

Another segment displayed the night side of planet Karkason: a swell of blackness pricked with intermittent little red pimples which were the mouths of its active volcanos—those, at least, which were not currently cloaked by smoke...

In a third segment, blurred by magnification, loomed the coaly bulge of the capital city from which searing threads of light lanced skywards, a shifting vertical mesh of beams issuing from the ground defence lasers. Even as Yeremi watched, an incoming diversionary frigate flared and disintegrated...

The fourth section of the screen was scanning a wrecked enemy orbital battle station that was tumbling slowly end over end, locked together with the ruptured cruiser which had finally rammed it to neutralise it. Debris and tiny bodies circled like a halo of scurf, brightening periodically as those metal shards and corpses tilted to catch the sunlight of space...

Another sacrifice frigate erupted into a gorgeous, noble orange fireball over the city.

"Seven minutes to Drop-zone." The pilot's emotionless voice issued from a brass loudspeaker wrought in the shape of a snake's gaping, fanged mouth. By now the bucking roar of entry had subsided into a sibilant trembling caress imperceptible against the engine throb except to possessors of Lyman's Ears. "Prepare to adjust to planetary gravity. Artificial gravity *off* in five seconds. *Off.*"

The floor tilted forwards, and Yeremi felt heavier.

"Right," snapped Sergeant Juron. "Wolverine Squad: why are we here on Karkason?"

"To skrag," said Tundrish before Yeremi could frame an answer, grinning with those sharpened teeth of his. "To mega-skrag." And indeed that reply was accurate enough, as regards the Scouts. Had the ex-scumnik's laboriously acquired veneer rubbed away, though, at the prospect of mayhem?

That crazy snob d'Arquebus curled his lip at such a response. "We're here because Lord Sagramoso is a damned heretic against the Emperor, stirring up other heretics."

"An infidel," agreed swarthy Omar Akbar, he whose cheeks were branded with curious symmetrical runes. "The Emperor is great." Akbar was from a desert land-train clan.

"And you, Valence, what do you think?"

"We're here to restore true universal law," said Yeremi. "But also... Karkason is a source of the best power crystals used in battle armour."

D'Arquebus chuckled. "Spoken like a true practical tech. One with a cosmic mission, too. You'll protect us from our own excesses down there, won't you?"

"Jus' don' try to spoil the fun," said Tundrish, slipping into argot.

Juron glanced at those two contentious spirits. Now that the ex-cadets were initiated Scouts, they could speak out of their own accord. Yet even so...

"I thought you three from Trazior were like Siamese triplets joined at the hearts," the Sergeant said. "Hauling each other from the Tunnel of Terror as you did..."

"Yeah," said Tundrish, "but our blood's poison to each other. Sort of *addictive* poison, though!"

Juron frowned. "I can visualize you three duelling many times till you inoculate yourselves against any trace of enmity."

D'Arquebus smiled ethereally. "Oh, I do not see *us* duelling... ever." Which part of him was saying so? The mystic devotee of Dorn? Or the residual high-hab swanker?

"All your answers are correct," said Juron, "and *yours*," he told Yeremi, "is strategically perceptive. But," and he nodded at Tundrish, "your reply best describes what our Scout squads must do now: help restore true law through wanton terrorism. The more inventive, the better. You few must seem to be many."

"*One minute to drop-zone. Fists: prepare.*" The vessel shook and rocked. Was it drawing fire?

The aim of this crusade was not to devastate, as such. Not as the prime objective, though that might well be a consequence. The desired result was the obliteration *ad extremum fetum*, down to the last foetus, of the entire entrenched Sagramaso clan, hereditary rulers of Karkason.

Karkason was—or had been—a sooty jewel in the Imperium. From certain of its volcanos poured rivers of lava rich in transuranic elements including psycurium, invaluable in the crafting of psychic hoods and force swords such as Marine Librarians could use. During other eruptions, power crystals forged in the deep magma were scattered far and wide across the lava plains, sometimes killing the harvesters. Many of those plains were made of purest vitrodur, the inky armour-glass from which vast Sagramoso City—the "black chandelier of the Imperium"—was largely carved.

Lord Sagramoso's writ had run to the other barren planets of Karka's Sun, and to those of its runtish red dwarf binary twin, Karka Secundus, including some small mining world in orbit around the twin.

In the effervescence of his accession as His Lordship thirty years earlier, Fulgor Sagramoso had declared himself to be an independent sovereign ruler and a god. He was prepared to conclude a trade pact with the Imperium on his own terms, a treaty of one god with another. To prove his divinity he had the praetorians of his planetary guard butcher all the Preachers of the Imperial Cult and all Administratum officials whom he could catch—while the Pontifex of the Imperial Cult was winched down into a volcano.

Ten years later, the Imperium registered that Karkason had lapsed into heresy. Fifteen years later, it became obvious that Lord Sagramoso was seducing the hereditary lords of neighbouring star systems—mainly agricultural ones—to turn preachers into compost and swear fealty to him rather than to a deity thirty thousand light years distant.

Twenty years after the vulcanization of the Pontifex, plans for Crusade began—for the wheels of the Imperium often ground slow; but certainly they must pulverize the Sagramoso clan to dust, to microns, and install a new loyal commanding dynasty. An upstart mini-emperor was anathema.

Orbital laser platforms aside, much of the surface of Karkason was undefended. Yet what virtue was there in capturing a whole chain of volcanos, or in subduing a lake of lava? Sagramoso City itself was heavily guarded by skyward laser batteries, and these could not easily be neutralised. Precision laser fire from an altitude would be reflected, scattered by the vitrodur shields of the city's architecture. The blazing inferno of a plasma package likewise would wreak little major havoc upon such volcano-forged material—while barrage bombs and thermonukes would leave precious little by way of city or population to command. Organs of the Imperium fed on psycurium and power crystals as a sickly gourmet on oysters. A dyspeptic, phlebitic, tuberculous—yet still bellicose—gourmet, to whom such rarified nourishment was as a staff of life...

Whilst the heart of that entity fed on... worship, which was being damnably denied.

The planetary guard of a godling despot must be assumed to be numerous and very well armed—though how well experienced? Hence the landing of the Imperial Guards to dilute the acid of resistance, and allow over seven hundred Space Marines led by Lord Vladimir Pugh to spearhead a fierce organised drive against the capital and the praetorian troopers, with whom they would cope.

While Scouts would skrag that city randomly—fleas with terrible bites...

The ship was down. Hauling himself higher up the brass serpent, Yeremi squinted over the helmets of Fists as three Land Raiders roared out across a ramp from the adjacent larger hold, on to a fossilised sea of undulating ebon lava.

Skidding somewhat, the broad tracks of the vehicles struck fire from the vitrified surface, as steel from flint. Their las-cannon ball turrets swivelled alertly but nothing else seemed to be in the vicinity.

Already the Fists were disembarking on the double. Streamers of smoke and ash streaked the night sky, obliterating most of the stars, though one of Karkason's egg-shaped moons shone through, reproducing its image some way off in the shiny lava as an illusory silver pool, a distorted cool medallion. Briefly Yeremi scented the char of combustion on the incoming breeze, then the hatch pistoned upward to seal the vessel again, and it powered aloft, to veer wildly—low and jinking—toward the outskirts of the city.

Those pitch-black skirts...

Within which, behind which, a multitude of lights lurked faintly, intrinsically bright lights filtered by obsidian and vitrodur so as to resemble a swarm of phosphorescent creatures seen mutedly afar in some great oceanic abysmal valley that was deep and very long and very wide...

Above which, an embroidery of light flickered in and out of existence, stitching hints of a sampler spelling out death.

The drop-ship had jarred down, skidding some way; the hatch-ramp slammed open. In a trice the Wolverines and the other four Scout squads were outside with their Sergeants, and scattering in different directions. Already the emptied drop-ship, lip still hanging open, that steel tongue lolling out like an imbecile's, was lifting off again, engine roaring, a burning blast-wind buffeting.

Initially the pilot may have been uncertain whether the surface—of black upon black, with deep-down submerged glowglobes—was solid or deceitful. Now the surrounding squat towers of glossy darkness, with dully glowing hearts resembling X-rayed organs, were perhaps disorienting him—while overhead the sky was cross-stitched with hundreds of thinnest pulsing lines of coherent light, appearing, disappearing, rendering incandescent whatever atmospheric dust they stabbed through. Their origin, the city; their goal, incoming ships. The laser mesh shifted constantly, those two-dimensional searchlights knitting a lethal, spasming cat's cradle, perhaps operated by computer-minded Lexmeks cyborged and slaved to their weapons.

As the drop-ship yawed away, fleeing, a hem of the cat's cradle dipped towards it. Threads of light gleamed. The ship flared, briefly brightening the scene below—whereas earlier the distorted reflections of that ethereal lacework strobing from the ebon city had only confused the eye. The vessel Yeremi had been riding in scant tens of seconds earlier erupted¿ disintegrated.

He and Tundrish, d'Arquebus, Akbar, and the Sergeant hunched by the base of a stubby vitreous tower.

Yeremi shook his head and rubbed his eyes. His surroundings were so suddenly and so totally *novel*. He saw so much and so keenly, his vision enhanced by his occulobe. Yet what *was* he seeing? What was the meaning of all the vast patterns and shapes, of this darkness visible? Of this great brooding complex *mineral creature* they had been dropped in the midst of—safely, yes, into a pocket of calm and inattention, locally barren of signs of life... though barren for how long?

And here was only a *human* place. This wasn't any alien habitat, where even geometry might be twisted out of shape.

Tundrish appeared dazed by the environment too. Yeremi almost clung to the former undercity dweller, whether out of strange fellow feeling or only for support he could not have said. Or whether mutually to reinforce their ability to perceive and understand this city—two viewpoints yielding a stereoscopic perspective.

Almost clung. Almost. The binding magnetism of their triadic relationship—his and Tundrish's and d'Arquebus's—was as ever fluxing between positive and negative, attraction and repulsion. Disdain for one another was a sticky, bittersweet glue. Rivalry was a rivet piercing through their bones, uniting those in a danse macabre, a shifting *pas de trois*. Like mantises that eat their mates, or are eaten by them during intimate congress—even knowing that such a fate must occur—they were fraternally drawn to one another, obeying a bizarre tropism.

The callous incident of the heat sink... but then: hands linked in the Tunnel of Terror... the upper-habber *had* come back for his two companions, for whatever reason... Atonement? Hardly! Condescension? Maybe...

D'Arquebus himself was at once sneering and praying for clarity.

"*Think what you see!*" urged Sergeant Juron.

Of a sudden, for Yeremi at least there was *law* in his surroundings. There was rule. There was order. He chanted an old Valence family incantation, an enigmatic invocation used by his clan when switching on machinery: "*Artifex armifer digitis dextris oculis occultis!*" For he was perceiving the *tech* of Sagramoso City.

Huge umbrellas of black vitrodur atop turrets... umbrellas that could, and indeed were closing up into cones and steeples. Obsidian-carapaced buildings, vitreous canopies, cupolas... Edifices resembling giant bells carved of jet... Sleek towers that were telescoping down into the undercity, leaving great smooth plazas where they had previously reared, chequerboard-patterned spaces with a hint of roof outlines. Other buildings contracting and infolding like armoured animals under attack, cubes becoming pyramids.

This city could reconfigure parts of itself, great vitrodur panels sliding smoothly, tilting, canting. Shafts opening up and closing... Roads that rolled over, twisting to become walls. Level below level of roads. Coiling ramps that corkscewed up and down.

A city-*machine*, of glossy black sliding glass...

And not absolutely black, oh no. Now that Yeremi perceived those shapes—some of which were shifting, as he watched—he also distinguished a rich spectrum of dark hues: purple, indigo, amethyst.

On the horizon a dull storm of light began to flash as though the edge of the world was short-circuiting. Muted thumps muttered of far explosions. Imperial Guards must already have encountered the rebel Planetary Defence Force—or the other way about.

The other three Scout squads had promptly vanished with their Sergeants, hastening off into the glossy dark entrails of the city-machine, but Juron seemed content to pause a while. Yeremi realized that during these precious moments Juron was allowing his Wolverine Squad to lose their umwelt-virginity, to embrace the shattering impact of the utterly *new*. Thereafter, Yeremi himself would never again be fazed by being decanted into any foreign environment. He would adjust to it automatically with deadly machine precision. Or so he hoped.

Yeremi sniffed the faintly singed air: a hint of ash smuts, scorched dust, the odour of the volcanic plains, a warm caustic balm.

"And understand what you hear!"

He heard the city's limbs, sucking and gliding hydraulically. And the mid-distant signature of boltgun fire. First, came the popping ejaculation of the bolt. Then a flaring swish as its propellant ignited, accelerating it helter-skelter accumulating redoubtable kinetic energy. As double finale, the thud of piercing impact followed a fraction of a second later by the blast of detonation...

A hissing swish was also evident, and intensifying, a sly hissing scherzando.

Ssssag-ram-ossso! Ssssag-ram-ossso! the sound seemed to say.

Up a nearby spiralling ramp, up from that funereal glassy whirlpool, skaters were speeding, sable silks fluttering like sails, shuriken catapults outstretched bowsprit-fashion.

"Shurikens," warned Akbar.

"So I can see." Yeremi had already recognized those still-distant weapons because of the magnetic vortex fins sweeping back from the muzzles, like twin wings tipped with engine pods, and the flat round top-mounted magazines.

At sight of those silken black figures rushing their way, d'Arquebus jerked forward as though mesmerised.

"Lordly Phantasms!" he cried out. "Raphaelo Florienborque!"

Kik! Kik! Kik! said the tower beside them as a spray of accelerated star discs impacted overhead. Most stars ricocheted wildly. Others actually sliced into the vitrodur with their monomolecular edges and lodged there like so many tiny pitons hammered in to a precipice—an irregular, minimal ladder of discs, a coinage with the face-value of death, leading back skyward.

Were their assailants aiming to kill? Or were they a security squad determined to drive some supposed gawping cluster of citizenry below, unsure as yet in the darkness of their rank or affiliation?

Or were they more intent on *capture* and rapid interrogation? Those shuriken stars could slice through armour and carapace and bone and might cripple Scouts yet would not inevitably kill a superhuman body.

More skaters were emerging, with graceful pumping scything thrusts of their legs. Were their boots equipped with tiny wheels, ball bearings, blades?

"Lordly Phantasms!" cried d'Arquebus into the night, as though in torment, vexed by spooks. He started forward.

As Akbar and Tundrish opened fire with bolts, Yeremi lunged to drag the impetuous, or hallucinating, fool back.

D'Arquebus evaded Yeremi's grasp and raced aslant of the line of fire, right out in the open, seemingly intent on matching the speed of the skaters. Now that they had emerged, they did not continue headlong towards the Scouts. Swiftly the skaters circled and arced and sashayed, firing their sprays of lethal stars.

D'Arquebus mimicked their motion mockingly. He too

arced and raced in ellipses. Perhaps thus to confuse the skaters—was this sprinter really one of them, even in his silkless, padded garb?

Or magically to copy the essence of their being and so to own them within himself? To own, and consume, digest and destroy.

Or was he inviting injury, to prove that he could fight, even filleted by shurikens?

Crouching, Yeremi contented himself with firing his bolt pistol at the athletically shifting targets. The pistol hardly jerked at all as each bolt ejaculated before incandescing and zipping away. Yet only by luck did he hit one of the skaters—who was blasted apart. His silk ballooned, ripping into shreds. His flesh and bone opened up like a bud deploying a blood-red, white-stamened flower from which the petals almost instantly fell. Other bolts raced away into the night or else caroomed off vitrodur surfaces.

D'Arquebus ice-danced on the roadway, spiralling, looping, serpentining. Somehow he had captured that foreign poise, for when he did fire his weapon...

Sergeant Juron had entrusted d'Arquebus with a heavy bolter that could loose a single hellfire shell as well as ordinary explosive bolts.

D'Arquebus did just that—exactly prior to the moment when, quite unexpectedly to Yeremi, perhaps even to those parabolically crisscrossing skaters themselves, they configured close to one another like planets swooping into conjunction.

Had d'Arquebus's dance in some fashion drawn them together unwittingly as they concentrated on him, on his bizarre behaviour?

The shell only needed to hit one of the skaters—though it *did* indeed need to strike a target and not be wasted, as might easily be the case when fired seemingly without aiming. That weapon could certainly continue to fire ordinary bolts yet not a second hellfire shell without a perilous pause for reloading...

Time seemed to halt for Yeremi as he saw d'Arquebus squeeze the trigger, and was sure that d'Arquebus was squandering that single shell, shooting his hellfire bolt off prematurely.

It was an ancient, historic weapon that d'Arquebus had been privileged to handle. Generations of Artificers had lovingly serviced and adorned the gun; and Yeremi had felt bitten by envy. Gilded panels of religious inscriptions enchased the foregrip. Strips of engraved antler from some rare combative rutting beast inlaid the casing, and mother-of-pearl the trigger guard.

Surely an ex-tech should tote such a fine tool! A tech possessing almost genetic rapport with antique devices which might jam or fracture. A tech knew the appropriate litanies to mutter.

However, it had been d'Arquebus who returned along that terrifying, tormenting tunnel... had it not?

The crystal missile impacted in a skater's chest, and erupted. Needles of razor-shrapnel sped outward. Fierce acids and neurotoxins engulfed almost all of the skaters in a caustic, nerve-convulsing fog.

Their silks and skin dissolved as if gobbled by a cloud of ravenous moths. The skaters skidded outward, their muscles convulsing. They were crashing, tumbling, writhing every which way.

Yeremi, Tundrish, and Akbar shot down others who had survived the crystal slivers and the death cloud but who had slowed in apparent shock.

D'Arquebus simply stood motionless, his zany rush abruptly halted. How nonchalantly he posed, letting his *menials* deal with the remaining, no longer so elegant riff-raff.

"You were *rash*," Yeremi called out to him. "You were lucky."

"I was blessed," replied d'Arquebus airily; and he

laughed.

Yeremi glanced at the Sergeant in case he might chastise d'Arquebus. However, Zed Juron simply nodded approvingly.

The route down that petrified whirlpool into the entrails of Sagramoso City invited them.

"It's skraggin' time," whooped Tundrish.

Chapter Eight

Biff rejoiced. The spider on his face smiled. Grinning, he showed the mandibles of his filed teeth, and sucked saliva to and fro through his pointed ivories.

The skraggin' o' the city was goin' good, from his point-a-view.

In swank zones, you wouldn't exakly a thunk there was a war goin' on – not till the Scouts arrived...

I mustn't slump into scum lingua just 'cos I'm excited, Biff told himself. *Because I'm excited*, he corrected mentally. For one thing, that was unworthy of Rogal Dorn, warrior and *courtier*. For another, it was unworthy of the transformed person Biff had become. For a third, d'Arquebus would look down that slim, ruby-ringed nose of his.

Valence might enjoy a squirm of... masochism, on account of d'Arquebus. The ex-tech might relish enduring the pain of minor humiliations, as though the flaw in his gene-seed had found a convenient outlet in that regard. But not Biff Tundrish.

Biff was rather a *basic* name, wasn't it? Biff himself

wasn't basic; never had been, not even down in the depth of ignorance that had been the undercity of Trazior. Tundrish sounded like a heap of turds. Biff Tundrish was someone who bashes piles of turds. Which suited okay for Scavvies who grazed on a hive's garbage, who supped on its polluted excretions—and skragged each other for the chance to do so.

There was magic in a name. Prayer-words made machines work, that was a fact. So was he a captive of his name—as d'Arquebus might well be of his?

No. Never.

You gave me your sludge, Universe, he told the cosmos, *and I'm turning it into gold.*

And other bits of you into debris, he added with a feral grin.

Those skragged bits were the sacrifices to his personal god of Transformation. Nothing high-falutin' about this, nothing d'Arquebus-like. Still, Biff sensed the imminence of a pattern, which one day he would fully perceive. He would discover a web, a network of creation and destruction, which the spider on his face would recognize, and know how to navigate—to arrive at what? At personal gold, at himself thoroughly transmuted—by way of the furnaces of pious warfare.

Then the name Biff would mean something really special. Someone would carve it on an adamantium monument.

Several city levels above, it would be mid-afteroon now, though the inhabitants of Sagramoso City plainly spurned the radiance of daylight, sheltering as they did under their immense, interlocking umbrellas of black glass. Whenever the volcanoes held their fusty ashen breath, the white sun cruelly baked the lava plains, from which polishing thermal winds whipped dust away towards the east, always eastward, to the Death Drifts, a shallow sea without liquid.

Sated by skragging, Wolverine Squad were preparing to doze on guard in a vast dim dusty vitrodur cellar crowded with a petrified army of lava sculptures. None of these sculptures was less than three metres in height. Some were slender, others bloated. All bore a distinct snub-nosed family resemblance to one another. Many, indeed, were duplicates. Their carved costumes varied: uniforms, togas, robes. Some were nude. A few were merely giant heads; for fashions changed. Here was a storeroom of statuary of deceased Sagramosos, exiled at the accession of a new Lord, though not condemned to be crushed to dust—their sheer enduring weight might act as anchor to the multi-thousand year dynasty.

A few electrolumens flickered, ensconced in nooks, though others were defunct. Scores of chained skeletons lay in the aisles—rivals, no doubt, of the regime, potential competitors for power who had been left here naked over the centuries, stripped of everything, to contemplate its monumental history while they starved.

The night before, and through the morning into the afternoon, the Wolverines had rampaged from level to level, always moving as quickly and confusingly as they could. Sometimes the Scouts took the initiative, and *in extremis* Sergeant Juron herded his squad hastily. The shuriken skaters of Sagramoso City were swift—if inclined to capricious flourishes and virtuoso displays, as though recognizing that the Scouts were providing some destructive harassment, but ultimately posed no major danger.

"I think they don't mind if we trash some areas," Biff had said. "Then people'll feel more loyal to their Lord... 'Course, they don't mind killing us neither." All four Scouts sported minor shuriken wounds, swiftly healed, their cinnabar blood closing up gashes like sealing wax. Only Zed Juron was wholly uninjured—that slab of a man was so nimble at dodging, as if he had second sight—though a ricocheting shuriken had smashed his communicator. Juron almost seemed to be enjoying a second adolescence in company with his Scouts, while yet remaining devoutly responsible.

The Scouts had skragged many gaiety pods. Those black ovoid lustres linked by slideways dangled beneath over-arching vitrodur umbrellas as though these were weeping solid sooty rain. The Scouts had rushed skiddingly from one pod to the next, annihilating languid swanky drugsters, warbling liquorites, squirming orgiasts who were respond-ing to the war in their own indulgent style, if they even heeded it at all.

Parts of the city which were more heedful had recessed into themselves, clearing great arena-spaces—although contracted routes through the internal organs of those zones were still negotiable.

The Wolverines had burst into a chapel to Fulgor Sagramoso Deified where a floodlit lava statue stood in place of the Emperor's altar. Aged heretics were hymning wailingly to their god-dictator, supervised by armed deacons. Perhaps the worshippers had no other choice but to sing Sagramoso's praises and sniff the victory-incense already so impertinently burning. The Wolverines threw offerings of frag grenades into the elderly congregation.

The Scouts had hellfired crowded transport sledges that slid at speed down glossy oiled vitrodur channels, diving from transit stations, canting along branch-lines, cork-screwing, swooping up to come to rest at other destina-tions...

Once, they came across a dead fellow Scout of the Wild Boar Squad, lying in a glassy cul-de-sac. He had been so butchered by shuriken stars that his corpse was a mere long mound of rashers glued by cinnabar. Later, from a nearby height Wolverine Squad spied many other corpses of Karkazon natives laid out in sinister rune patterns along one dismal lacquered boulevard—spoor of the Boars, now being exorcised with burning incense and sprinkled acid by some raving Sagramoso cultist guarded by skaters.

So the Boars had been busy... while the real battle raged closer to the black chandelier of the Imperium, to set those parts which had not contracted a-tinkling and a-rattling.

And the Wolverines had likewise been busy—though they had not thought of that rune trick...

Sergeant Juron seemed dubious of its merits. Swapping speed for japery may well have resulted in the conversion of that fallen Boar into bacon.

And now they should rest a while.

Where better than this great vault of abandoned statuary and skeletons, to avail themselves of their Catalepsean Nodes for a couple of hours?

So the Scouts sat deep in that cellar amidst the jumbled dusty lava-carved genealogy of the Sagramosos.

So they switched off one side of their brains in order to purge fatigue poisons from their systems while the other cerebral hemisphere remained alert for intruders...

Logic and speech slumbered in Biff, and dreamed; for the left half of his brain was asleep now.

In that half-dream, of which he was less than half-aware, regiments of rubbery words marched to war with one another. Nouns and verbs armed with chainswords and power-axes paraded on elasticated feet. As each side manoeuvred, they sought to spell out some seemingly important message—conflicting messages over which they were about to fight.

The Emperor's Will is Supreme, Blessed, and Eternal.

The Emperor's Name is Death; his Throne is the Grave.

These sentences, and others, clashed. They hacked and sliced at one another till there was no meaning left, only a confusion of bloodthirsty syllables spelling out absurdity.

The alert, conscious right side of Biff's brain registered the faint odour of ancient dust. It noted the faded fustiness of death from the many skeletons, and the drying sweat of his comrades spiced with hints of their precious superhuman hormonal secretions. It savoured the tang of Biff's own saliva, similarly flavoured, like a waxing and ebbing tide inside his mouth. It detected the twin heartbeats around him and the mingled sigh of breath. It scanned the gloomy pattern of piers and arches which sustained the fan-vaulting above. Configured like the reticulated rib-cage of some enormous alien creature, long dead and looming over them, the vault appeared not to have been carved but rather *rubbed* into shape painstakingly, no doubt by the labour of slaves over many decades, millennia earlier.

The right hemisphere of his brain could not articulate what it registered. Words and logic had deserted. They had fled away to war, to that dream of a ghostly battle elsewhere. Raw sensory impact was what that hemisphere knew of—moods and intuitions, the immanence of *patterns* and *rhythms* founded upon survival. It was as though Biff had devolved into an animal, even a reptile, temporarily torpid since there was no spur to action, yet springloaded to respond...

Something *itched*...

Some oddity.

Some anomaly in the echo of breath and heartbeat within that vault of monumental ozymandian arrogance and slow chained doom.

The right brain noted something amiss...

Meanwhile, Yeremi's logical tech-side dreamed.

It dreamed a ghostly dance of rune-scribed tools. With their assistance, gears and warped carburettor components and portions of armour major and minor were assembling themselves into an enormous baroque weapon.

Elephantine wheels supported a caged chassis of wrought adamantium. Hydraulic recoil buffers were worthy of a sewage pumping station. Presently a hugely long brass-hooped barrel jutted up towards the heart of the galaxy.

That gun would fire an armoured human missile, namely Yeremi himself, brandishing in his outstretched hands a huge volume bound in luminescent human skin inscribed with the spidery title *Codex Lex*, the Book of Law...

Unless the barrel exploded.

Meantime, Yeremi's wakeful passion-mind was heedful of his environs and his comrades, in particular Lexandro d'Arquebus...

Yeremi did not think logically. He could not. His rationality was exiled to that other phantom domain where the Weapon of Law was being constructed according to dream-logic.

He experienced hormonal surges—an equation of wordless emotions. Jealousy. Hatred. Piety. Fraternity.

Each value circled around the d'Arquebus enigma like a shark seeking its supper.

Until he knew deep in his belly that he would only ever excel and humble that damnable "brother" of his by making himself into a *devotee* of Lexandro's existence, akin to a cultist, a protector and preserver of d'Arquebus in his ostentatious recklessness.

Yes, Yeremi would hone his senses to detect *danger* to d'Arquebus, to avert the threat of death from him. Yeremi must become Lexandro's beneficial leech or remora, his benevolent vampire, sucking away the poison of peril into himself, and thus leeching away also—parasitically—at Lexandro's spirit. Aye, until d'Arquebus knew bitterly— and until others recognized scornfully—the sham of his valour, which came not from Dorn at all, but was really no more than the flip-side of his former high-hab extra-vagance...

Thus vowed Yeremi's passion-hemisphere—not in so many words, but rather in the form of emotive emblems that lodged within his heart and guts, to flourish there like tumours.

Lexandro's own schismed mind dreamed of himself ennobled. Blazons of heraldry tattooed the whole surface of his skin—he seemed to be a living shield armoured in righteousness. He was wearing a translucent gossamer pain-glove that hardly anyone else could see. High up on a wrought-plasteel balcony he posed implacably, beholding the execution by Fists of an unending stream of aliens and heretics. And enjoying his own agonizing neverending penance, of which his Marines could only whisper with awe.

Simultaneously his senses scrutinised that vault, every grim shadow of which was luminous to him, pierced by a light of purity which Rogal Dorn focused through the lens of his being...

Biff roused from the split-brain trance.

He was still pure animal. For a moment longer, raw gaze and taste and smell were his sole sources of wisdom.

He was scumnik devolved into beast.

Then words trooped back into his reunifying consciousness. Unmangled, resurrected words.

"Someone else here," he warned. "Someone been here all along."

Mustn't over-educate myself, he thought. Else I'll rob myself of those animal-like perceptions, of the old scum instincts... I'll cheat myself of the patterns that a beast can register, with its robot-wired mind alert to supernatural vibrations.

Perhaps the swank had been right in that one respect when he jeered at Biff's diligent efforts in the Scriptory...

Deep in the cellar they found a quadruply amputated prisoner. Bereft of arms and legs, his massive torso was planted upright in a heavy bronze cauldron. He was sealed into that ample vessel with lead—the metal must have been poured whilst molten, then had hardened around his butt.

His eyes were wired open so that he must stare unblinkingly at a giant Sagramoso head, and his own body had been reduced to roughly the same contours. His former arm sockets were mere stumps of cinnabar. His lips were sewn shut with the thong of a thin black leathery whip, the tied ends of which drooped like a moustache.

As the Scouts approached the amputee, he was attempting to rock the weight of the cauldron. The faint grating caused by that supreme effort was what Biff had detected in his beast-brain.

The man—or what had been a man—was staring; he was breathing. His mastiff jaw jutted.

A faint feathering of ancient surgical scars on his trunk... Three holes in his forehead where *studs* had seemingly been pulled out with pincers...

This was—must once have been—a *Marine*.

The man's cheeks were tattooed with little vermilion chalices brimming with gore.

Sergeant Juron demanded Biff's combat knife. The looping whip that shoelaced the mouth of the mutilated Marine was branded with a frieze of miniature cabalistic hexes. Muttering a prayer to render those impotent, Juron slid the monomolecular blade between the man's lips and sliced the edge easily through the whip.

The mouth yawned open. Canines and incisors were long sharp fangs, the canines hollow like hypodermic syringes carved of ivory.

The man croaked a few hardly comprehensible syllables. His tongue had not been cut out—it loomed thick and purple behind those savage teeth and the thick whiskers of severed whip—however his throat was dry as dust.

Juron squirted his water canteen into that arid gob again and again. The man stretched his head forward, teeth wide now, as if impelled to fasten those upon the Sergeant's gauntlet and pierce right through to bite; but he desisted.

"*Who are you?*" demanded Juron.

Painfully the answer came: "Blood Drinker... Marine...
Lieutenant... Tezla..."

Biff glanced at his Sergeant, who nodded confirmation.

"An honourable Marine Chapter—I've heard tell of
them. How did you come here... Sir?" he asked the
amputee whose buttocks and groin were embedded in grey
plumbum.

The Blood Drinker struggled to talk.

"Exploration ship... Squad of ten... Alien battle
damage... Navigator dying... We land on this loyal world
for salvation... World not loyal... They hoax us... They
pit us against a *Titan*... in an armour-glass arena. Titans!
Have Titans here!"

Juron murmured an oath.

"How many Titans?"

"I think... six Warlord class, and one Emperor Titan...
You don't know of this?"

"Damned right we don't." The Sergeant clutched the
ruined communicator on his equipment harness, muttering
anathema. Of course as a shepherd of Scouts he wore no
helmet, with inbuilt primary communicator... "*Mea
culpa!*" he swore. "Dorn forgive me."

Thanks to study in the Scriptories, Biff appreciated the
seriousness of the situation as fully as Valence may have
done. Titans were those heavily shielded, fearsomely armed
mechanical warriors seventy feet tall and more, whose
crews of three or four marched the armoured robotic
monsters and targeted their heavy weapons by mind-
impulse... Now seven such dire devices lurked within
Sagramoso City, ready to erupt against the Marines when
the hundreds of suited Fists came flooding in—*to a trap*.

A trap: yes. Biff thunk... Biff *thought* he could perceive
the pattern well enough. The thousands of invading
Imperial Guards and the possible tens of thousands of
Planetary Defence Force troopers loyal to Fulgor Sagramoso would pretty much neutralise one another. Led by

Lord Pugh, the Fists would punch their way through into the city, the *treacherous* city which would reconfigure itself like a machine so as to funnel them unwittingly. The seven Titans would be loosed from ambush, rising up like volcanic doom on a vitrodur platform or else stepping from behind some giant black wall that slid slyly aside.

How many Marines could seven Titans destroy with their plasma guns, macro cannons, missiles, even with their power fists alone?

Perhaps too many... The Marines would be like fire-ants attacking a Cudbear. The cost even of victory might be far too great.

"How well do they operate their Titans?" Juron demanded.

"One Battle Titan... easily killed nine Blood Drinkers in armour... Me, it simply seized and held... out to Lord Sagramoso... as an offering... My armour was stripped..." Juron made to squeeze more water into the Lieutenant's mouth, but the Marine shook his head. "Too much... I cannot urinate... With power swords they sawed off my limbs..." The man grinned crazily. "*Difficult*, even so! Thirty seconds each, it took them... Brought me here... Sewed my lips with hexes so I should not blaspheme against their godling... Poured molten lead to fix me... Left me solitary to adore his ancestors and starve..."

"How long ago did this happen?"

"Don't know... They're ignorant of... Sus-an. After they left I suspended my animation... till my sub-mind, dreaming of blood, sensed the odour of your wounds... and roused me..."

"How did they come by Titans... Sir?"

The Blood Drinker shook his head. "Not from the Collegia Titanica!"

"Of course not... Who could have serviced Titans? Who has the *tech* here?" The Sergeant frowned. "That's irrelevant. We'll have to leave you here, Lieutenant. An invasion's under way. But we'll free your eyes. So you can shut them. So you shan't have to watch Sagramoso.'' Juron shook his communicator in a fury of frustration.

"Maybe I can fix that," suggested Yeremi. "I know a litany. I'm of tech stock."

"The thing's too injured, Valence. *Mea culpa!* We must fight our way to meet our Brothers to warn them."

"We're deep in the city," said d'Arquebus, licking his lips. "Maybe we're *behind* those Titans."

"Can you describe exactly where they're kept in relation to here, Lieutenant?"

Tezla could. Tezla did. He had kept his eyes peeled. And yes, d'Arquebus's guess was correct.

"An obsidian arena that opens and closes..." mused Juron. "Waiting to gape once our Brothers appear..."

"Could we try to sneak in there and reach a Titan?" interrupted d'Arquebus. The Sergeant stared at him disbelievingly. "To disable at least one, Sir—or even *make use* of it?"

"*Make use of...*" Obviously d'Arquebus was oblivious to the *training* of the elite Moderati who controlled a Titan.

"How many of you... Scouts... *are* there?" moaned Tezla.

"Four here," said the Sergeant, "and there's myself."

Tezla laughed throatily.

This offended Juron. "We're Imperial Fists... Sir. We aren't suicide zombies. We're a Chapter that calculates carefully."

"You didn't calculate Titans."

"Cousin, kindly describe the arena to me in detail."

Tezla obliged, and Juron digested the information, glazed-eyed like some Lexomat, some data-sponge.

He thought. He envisaged. He calculated.

At last he said slowly, "Maybe there is one way we could use a Titan. If only we can reach it stealthily... It'll be disguises and knives, lads, no noisy bolts... No antics.

Silks and blades. We'll need the luck of Dorn Himself. We'll almost certainly die. Almost certainly. Ninety per cent.''

"Death in the Emperor's name," hissed Biff. Or did he say, "Death *is* the Emperor's name"?

"Knowing what we know, do we have any other choice but to go there? To sacrifice ourselves, even if we only buy our Brothers extra moments?"

Tezla stared at Juron, still wide-eyed.

"You, Lieutenant: shall we kill you? Since no one else may find you?"

Tezla considered. "No...," he decided. "I may yet be of some temporary use to my Chapter if I can be salvaged. I'll wait, with my eyes shut."

Chapter Nine

As camouflage they must obtain local clothing. Yet in quest of such, boltguns would be of no assistance. One could hardly wear garments that were ripped to shreds and spattered with blood.

Yeremi felt a flutter of perverse delight when Sergeant Juron decided that they must cache their weapons—other than combat knives and mini-grenades—in the cellar. How delightful to behold Lexandro's chagrin as he was obliged to lay down that antique heavy bolter inlaid with antler and mother of pearl...

The Wolverines' stock of blast and frag grenades would likewise be of little avail, though since each grenade hardly bulked larger than a coin the Scouts could at least retain their pursefuls of those in case they needed to kill at a distance.

If only they had some grenades of the gas or choke or knock-out variety! But then, the Scouts were lacking respirators. Mayhem had been the aim, not tranquillization.

So as not to appear over-conspicuous they must unclip their bulky shoulder pauldrons, unstrap their greaves, and discard their eagle-plastrons.

"What if we run into Boar Squad?" asked d'Arquebus with a mad gleam in his eye.

This prospect pressed a peril button in Yeremi's brain. The other Scouts might easily fail to recognize Lexandro and Brothers; they might fire first and ask questions later, if they bothered to ask at all. They might kill Lexandro if he played the fool.

"I guess we steer well clear of our Brothers," Yeremi said.

"Oh yes!" d'Arquebus agreed fervently—and Yeremi realised how enraptured Lexandro was with the heroic fate in store for them. Now that their crazy mission was mooted, he didn't wish it to be diluted with extra personnel.

"But the other Sergeants have got *communicators*—" began Akbar.

"Communicators that *work*," growled Sergeant Juron, in the bitter tone of one who didn't need to be reminded. "If we do run into the others, you, Akbar, will strip naked to maximize their chance of recognizing a fellow Brother. You'll go to them. First priority is to warn the Fists. But *that*," and he eyed d'Arquebus levelly, "don't mean we ain't gonna try for the Titans too. Be better we had more Scouts and a couple more Vet Sergeants on our side, is all."

D'Arquebus wrinkled his nose, whether disapproving of Juron's lapses of grammar in this time of stress, or simply of involving others on this enterprise, who could say?

Stripped naked, thought Yeremi. Lacking even plastrons or greaves to protect chests or calves, this part of the mission would be somewhat akin to a dash through a tunnel of terror...

Juron also seemed conscious of the exposure factor. "Remember, Lads," he said, "you ain't got chicken-ribs. You got a figging breastplate o' solid bone inside you. And you got the carapace, an' all." He cleared his throat. "We have time for one quick prayer to Rogal Dorn.'' Prayer would restore formality.

Henceforth they did not rampage—they sneaked. They slunk. They crept—through a city that was continuing to recoil in face of invasion. Buildings, black as anthracite, were receding or telescoping down, rumbling as they moved, clearing a field for battle. Avenues broadened to lure attackers along them. Troopers of the rearguard were already falling back in reasonable order. Refugees, herded by shuriken skaters, were streaming inward. The irregular heartbeat of battle was distant as yet but throbbing closer.

A while later, the Wolverines seized their chance. Springing from behind fat fluted columns, they seized two skaters and snapped their necks.

D'Arquebus snatched one shroud of black silk as if it was his birthright. The Sergeant availed himself of the other.

Those roller-boots proved to have vitrodur balls inset along the soles. Predictably the skaters' boots were several sizes smaller than Marine footwear. So the camouflaged couple must sprint in a semblance of skating motion—to lure another shuriken-starman with urgent gestures, and snuff him. ''He'' proved to be something more alien: a dark-haired dusky woman. D'Aquebus sniggered as Yeremi adopted her garb. Yet then his attitude altered abruptly.

''Lordly,'' he nodded approvingly. ''Phantasmic!'' For the moment Yeremi was a mirror he could admire himself in.

Next, the disguised trio snagged a couple of silk-clad refugees, strangled and then stripped them. Hugging the blackest shadows, all five mimers headed in the direction that the amputated Blood Drinker had outlined. Migrants flocking in panic from the battle zone provided a useful veil of confusion. Lights were dimming throughout the city, plunging whole districts into sombre murk. Scarcely any smoky sunshine from above filtered through the many dark glass shields.

Balloon-wheeled vehicles blocked a certain crepuscular boulevard. Macro-cannons were mounted upon those, and multi-meltas. Heavily armed troopers swarmed—outriders of Lord Sagramoso's palace guard. At the end of that avenue rose the coaly tiers of the palace itself: a great glooming glass-petalled ziggurat with telescoping spires from which vast vitrodur umbrellas unfolded, interlocking.

An obsidian plaza close by the road-block was almost deserted. Only a few shuriken skaters circled lazily—while refugees shunned that area as if it was mined. Golden silhouettes of phoenixes indented the paving, suggestive of mighty, three-clawed footprints.

As promised, the nigrescent domes of the arena loomed behind that not-so-public square.

The edifice resembled an enormous clump of towering vitrified black fungi. Yet merry silver and azure pennants flew from those domes, stretched out on wires to suggest the presence of a fresh breeze. Within, that arena might well harbour some exhibition or pageant, and thus be of no significance in a war. The place was hardly cordoned by guards, as if to emphasize its innocuous character.

As the Wolverines sashayed closer, the percussion concert of battle to the north became more insistent. Amplified by the vitrodur soundboards of the city, the crackle of fire and drumbeat of explosions rolled closer—impelling a flux of refugees to eddy towards the troopers and the seeming sanctuary of the palace region beyond.

This would not be allowed.

Was it a certain gunnery officer's intention to clear his field of view in Draconian style? Did he simply want to test the weapon? Perhaps he only aimed to chivvy those civilians in another direction, but was inexpert in the settings of the weapon.

A multi-melta opened fire.

Superheat surged from the quadruple nozzles, liquifying the flesh and fat of the nearest targets—boiling those liquids so that greasy steam rose from a pool of slumped steaming bones. More distant victims burst into flames. Others flared like candles as they tried to flee.

This distraction allowed the Wolverines to close in on the flanged skirts of the arena.

An access ramp corkscrewed down.

At the bottom, a trio of guards were on duty, armed with flamers. The Wolverines' borrowed silks lent them invaluable seconds wherein to close with those guards and sever their throats before they could fire or even cry a warning.

Branching tunnels led away underground, lit by the occasional electroflambeau. Figures scurried in the distance. Here was a manhole down which to stuff the bodies.

And here was an inspection panel of close-set steel mesh embedded in the wall, sealed with waxen evil-eye hexes and painted with a faded inscription in the hieratic tongue: *Hoc sacrificium consecrat nos muros.*

Muttering some vulgar exorcism to avert the jinx, Juron tore the panel open. Behind, lay a pile of chained human bones, a slumped fettered skeleton. A shinbone was broken, twisted—as was the ulna in one arm, and several ribs.

Above, a Stygian tubeway arched upward like some intestine within the wall.

One of the slave-builders must have been incarcerated behind this hatch as a sacrifice to good fortune—with the chance of squirming his way up that curving conduit to some high exit point, a well-nigh impossible task when fettered. He must have tried in the darkness; perhaps tried many times. And slid down, unable to brake himself, breaking one bone then another. How he must have stared through the grid at freedom, and squinted hopelessly at the waxed wingnuts securing the gate of his oubliette. How he must have aspired to rise up forcefully, his yearning impregnating the walls with a similar passion.

Juron stared up the tube as far as he could see, and nodded.

"You first, d'Arquebus."

Bones crumbled as d'Arquebus crouched upon them. He braced himself against the sides of that smooth slanting chimney in almost foetal position and began to force his way upward by flexing.

As Yeremi followed him, he breathed in the dust of death, motes from the pulverized bones.

Tundrish came next, then Akbar. Juron managed to heave the access panel back into position behind him, and what little light there had been diminished even more. Yeremi could still see the tube wall quite clearly with his enhanced vision. However, he did not bother to look. He shut his eyes—the better to concentrate upon the cramped flexing of his muscles; upon that monotonous, peristaltic thrust upwards as of some gross mutant baby ascending a vertical birth canal in defiance both of gravity and of sane obstetrics.

The way in which the relative positions of the three "brothers" mimicked the old hierarchy of Trazior became ruefully evident to Yeremi as they pressed their way upward. Compression of the guts caused inevitable farting. D'Arquebus vented through his tunic and his silks virtually into Yeremi's face. Nor did Yeremi have much option but to gas Tundrish in turn.

Yeremi at least gasped out an apology to the body below him.

"Pardon me, Brother."

"S'all right," panted Tundrish. "Reminds me of home in the underhive..."

"Did you just stand on his face?" piped a nonchalant

voice from above. Was d'Arquebus oblivious to the reason for Yeremi's courtesy?

Ah, d'Arquebus was the bold trailblazer, was he not? Right in the lead, where the air was stale but not otherwise malodorous.

Peeved, Yeremi's attention lapsed. He slipped. He butted down upon Tundrish—who in turn slumped heavily upon Akbar, who lost his adhesion. For a moment it seemed as though everyone but d'Arquebus would career back down fifty metres to the base of the tube.

But the Scouts fell no further. "Brace, you limp bastards!" roared a voice from below. With a Herculean effort, Juron had stemmed the little avalanche of bodies.

"Brace and squeeze! Brace and squeeze!"

They did; oh they did.

The steep ascent continued.

Yeremi found himself thinking passionately of that anonymous slave abandoned in the pitch-dark tube, with none of the superhuman muscle power of a Scout to help him, and fetters to mock his efforts. Had the death-dust breathed in by Yeremi conveyed a molecular message into his brain?

What if that slave could have triumphed over the tube that confined him? What if he could have emerged from the summit of this chimney?

How could he possibly have done so? The slave had enjoyed no real hope. Even less, after he broke his first bone. Yet how his spirit had yearned upward, despairingly. Now the slave's ghost was helping push Yeremi upward...

Yeremi would avenge that victim on those who roosted at the summit. He would bring justice to them.

At last they emerged between two giant ventilator gargoyles with dinosaurian mouths. Massive gantries illuminated by electroflambeaux jutted from a high balustraded parapet-deck. This harboured an array of towering, rune-painted servicing machines, and piles of ordnance: racks of macro-cannon shells and multi-launcher rockets. A spare chainsword-fist the size of a Land Raider dangled from the chains of a jib crane...

Beyond deck and gantries and derricks yawned the darkened abyss of the arena—where the Blood Drinker Marines had met their fate.

Between catwalks loomed the stooped carapaces of the Titans. Those rugged plasteel islands of black and purple flew Lord Sagramoso's vermilion volcano banner, and bore dire bulky weapons.

Yeremi recognized plasma cannons, macro-cannons, defence lasers—artillery which could melt fully armoured Marines, which could blow them away in scraps like chaff.

Overtopping the six waiting Titans of the Warlord class stood the solitary Emperor Titan—turtle head protruding, one plasma cannon held rampant.

Juron whistled softly at the sight.

Just then the high deck vibrated. Servomotors whirred. One of the Warlords took several thudding steps forward.

A party of techs hastened past the Wolverines' hiding place. They wore helmets suggestive of the heads of flies, and their black silks were embroidered with arcane silver hieroglyphics. Herded by a robed priest, other techs decamped from the catwalks. A second Warlord thundered forward, and halted. It swung an auto-cannon arm to left then right underneath its ratcheted neck, as if executing a derisive menacing bow.

The main flambeaux along the deck all died out suddenly so as not to backlight the fighting machines.

The techs' eyes would take far longer than any Wolverine's to accommodate to the profound gloom. Moreover, those techs were kneeling and bowing their heads—while the priest began to rant, his eyeballs rolling up whitely as though to stare inside his own skull.

"The Emperor!" snapped Juron. He meant Him on

Earth. He also meant that tallest of the Titans. Seizing their opportunity, the Wolverines sprinted, scrambled, ducked.

Now they were on the catwalk, deep underneath the carapace.

Now they stood beside the adamantium hatch. Gabbling a canticle as he tore loose a bundle of eerie fetishes knotted from dried ligament, Juron undogged that door.

The back of the Titan's head housed a red-lit escape chamber, equipped with anti-gravitics. From this chamber, short fat tunnels led to the control bubbles in the shoulders and in the forward head-cabin. In emergency those bubbles could be hurled back pneumatically, and the whole head would blast clear. The air reeked of sweet resinous balm, no doubt sprayed by that priest as a prophylactic against battle injuries.

Yeremi crept into the leftward shoulder-bubble, where a Moderatus sat strapped in his fire-seat, staring ahead, waiting. The earphones of his mind-impulse helmet blotted out any whisper of intrusion.

Thick metal cables curved up from that helmet into the ducted roof as though the man had sprouted banded antlers. Similar cables writhed from the sockets in his sheathed left arm. Those, to direct the servo-motorised fibre-bundles which were the muscles of the Titan's gargantuan arm. His gauntleted right hand rested on the gimballed firing handle.

Before him, tell-tales winked in a dance of fireflies. Ikons marched across data screens, processions of iridescent beetles. A gridded forward viewscreen, framed with bronze bones, displayed in subdued ginger hues—metamorphosis of infra-red—the expanse of the arena and the vast closed petals of the dome which presently would unfold to let monsters out of its cave.

Conical pauldrons, from which yet more cables coiled like the tentacles of a cuttlefish, protected the shoulders of the Moderatus. He was padded and armoured.

Below his goggle-visor his nose and mouth were exposed, though.

The first he knew of his death was when Yeremi plunged the monomolecular knifeblade up his severing nostril through bone into his cerebrum.

The dying man's right hand spasmed open. Yeremi snatched it clear of the firing handle. The plasma gun slewed askew, however, obscuring part of the rusty view.

A moment later, the whole massive body of the Titan itself lurched and tottered. The shock threw Yeremi against a luridly graffitied bulkhead. Somewhere below, angry serpents of stabilising jets hissed as automatics restored the balance. The Princeps in the head, whose thoughts impelled the Titan into motion, had obviously met his death.

Yeremi began stripping the corpse, whose face was a gash of blood...

In the control-head two great slanted eye-screens scanned the arena. Sergeant Juron was slurring lies into a helmet microphone torn from the head of the dead Princeps as Yeremi returned.

"Problem," he mumbled. "Plasma reactor... Tryin' to fix the flux... Evacuate area now... Power's goin'..." He switched off.

"They comprend?" Akbar asked.

"Karks use standard ImpGoth," Tundrish told him impatiently. "Weren't you heeding when we skragged that chapel?"

"We grenaded 'em all so fast."

"Listen, you all," snapped Juron, "these controls—" He gestured at the slumped mind-impulse suit with its spaghetti of cables. "They mean shit right now. *So get to your posts and open those guys' heads up and eat! And figging concentrate on controls!*"

Of course. But of course.

Use your Omophagea organ.

The remaining Warlord Titans were moving out from their berths alongside, striding away from the Emperor in lumbering haste.

"Pray we can all learn enough, soon enough!" Juron held his knife to the dead man's brow and began sawing the monomolecular edge through bone.

Yeremi soon discovered that while a monomolecular blade was excellent for *bisecting* a skull as such, when it came to dissecting the contents the knife was, if anything, too keen a scalpel—its cuts so wafer-thin that the warm brain matter seemed to seal together again as if glued. Nor could he safely convey tissue to his mouth on such a blade; which could easily sever his own tongue.

So he ungloved, and rummaged with his fingers, sucking vigorously on those till the lower half of the skull, still attached to the spinal column, was quite empty. Then he supped hastily from the bone cup of the cranium.

Even in his haste he noted subtle distinctions of taste between cerebellum and cortex, between frontal lobes and limbic system. Here was a hint of bitter almond, and here of truffle. This glob of tissue tasted of boiled mushroom; and that of bland fish roe...

Concluding his hasty feast, he tossed the bone cup aside. It fell where a chained skull-amulet lay forlornly, having utterly failed to protect its wearer from radical craniotomy.

He wriggled into the impulse-suit, ducked his head into the helmet. Strapping himself into the vacated chair, he entreated Rogal Dorn to guide him—then emptied his mind of all but titanic tech thoughts.

My plasma gun, he thought, and his muscles twitched. It works by... by...

...by a discharge of super-heated ionized matter in its fourth state, as in the inferno of a blazing sun. The accumulator vanes within the hood energize the conductors and insulators of the capacitor to power this incandescent

discharge. After each venting, this ancient capacitor recharges its energy briefly while the frontal hood ventilates. During that short pause I am vulnerable unless I draw booster power from our Titan's plasma reactor and opt for maximal fire. But then I may fuse my gun...

Thoughts were welling up like globules of oil through water to form a glutinous slick upon the surface of Yeremi's consciousness.

He ignored all intruding hints of the personality whose thoughts those had been. He let such irrelevancies disperse, cracking the discharge for useful data, refining it.

Much was murky and indistinct, confused by those very irrelevancies. Really, he could use half an hour to *digest* the gobbets of this person.

He only had minutes. Combat-cannibalism wasn't a gastronomic indulgence.

...and my right-hand Moderatus controls a power-fist for close quarter work, for scooping and crushing those miniscule Marines whose explosive bolts will be like stings...

However, the Moderati of the Clavicles between them control a macro-cannon riding high on our carapace, and a defence laser too...

Still, our body is relatively exposed...

This deployment of weapons, with the fast-firers mounted high, is because we are the tallest Titan, and will aim over the Warlords' shoulders...

Yeremi's sheathed right arm unflexed. He felt power pulse through the hydroplastics by way of the actuators to the fibre-bundle muscles—and outside, the great plasma gun swung aside.

Yes, ah yes... This must be a taste of how it was to be a Marine in armour, whose servo-suit responded to the motions of his body, magnifying these...

The scene without shimmered faintly.

And Yeremi knew without question that void shields

were up, to cushion the impact of any hostile fire.

...If incoming fire shall overload our void shields and damage our Titan, if the feedback dampers shall fail too, then a Moderatus will suffer the intense agony of pseudo-injury. He will experience his own body as broken, ruptured, or burned...

These Titans are old. Old.

Reconditioned, but old. The systems are old.

We are not the maniac Moderati of the vile Imperium with their Mars-made machines—though maybe ours were assembled on fabled Mars millennia ago. We are Lord Sagramoso's claws, talons of the New God who will tear loose a great sphere of space and stars for Himself, and for us...

Our plasma reactor is old, though...

So Sergeant Juron's excuse might indeed have seemed only too plausible...

For a moment, Yeremi felt a spark of hope.

"Internal command radio," Juron's voice said in Yeremi's ear, startling him with the recognition that they were all parts of one united body now. "All acknowledge. State capacity and battle readiness."

"Valence. Left arm plasma cannon. I think I got the hang of it."

"D'Arquebus in the left shoulder. Carapace macro-cannon. Tasty brain. Sweet, sooo sweeeet to me."

"Tundrish. Right arm. Power fist. Feels mega!"

("Though not much *use* in the circumstances!" d'Arqebus cooed softly.)

"No firing till I say, d'you hear! When I *do* say, open up on the one Warlord I designate. Figging, full salvo. Overload its shields—that's how to cripple it. Then we'll target another. Let's sell ourselves dear."

("And what will Tundrish do, poor thing, but clench his great big fist in frustration?")

"Tundrish: your turn will come if all the other weapons

go down. If we're still alive. D'Arquebus: cut the chatter. *Imperial* Fists do not succumb to frustration. Akbar!''

"Right shoulder. Carapace defence laser. I'm not... sure. Feels... cramped, heavy. Can't get the feel. Can't swivel easily."

("Why not nip up top and grease it?") Only Lyman's Ear could have detected such a sly whisper.

"I don't feel ... merged properly."

"Just *try* to fire where your Brothers fire, Akbar."

In the distance, one of the Warlords half-turned...

...as the Emperor Titan jerked, its spastic tremors caused by an untrained, amateur Princeps. A rocket atop the Warlord tracked tentatively towards the shuddering Emperor.

Vortex missile...

...creates a whirlpool of seething energy...

...our only vortex missile. Will it work...?

"Oh Dorn, dawn of our being, be with us, illuminate us," prayed Juron.

Engines thrumming now, the Emperor Titan lurched forward roughly, crashing its right foot down, then its left, so that Yeremi's seat bounced violently on its hydraulic suspension, and he almost fired plasma prematurely. The corpse of the rebel Moderatus rolled to and fro, and somehow the amulet had slid into the rocking skull cup.

How the giant machine swayed and staggered—until Juron gained a semblance of proper rhythm.

The far end of the arena was opening, however. Vast vitrodur panels pistoned upward to reveal a battle-torn vista beyond. The inquisitive Warlord turned to realign itself with its mechanical peers—which strode onward together in line abreast, to massacre Marines.

Chapter Ten

Biff's whole right arm was encased in a flexible sleeve of slim sensor-studded steel hoops embedded in flexiplast, and his hand in a glove of the same. The weight of the ensemble was counterbalanced by the tug of transmission cables snaking up into the ceiling. In repose Biff's arm hung in mid-air; he might have been recuperating in a wing of the Apothacarion with his limb in traction...

He clenched his fist in frustration.

On a light-amplifying side-screen, the huge power fist outside—size of an assault tank—obediently clenched itself too, becoming an adamantium wrecking ball. The outline of its fibre-sinews flickered in viridian, while diagnostic ikons marched across the bottom of the screen. The system was checking itself, though Biff was unsure what answers it was coming up with.

Limit to what you can get by gobblin' a guy's raw brain.

Wearing the fist felt mega indeed. The previous user had painted a snarling beast's mouth across the palm. Big teeth dripping red goo.

Felt bad, too. Frustrating.

'Cos when was he going to get to use it?

The Warlords had already marched right out of the arena. But so far Sergeant Juron had done nothing except walk the Emperor along, swaying, in their wake.

Heave, *thump*; heave, *thump*.

"We don't want the arena closing up afore we're out of it, Lads," he explained.

Sure. Of course not.

Even when their Emperor did emerge into the fire-streaked gloom, Juron let the Warlords cross right over that plaza.

Warlords shoulder to shoulder, unmissable targets. The inlaid phoenix silhouettes seemed to be their great golden, alchemical footprints.

("*Sir,*" d'Arquebus spoke up from his control bubble. "How soon, Sir?") The swank sounded to be on a knife edge, barely controlling himself.

("Not yet!")

Deliberately, Biff relaxed his fist.

In his main screen, on high magnification, he saw beyond the Warlords to where the squad upon squad of Imperial Fists were advancing, some under cover of Land Raiders and Rhinos, others leapfrogging squad by squad from one hard-fought nook to the next.

A whole zone of the city had flattened itself into a vitrodur plain. Slim spires still soared to support the ebon umbrella shields. Otherwise, architecture was largely reduced to stubby tower-tops, inky and indigo, from which hostile fire poured. Local troopers crouched in ambush in a maze of low black glassite trenches—wrinkles in the telescoped city's jointed carapace—and emerged from armoured hatches in what had previously been rooftops.

The defending troopers were being beaten back steadily. Momentarily, in the jolting muzz of magnification, Biff thought he glimpsed the battle standard of the Fists.

Commander Pugh would be right there in the thick, tasting the heart-fires of battle—he who could taste nothing else.

(*"But their backs are to us!"*)

("And their void shields are overlapping because they're so figging close together! I don't know whether that multiplies the shielding—I can't regurge that info—but sure as hell they'll cover for each other! They must move apart. They *must*.)

"Can't we charge inside the shielding?" Biff asked. Without quite realizing he clenched his fist again, crushing empty air.

("If they open fire without moving apart, we *shall*.")

("Our Sergeant's being a tactician," d'Arquebus commented wryly.)

("Pain-glove for that comment! Afterwards... Understood?")

If there was any afterwards.

Which seemed unlikely.

At least they would die in a disciplined mood.

The previous user had also daubed the ducts along the roof of Biff's control bubble with vermilion slogans. *Ego Atrox. Ego Ferox.*

Whatever those meant.

The author of those words lay slaughtered beside the gimballed plasteel chair. Brainless now. Dumb, speechless, senseless, blind. Biff had swallowed his eyes too, as an afterthought.

But yes, yes... now the Warlords were angling away from one another as they tramped thunderously towards the Marines—who could certainly see them now through veils of smoke in the darkness riven by the lightning of explosions. No, dear Marines, these aren't mobile buildings looming out of the obscurity—but six of the mightiest war machines ever crafted! With one other lagging behind... That's what the Imperial Fists would be seeing, staunch horror in their hearts.

And what would Lord Pugh, that purified man, be feeling? Surely, a certain consternation.

Biff sympathised.

And he raged because he could not reach out to interpose his power fist.

And he sought to still his soul with a prayer.

Many of those stubby towers out on the field of battle were recessing further to sink flush with the surface. All those that could. A few were damaged, their mechanism jammed or their power supply shorted out.

Many Kark troopers and vehicles were left exposed, yet what of that? The advancing Imperial Fists, and their surviving Land Raiders and Rhinos, were soon likewise denuded of any significant cover—whereupon the Warlord Titans opened fire from their lofty eminence to rake the terrain with laser beams, heat-beams, plasma, and cannon shells.

(*"That Titan with the missile! Destroy it!"*) At last Juron had given the order.

As their striding Emperor quivered with the unleashing of its weaponry, Biff sat impotently for only a few moments.

Rotating his power fist, he gave the finger to the Warlords: an adamantium finger bigger than any armoured Marine.

He hoped some of the Fists might perhaps behold that gesture with joy.

Whistling a half-forgotten high-hab melody, *Necromundan Nightclub*, Lexandro pumped cannon shells at the arse of the Warlord swaying there in the cross hair graticule of his aiming screen. Explosion followed explosion. Damnably, gouts of plasma from Valence often interfered, detonating shells before they even reached the target's void shield. Valence the void-brain, Valence the virtuous valet. Why couldn't the figger choose his own portion of titanic

anatomy to shaft? Did he think he was helping? Akbar the
sand-flea at least was pulsing laser beams at that missile
atop the carapace.

Still, the Titan's void shields were starting to flush
visibly. Blotches of orange and electric blue energy
coruscated, mantling the monster in wraiths of electro-
magnetic disease.

The Titan was turning back, its missile swivelling.

A neighbouring Warlord was turning too...

The great splayed fairings of their target's legs were
painted with ochre volcanoes spraying hot scarlet lava like
blood from an artery. It sought to steady itself amidst
plasma and shell-blast...

...and the missile erupted. More than one of the void
screens had at last been overloaded. Just before the missile
could be launched Akbar's laser had tickled it to detonate.

Lexandro's eyes ached as energy whirlpooled. A local
region of space itself seemed to writhe in superheated
paroxysm, tearing the Titan apart into a maelstrom of
spinning vapour.

The nearby Titan lurched askew, its banner on fire, the
multi-melta of its right arm warped and sputtering. Its left
arm aimed a las-cannon at the Emperor's carapace.
Lexandro's vision blurred momentarily as their void
screens fluoresced, soaking up incoming lances of light.

Yet another Titan was turning to confront the enemy at
their backs.

And a third.

A fourth hesitated.

Obviously they must destroy this threat which was so
much more puissant than that posed by the Land Raiders.

However, those assault tanks were now concentrating
las-cannon fire on the other Titans, raking upwards as high
as they could—at fairings, legs, and belly—so that those
Titans marched through a dancing aurora of writhing
spider-lightning.

One Titan's lower shield flared and failed.

Land Raiders closest to the exposed Warlord redoubled their efforts, scalpelling away at its right knee-joint just above the fairing.

The offended Titan lumbered forward and stamped upon one Raider, crushing it underfoot. It gushed plasma at a small knot of Marines who were storming a trench crowded with troopers. Suited bodies were thrown head over heel.

Yet then the Titan began to lurch arthritically; its right leg had locked up. . .

Its Princeps still tried to walk it, thusting the rigid leg out—in vain. The Warlord toppled backwards—slowly at first, then avalanching down on to the vitrodur surface. Marines raced at power-speed to empty their boltguns into its heavy weapons, now laid low, so as to pierce casings and blast actuators lest the Moderati recover from the stun and injuries of the fall. . .

Even before Juron ordered the targetting of the Titan that had been touched by the vortex implosion, Lexandro wrenched his attention back to the immediate peril. He pumped cannon shells at the las-cannon on that Titan's carapace—while searing light pulsed from it towards theirs.

From other quarters too. Those other Titans which had turned were hurling shells and plasma and bolts of heat.

Exhilaration pulsed through Lexandro's being.

"Though you fly through the ultimate fire—" he seemed to hear. . .

Yes, he was almost flying—so high above the ground was he. Explosions and convulsions of heat clawed at the energy shields—an unending succession of ravenous monsters springing into existence just outside, only to die because they could not feed *yet*, yet being born again instantly.

Lexandro wasn't going to die in this battle. Not *die*, but be transfigured. Soon his shield must fail. Soon those eruptive, blinding spasms of violence outside must reach in to snatch him, to tear him apart, and vaporise his fabric. His flesh would become boiling plasma.

Yet his spirit, united with Dorn's in that exquisite agonizing pang, in that orgasmus of death, would transmigrate into a being of boiling ionized gas. In this form he would hover over the battlefield, dipping down to engulf enemy troopers, to consume these like fat in a furnace so that their smoke would rise up as incense into Dorn's amber nostrils and by way of that conduit across time and space—beyond mortality itself—into the God-Emperor's seered olfactory lobes so that the Divine Person would pause for a microsecond in his eternal scrutiny of the cosmos from his golden throne and would exclaim inwardly, ''What sweet fragrance is that? Why, it is the odour of the enemies of the human Imperium, blazing.'' For a moment the Emperor would notice at least the aftermath of Lexandro's existence... before what had been Lexandro dispersed.

Reality reasserted itself as, in Lexandro's headphones, a voice screamed in torment. Or was it in sheer surprise?

The screech died away to a strangulated hissing as though the victim had clamped his lower lip with his teeth, biting with all the force of a steel beast-trap.

''Right dorsal shield collapse,'' announced Juron bleakly. ''Feedback damper failure. Defence laser is slag. Cutting Akbar out of circuit.''

The strident, static-like hiss ceased abruptly.

Though that did not mean that, in his bubble chamber, Akbar was not still writhing in the agony of pseudo-injury—terrible burns and blindness—as he struggled to master such huge referred pain. He was feeling what the laser would have felt, had it been of flesh and bone. He was enduring. Unless he was already dead.

The caustic reek of smouldering insulation...

The bitter lemon tang of melted plasteel...

Fishy whiffs of liquefied adamantium... The bite of

ozone from air molecules fused by fierce discharges of energy...

And the heat, the scorching heat. The remaining void shields were doing their best to bleed hostile energies away as heat, but there wasn't time for it to radiate away. The interior of the Emperor was beginning to resemble a hell.

A ceiling gargoyle sucked in furnace breath. A floor gargoyle exhaled air that was cooler, yet the refrigeration unit was thumping in distress. Lexandro coughed and spat at the partly crippled Titan on his target-screen. His gob of saliva dribbled down then clung, warping the image of the turtle head as though the corresponding section of the enemy Titan was bubbling, rheum leaking from its right eye.

He fired again and again at that phantom weakness, divined by spuomancy, targeted by phlegm.

The Titan with the blazing banner shook its head from side to side like some grazing beast tormented by stinging flies, by the hornets of his cannon shells.

Abruptly one slanted eye exploded.

The Titan gyrated, swinging around in spasm. Its injured Princeps must be convulsing. Bright spears from its las-cannon and plasma from its carapace cannon washed briefly across its neighbouring Warlord before the erring Moderati realized.

The metal giant danced then crashed over.

Lexandro's macro cannon must have overheated and jammed. In his hooded hand he felt a terrible clutching cramp that would not allow him to move his fingers.

Maybe there were no more shells left in the cannon's magazine. He had been prodigal with them.

"Macro cannon dead," he reported.

Targeting the nearest Warlord, he spat again vehemently at the screen.

And sat.

Awaiting the dying of his void shield.

And his own dazzling transfiguration into plasma.

Yeremi peered every which where for weapons which might be aiming at the now-inactive macro cannon on their carapace, or at their left shoulder where d'Arquebus was ensconced.

D'Arquebus mustn't die prematurely.

Oh no.

Inspired, Yeremi sprayed a stream of incandescent rainbow plasma gobbets at a defence laser which was tracking in that forbidden direction, and rejoiced to see its shield fail and the shark-snouted gun warp and drip like a lugubrious runny nose.

"Ha! Saved you there, Lexy!" he exclaimed to himself, forgetful that he was on an open channel.

("Saved me?" came an ethereal voice. "What, from my golden transmigration?")

What on Necromunda was d'Arquebus rhapsodizing about?

("You villein! You valet!") Those insults were virtually meaningless nonsense—yet at least it seemed that d'Arquebus had been *stung*.

("Lucky shooting, Valence," snapped Juron. "Ain't enough, though. We're down to your gun alone. I'm gonna run. Try to get inside the next one's shields. Wake up, Tundrish. Time to earn your living.")

Given the bulk of the Emperor and the weight of its weaponry, it could not actually *run*, yet it could certainly lumber forward more quickly. Some onboard klaxon wailed as though in pain at the effort. Rocking buffetingly in the gimballed seat, Yeremi returned fire wildly to divert attention away from d'Arquebus. Missing, missing alas because of the lurching, even if the target loomed vaster by the moment.

"Drawing booster power for max fire," Yeremi shouted

to warn his Sergeant. "Good plasma cannon," he prayed, "best ever weapon, do not quit on me! *Artifex armifer digitis dextris oculis occultis!*" he chanted.

("What you doing?" shouted Juron.)

"Drawing booster power for max fire, Sir." The heat in the control bubble was almost unbearable. Sweat slicked Yeremi's flesh within his servomech sleeve. It was as though his hand and his whole arm were plunged deep within the hot tight birth-canal of some angry animal to manipulate the contents of a packed, pulsing womb.

("*What you doing?* We're slowing. Gotta be some override... Dorn, the reactor's red-line already! *I can blow it... Set it to figging explode!*")

("Incandesce us," prayed d'Arquebus. "Oh holy light, oh holy heat.")

Many things were happening at once. Yeremi's stream of plasma ceased abruptly as his hand cramped within that fervid womb. On the small monitor screen his great external weapon was white-hot, seething, dripping molten metal on to the carapace below. Doom-ikons flashed in panic. Tell-tales glared red. Pushed to the limits, their remaining void shields failed. Fumes from the charring generators swirled to choke the filters in the gargoyles' throats.

Then their Emperor collided with the Warlord in a teeth-jarring, bone-shaking impact of metallic mountains. Which teetered, rocking back on their adamantium heels.

Had the Emperor Titan been moving any more swiftly— had Yeremi not drained power and slowed the lumbering charge—both great robots might have toppled over devastatingly.

This did not happen.

And in that moment of recoil from collision...

"It's *biffing* time!"

Biff swung his power fist upwards into the turtle head of

136

the Warlord, staving in its slanted eyes, crushing through adamantium into the Princeps' cabin, pulverizing the softer contents within.

His power fist was locked in wreckage... as Juron swung the body of the Emperor about so that its carapace faced the fury of the surviving Warlords. Some shells caromed off their back. Others erupted on it, while hostile lances of light sought the gaping wounds those explosions had opened...

Their turtle head strained clear of the almost decapitated Warlord.

("Emergency evac! Overloading reactor!")

Of a sudden Biff was propelled sidelong then forward in his bubble, to crash into the escape chamber.

Yeremi, in his bubble, likewise cannoned askew into the occipital portion of the head.

And Lexandro was hurled from dreams of incandescence into that now sooty cavity.

Blind, burned Akbar was not salvaged, though. Some guidance unit must have failed. And perhaps this was a blessing.

A moment later the head blasted free.

It soared close past another Titan which was already turning around again—limping mightily—to answer the las-pulses of the Land Raiders.

Over the vitrodur battlescape the Emperor's detached head veered. It rocked and yawed.

("Brace yourselves! Brace!")

Presently, the flying head touched down in a crash which was at least semi-controlled. Onwards it skidded on its side across sleek vitrodur through corpses and burning husks of vehicles for almost half a kilometre before finally coming to rest...

With the exception of the Sergeant in the Princeps' seat, those inside the head had not been able to notice the fireball behind them, though the blast wave contributed somewhat to their sway.

Within the hour, from the Fists' rearguard, the bruised and battered Scouts were to watch a greater detonation—when the ziggurat of Lord Sagaramoso's besieged palace erupted volcanically.

The explosion hurled a black ship upwards on a tail of fire. Simultaneously, coaly umbrellas flew apart so that smoky sunlight bathed the devastation below.

The fleeing ship shrank as it climbed a column of billowing grey cloud. It became a mote, a shining point.

Then this point blossomed silently.

An orbiting imperial battleship must have noted the attempted escape.

Chapter Eleven

The crusaders had returned to their interstellar castle—which flew onward from nowhere to nowhere just as it had done for many millennia, and must continue to do for many millennia more.

The Sagramoso dynasty had been duly expunged from Karkason *ad extremum fetum*. The cult of that false god was purged and all of its images and statuary pulverized. A new loyal planetary governor of the Capreolo clan had been installed to supervize the export of power crystals and psycurium; and perhaps even more importantly, the offering up of devout prayer.

So the Battle Brothers gathered in the Assimularum to feast on a tithe of succulent smoked blindfish from the warm subterranean culture lakes of Karkason.

All of those who had travelled through the warp to Karka's Sun and returned alive crowded the carved benches; and Lord Pugh partook too—enthroned at high table on a dais in front of the enamelled rood-screen—even though the pink piscine flesh was less than ashes in his mouth. On either side of his own silver plate, like some massive array of bone cutlery, were ranged the amputated hands of those who had died in the campaign, shorn of flesh and muscle and tendons.

Many more Brothers had returned than might otherwise have been the case, had the Wolverine Squad not commandeered that Emperor Titan...

Fresh from punishment in the pain-glove, glowing pink himself, Lexandro sat with his brother Scouts, regarded with some awe by those not of Wolverine Squad.

The feast proceeded in dainty silence until a bare fish skeleton the size of a heavy bolter lay on the platter before each celebrant, and their stone steins stood empty.

Then Battle Chaplain Lo Chang preached...

...and Lexandro heard of such incidents of the campaign as the Battle of the Glass Bell Temple, and of the Sixty Suicide Skaters who had swooped on Brothers of the Fourth Company clutching melta-bombs, and how the Fifth and Seventh and Eighth Companies had found themselves confronted, to their astonishment, by Titans...

...which Wolverine Scout Squad led by Sergeant Zed Juron had proceeded to savage, at the cost of one dead Scout—a sacred event which must forever be commemorated. Even now a Master Artificer was engraving a wall-tablet to be mounted in the Teuton Chapel. After twenty years' exposure to religious scrutiny, if deemed worthy and untarnished, this votive tablet would be transferred to the Reclusiam itself.

Stern, ascetic Lord Pugh signalled to Lo Chang, and the Chaplain's cratered moon-face shone with joy.

Chang proclaimed: "*Nos honoremus mortuum Omar Akbar, cuius osses sunt perditos, in pleno grado Pugni Imperatorii!*"

In his death the sand-flea had been raised to the status of a full Marine...

The Brothers banged their steins upon the table-tops in a quickening rhythm till the fish skeletons quivered and seemed about to swim.

Lexandro grinned wildly, for within but a few more weeks he was to have holes drilled through his carapace so that he could jack in to power armour. Whereupon he would be enrolled forthwith as a tyro marine of full status.

As would Valence be, and Tundrish.

Lexandro directed his grin at them. All three "brothers" had earned their rapid elevation from the Scouts.

Tundrish leered back—a smirk generally twisted his spider tattoo into a predatory posture. Clenching his fist to deliver an imaginary uppercut, he sketched the very blow he had used to crush the Warlord's face.

Valence also smiled, though his was a pensive smile, a smile of reverie. He regarded Lexandro musingly as a brother might a sister whose honour he must protect—a sentiment which Lexandro had purged from his own soul, though he recognized the symptoms. Aye, in warped guise.

Briefly, the image of Lexandro's own two indulged foolish siblings, Andria and Phoeba, flitted through his consciousness for what seemed the first time in years. He had rightly abandoned them, since the only way that honour could be restored was the path he had chosen; or rather, the path on to which he had been propelled. The path of the Legiones Astartes, the star warriors. In the intricate weave of the universe, his was the golden strand, and his sisters' was dross, part of the vast lumpen-knot of the ordinary, the confined mortal mass that bred and died on a million worlds like some foetid yeast in order to ferment a spirit such as his, a spirit which a God-Emperor could sip.

Marines *defended* that yeast from pollution and corruption...

They defended with fire and explosive bolts.

Was this the "higher justice" that Valence sometimes babbled about? Aye, babbled *sanctimoniously!* When, for its sake, Valence himself had abandoned his own tech kin! Brother Yeremi must be a hypocrite.

In that pensive pucker of Brother Yeremi's lips Lexandro sensed that he himself was now becoming a focus for Valence's hypocrisy...

Phoeba and Andria... A comely pair, resembling Lexandro himself in countenance... Refined...

Even now that he was so brawny with musculature, rooted over ceramically reinforced bones, Lexandro remained personable.

Andria and Phoeba... Faces... Names... Yet not whole bodies, in the way that his own was whole—enhanced and complete. In his mind's eyes Lexandro could no longer quite capture nor comprehend the essentially alien anatomy of his quondam sisters. The anatomy of... woman...

Sister... Mother... high-hab whores whom the Lordly Phantasms had amused themselves with... those were mere spectres now, white ghosts.

Abandoned ghosts.

Lexandro stared at Valence, and it was as if their minds conjoined for an instant—Valence would never *abandon* Lexandro. He would haunt him, so as to complete some aberrant equation within his own brain which allowed Brother Yeremi to pursue his exalted, disingenuous ideal.

The Chaplain processed to a lectern. From an aumbry cupboard beside it, repository for sacred vessels, he removed a gilded holo-projector into which he slipped a data-cube.

In the looming vacancy above the tables appeared the tableau of Lord Sagramoso's palace... erupting, throwing upward once again that black ship.

The very next scene must have been recorded from an imperial battleship in orbit. The view was distant and distorted. A large ship climbed from the orb of Karkason. A ship erupted. Wreckage flew afar, diminishing out of sight.

This scene segued into the smoking wreckage of a fallen Warlord in Sagramoso City—now renamed Fidelis—up which an armoured Fist was climbing to plant a charred torn victory banner...

Battle Brothers sang a psalm, hundreds of bass voices throbbing with emotion. Tears trickled down the cheeks of some stout veterans.

And then Lord Pugh distributed the hands of the dead to those who had most distinguished themselves—to be wrought upon patiently over many years in their cells with scrimshaw designs.

Sergeant Juron received one such hand, which he placed tenderly inside a velvet-lined brazen case presented to him by a Medic Captain for the purpose.

The three Scouts could not, of course, be so honoured since they were not quite yet full Brothers. Nor was the itch yet in them to engrave finger bones—though that would come with the passage of time. Very likely it would come. The pastime was contagious, as itches often are... that yearning to honour by meticulous craftsmanship—and in a very real sense to shake hands with—the glorious dead...

Afterwards, Lexandro—still thinking fitfully of the bodies of women and of Brother Yeremi's ambivalent attitude towards him—said to his fellow Scout, "Shall we see how *part* of a person thrives?"

Valence understood Lexandro's meaning well enough.

So they turned their footsteps in the direction of the dropshaft which led down to the Solitorium.

Tundrish caught up with the two of them before they descended—whether filled with an access of comradeship, or leery of why they should seemingly wish to seclude themselves together, who could say?

Down, down the trio dropped, to step out into that long starlit gallery at the base of the fortress-monastery where Brothers would cloister themselves to meditate.

Oriel windows projected over a void which fell away forever to the very edge of the universe itself, if such an edge existed. Perhaps, in some unimaginably distant region, the cosmos simply melted away into Chaos without sane dimensions—so that all the immensity of physical reality, all the billions of light years of stars and galaxies without number, amounted to no more than a tiny archipelago within a dire and senseless ocean of absurdity.

Plasteel mullions divided the narrow, high lancet windows of stained armour-glass. Those panes lent spurious colours to the drifts of stars and lakes of nebulae. Here, a wash of azure suns. Further along, a pool of bilious gas pricked by glittering young luminaries. Necklaces of florid carbuncles... Cyanotic tiaras... An emerald zodiac... The dagger-shaped trefoils in the parabolic arches above were uniformly of blood hue.

Steadfastly beholding one jaundiced sector of the cosmos, there lolled Kroff Tezla, Lieutenant of the Blood Drinkers.

That heroic total-amputee had been rescued at the same time as the sculpts of the Sagramoso dynasty were all reduced to dust. The limbless barrel of a man had been removed from his bronze flowerpot, freed from the loam of lead. Now his torso rested in a cup-shaped cart adorned with valour tassles and therapeutic seals. Two speechless simian Servitors attended him, one to ingest his waste and cleanse him, the other to nourish him with its own enriched blood and shift his cart from window to window—from which he gazed out, praying for an exploration vessel of his Chapter to pass this way.

An Astropath in the Librarium had messaged to Tezla's own fortress-monastery on San Guisuga, a jungle world five thousand light years away, though it might be some years yet till that cousinly Chapter retrieved their Lieutenant. Meanwhile he remained a guest of the Fists, whose Chirurgeons deemed his scapular and hip scars too throughly cauterized to allow them to cyborg him. His vampiric metabolism—the gene flaw of his Chapter—was somewhat peculiar, besides. The Lieutenant had opted for seclusion in the Solitorium.

"Greetings," Lexandro addressed Tezla as one of the apish customized Servitors licked the Blood Drinker with its long tongue.

Melancholy rheumy eyes regard the trio. The chalices on Tezla's cheeks wept tattooed gore. A double line of cicatrices along his lips marked where the whip-thong had been laced.

His long sharp canines jutted as he replied, "You have some enquiry...?" He blinked. "...Ah, I recognize you. You were my discoverers."

"Do you regret your survival?" asked Valence curiously.

"There's no shame, while I still have my teeth. If Sagramoso's lackeys had pulled out my teeth, though! They did not think of that..."

"We're glad you endured," said Valence. "We're all in your debt."

"Go ahead," Lexandro invited. "Why don't you offer him your arm to bite? Let him suck you."

"I would not," the Lieutenant said with cold courtesy, "wish to feast on a Battle Brother who was not of my Chapter."

This remark intrigued Lexandro. "So do you sup each other's blood?"

"Did you come here to taunt me politely? But really like children at a freak fair mocking mutants?"

"I do wonder," interrupted Tundrish, "how the Karks got hold of those Titans? What manner of clever techs reconditioned those Warlords?"

"I have already been asked that question several times under druggings of Veritas. I had no opportunity to learn, and none of Fulgor Sagramoso's excruciators teased me by telling. I don't know. Our galaxy is vast and filled with mystery."

Tundrish nodded. "And no informants survived, to

Ian Watson

question.''

Numerous senior rebels and injured Moderati had committed suicide to avoid just such an outcome...

"Do you want for anything, Sir?" asked Valence.

"Do I want for anything?" echoed Tezla gloomily. "Arms?" he suggested. "Legs?"

At last, came the joyful day when the holes were carefully bored into the three Scouts' dorsal flesh in the Apothacarion, and through their subcutaneous carapaces which were now fully fledged...

Armour! Power armour!

Lexandro waited patiently within the suit which made him so much more awesome a giant while armiger techs and biomedics, uttering incantations, completed their checks on the trio of warriors in a rib-vaulted barbican giving access to the practice deck. The plasteel door of the airlock was a grim grin of great interlocking teeth, surrounded by tubular lips from which ducts ran to pressure gauges.

Vacuum pumps sweated chilly condensation. Compressors attached to rune-stippled air tanks thumped with the beat of a hyperactive heart. Vent valves along serpentine pipes hissed.

He waited *in* his armour? Nay, he *was* his battle suit. Through the interface of the black carapace the suit plugged into his spine with nerve electrodes and into his motor nervous system.

As soon as Lexandro flexed a finger, his power gauntlet twitched in rapport. He shifted his foot a fraction; immediately electronic signals through fibre bundles amplified his motion so that the weight of his boot and the flared greave obeyed effortlessly. He blinked, and projected before himself a read-out monitoring his life-support systems.

He was not viewing his snout-visored companions with his actual eyes, though. The optic sensors in his visor transmitted the scene through the suit's calculator directly to his brain. Thus no flash, however bright, should blind him. Thus, using infra-red, he would be able to stare through smoke or darkness.

In the Titan he had only been a partial paladin—merely part of a vaster amplified body which also comprised Tundrish and Valence and Zed Juron and, oh yes, Akbar too. Now Lexandro was complete in himself.

"Fists of Dorn, about turn!" a voice ordered over the radio. A voice that grated mechanically. Faust Stossen, their new Squad Sergeant, had once been lasered through the throat and wore a damascened silver voice box in place of his Adam's Apple.

The gargantuan teeth of the airlock unclenched.

Stars burned unblinkingly in the inky void like tiny hostile eyes. A nearby nebula, orange and pink, was the lurid gaseous residue of an explosion. The towers of the home-base soared, pennants and banners glittering in the light from illuminated galleries. Those metal flags never stirred, nor ever would. Perhaps a single atom of interstellar hydrogen might strike each once a year; such was the only breeze here between the stars. The trio spread out across the acres of plasteel, holding their lasguns ready—three hunters awaiting the flushing of birds that could fly through the void.

"Targets incoming any time from now—"

Now the faint hint of an energy shield encompassed towers and galleries, in case any laser fire flew astray. The initiate Marines would not of course practice with boltguns here, where shells could speed onward unimpeded by atmosphere or gravity, perhaps striking some incoming ship. Nor did one put shrapnel into orbit around the base. Thus, too, no target drones could be destroyed. The lasguns were at their lowest setting; though mistakes might still occur.

Lexandro and his companions were simply about to test their reflexes, their accuracy, their control of the power suits. Many weeks of such training must follow, in the target ranges beside the Foundries, and in cleverly designed menacing environments, using live ammunition.

A speck of light caught Lexandro's attention. He pivoted, aimed, fired. Fired again.

"*Drone hit*," reported his calculator, assessing the reflected light.

The target swooped overhead, twisting and turning. Other little drones were rushing by, some of which were only decoys. Faint pencils of light rose from Valence and Tundrish.

Lexandro's drone returned, corkscrewing above him. He twisted to track it. Unexpectedly light leapt from the drone itself. A searching spot snaked across the deck towards him.

This, he hadn't expected. Not that the drones would fire back. He ran aside, firing upward on the run. The beam from the drone didn't heat the deck, consequently it was low-powered too. If it touched him presumably *he* would be registered as hit. A black mark against him!

"*Drone hit*." The target veered away; spiralled back.

It fired. The deck glowed between his feet. Lexandro leapt aside.

He leapt so easily, so mightily in the minimal gravity prevailing outside the fortress-monastery. He leapt with both feet.

And left the deck behind.

He drifted on upwards at an angle. He had lost his magnetic grapple on the deck. His exhaust pipes were pushing him away too.

He increased the magnetism of his boots to maximum so as to draw himself down. Ach, the deck was already metres below! His method would fail. Use the stabilising jets, of course...!

"We are hit. Jets deactivated." Fury filled Lexandro; and he stilled that fury. He fired at the drone. Again, again.

"Drone hit. Drone hit. Drone hit." His robot attacker fled away, and seemed to lose interest in Lexandro. Perhaps he had "killed" it. But perhaps it classified him as out of action, impotent despite his puissant armour. Neutralised. There was no way back to the deck. On the contrary, he was slowly drifting higher, and sternwards. Given his rate of drift, within ten or fifteen minutes the home-base would pass onward beneath him. He would seem a fool.

The two other mock-combatants were still tilting with lances of light at the quintains of other drones.

One of them fired, fired, fired... and presently trotted towards Lexandro, to keep pace beneath him, peering up facelessly—while Lexandro floated, vulnerable. Inspecting Lexandro speculatively, so it seemed.

Which of the two was it? Valence—or Tundrish?

The figure held his lasgun upright, the nozzle against the tip of his visor, as if sniffing or kissing the weapon.

Surely his fraternal rival couldn't be contemplating shooting Lexandro? Not while scrutineers watched, and calculators assessed?

Yet the yawning emptiness out here upon the vast deck already seemed to be swallowing any sense of *connection* with the interior of the fortress-monastery...

As covertly as he could, Lexandro adjusted the setting on his own lasgun to maximum. Just in case. A lucky lasgun shot at max could sheer through a flexible joint in armour.

Was Lexandro being tempted—taunted—to do exactly that? To menace, and even to fire on a comrade? Was a malicious trap being laid for him, to discredit and disgrace him? The figure might wait till a drone swooped nearby and fire up at it—just as if shooting at Lexandro. Lexandro would fire back at the figure mistakenly... He'd be lucky if he was merely broken back into the Scouts for ten or twenty years. More likely he'd be executed—or left to drift till he died...

No, the Chapter would never abandon the armour.

Lexandro imagined his whole skeleton being presented to his enemy so that execrations could be carved upon Lexandro's bones, anathemas and runes of excommunication whereby his spirit would writhe forever—if a spirit there be—eternally separated from Rogal Dorn...

With its free power glove, the figure below made a sign as of a leaping spider.

That must be Tundrish! The scumnik had reverted to vengeful type.

Stabilising jets pulsed. The figure jumped gently, rising up alongside Lexandro, and gripped him with one metalled hand.

Both knights hung, stabilised.

The vibration of the other's voice communicated itself to Lexandro's Lyman's Ear.

Valence's voice. Valence must have tongued his radio off.

"You almost shot me, didn't you? Such restraint... Unlike your impulsive blundering leap. I see that I need to be your shadow. Yes indeed, by the Emperor's blood! 'Look,' other Marines will say, 'how that son of Trazior protects his rash brother, yet how his brother scorns him...!'"

"I ken your perversity already," retorted Lexandro. "Your cursed amor-odium fixation. Yet how typical of a tech to spell this all out so literally. Have you no finesse?"

"Shall I leave you... alone... brother? Alone, *now*?"

Lexandro considered.

"Oh you're really flying right now. You're hovering like some void-bird... Transcendent!" Had Valence trespassed on Lexandro's visionary dream? Had he invaded his very mind?

"But what use is it to you right now? Shall I leave you all alone?"

How haughty it would seem to refuse the aid of a Brother... so that others must inconvenience themselves by fishing him from the void.

"Shall I leave you alone... brother?"

"No," Lexandro said quietly. "Damn you."

Gently, Valence jetted the two suits back down to the training deck.

"Exercise completed," radioed Sergeant Stossen. "Double around the perimeter and return."

Valence promptly set off... However, for several seconds Lexandro's boots clamped him inflexibly to the plasteel surface like two puppies clinging to their bitch mother's teats—till he remembered to lower the magnetism.

Already some distance away by now, Valence looked back and rotated his power gauntlet, making a mocking spider sign.

The myriad of tiny far stars regarded the scene unflinchingly. Compared with those, the whole mighty base was but a jagged grain of crystal dust...

Only weeks after they had been initiated *in primo grado* by the Reclusiarch during a ceremony forbidden to describe, a message of alarm from Fidelis City reverberated through the fortress-monastery.

An Astropath on board a barge bound on the long slow haul from Karkason to the dwarf partner star, Karka Secundus, had chanced to eavesdrop on a telepathic message from the mining world to one of those agric planets that Sagramoso had seduced, using pirates paid with power crystals as his emissaries—pirates who had made themselves scarce with their illicit starships when the crusade had come through the Warp to Karka's Sun.

Lord Fulgor Sagramoso had *escaped* to that insignificant

mining world apparently known as Antro.

The ship which had blasted upward out of the ziggurat palace only to explode, had propelled a life-capsule onwards, a stasis casket disguised as wreckage...

The crusade was incomplete. Fists must punch their way through the Warp once more.

Yet this was very life itself. What other life was there?

To pray was to slay.

Righteously.

That the human galaxy might be free from all manner of evil, both of alien and of corrupted human origin, and also of unmentionable source.

The yeast must be pure, or the stars would be poisoned.

Chapter Twelve

Biff awoke from his demi-brain dream of the tunnels.

Instantly he checked his bolter, confirming that the magazine was indeed half empty. The cracketty sound he'd heard in his trance wasn't issuing from either entrance to the little cave his reconnaissance squad was sheltering in, but was propagating through the solid rock from roughly mid-way along, up by the roof.

Perhaps it was the sound of a fire-fight on another level. Perhaps not...

Maybe another cyborged Ambull was coming their way, clawing its way through the stone with one of the damned dwarfs saddled on its back, operating it.

The dream! What did it mean?

In a vast dream-cavern, squads of the Imperial Fists in their pus-yellow, blue-chevroned armour had been fighting with red-bearded dwarfs wearing quilted red flak-jackets and coveralls. At the selfsame time, in that selfsame place, Marines from a different Chapter entirely, who wore blood-red armour with black flashings, were in conflict with green-clad dwarfs. All four contending groups milled in

fury. Innumerable stalagmites reared, defining criss-cross-
ing routes. Yet Fists only fought the dwarfs in red—and
vice-versa—while those Blood Marines only fought green-
costumed dwarfs.

It was as though two entirely different battles were
superimposed chaotically; or perhaps as if one single battle
was utterly out of focus, stereoscopically ruptured, so that
the pattern of events was a nonsense...

Thus, in the dream.

Likewise in reality the three-dimensional pattern of all
these twisting tunnels and sudden caverns and shafts and
abysms eluded any easy comprehension. The subterranean
maze must sprawl for hundreds of kilometres laterally as
well as for several vertical kilometres.

Damn this treacherous world of Antro where Lord
Sagramoso lurked.

Did Biff need a dream to tell him of danger and deceitful
labyrinths?

No... The dream was more urgent in its prompting.

Of a sudden he felt convinced that those hypermobile
Marines and darting dwarfs in that phantasmal cavern were
ikons representing *processes* in his own grey matter as his
brain cells tried to come to terms with this place. Tried to
intuit its likely map.

In effect it was an *undercity*—not consisting of bowing
plasteel vaults choked with dreck and polluted wastes and
drifts of metallic scurf and broken rusted machines, to be
sure—no, but buried underground nonetheless: a maze of
stone intestines and bowels. These must possess a pattern
that the bearded little troglodytes understood like the hairy
backs of their hands, like the lines of their tough palms...

But not Biff. Not yet. Though the right hemisphere of his
brain was struggling to savvy.

That cracketty sound was becoming louder; and Biff's
armoured companions were alert too. Lex and Yeri and
Sarge Stossen. No peace for the virtuous.

A crunching, pulverizing noise...

Stossen signalled for silence with his power glove, and cocked his heavy bolter.

Something was going to break through into the cave—unless whatever it was altered direction.

And they would destroy the something.

Maybe this would prove to be a diversion to mask an onslaught into the cave from either existing entry...

Biff noted that Yeri was at least keeping watch to the leftward, and Lex to the rightward.

Maybe a new tunnel was simply being bored slyly, to increase the already labyrinthine complexities and provide a new route for ambush and attack... In which case, their reconnaissance squad might seize an advantage and penetrate through to a new, forward position. Beyond, above, or below.

So long as the new route didn't prove too narrow. So long as it didn't kink and cramp after starting out adequately.

Power armour was invaluable here. Booby-traps menaced the Marines. Dead-falls and pitfalls abounded. Even doughty Eagle Armour could be buckled or imprisoned by a ton of rock falling down a shaft upon it. Camouflaged hatches of rock could spring open, to disgorge dwarfs.

Electroflambeaux that lined the tunnel walls were being kept doused by some distant engineers—though those illuminations might blaze up selectively to spotlight Marines at a moment of attack from out of deeper darkness. Generally darkness prevailed, redeemed only by phosphorescent violet lichens faintly blotching the walls. Even a Marine's keen eyesight might have grown weary but for the extra enhancements afforded by the helmet.

Without oxygen tanks, the air would often have been far from breathable. Some tunnels contained mere stale nitrogen. Poison gas choked others. Arcane, treacherous machinery would exhaust the atmosphere from some areas, and pour caustic vapours into others as the Marines advanced.

Yet power armour was *bulky* in such confined spaces. Main galleries, with railway lines laid along them, were wide—yet also deserted. Most passages were considerably narrower. A while since, they had come across one Battle Brother who, through over-eagerness or due to enemy deceit, had become jammed in a cleft. His boots—and feet—had been burnt off wickedly from behind, crippling him.

Up above, in the ruddy light of Karka Secundus, the surface of Antro was a harsh, barren wasteland of scree and talus and spoil heaps from which rocky pinnacles soared. Very little of attackable value was up there, beside a small spaceport for ore freighters and various shafthead buildings, which the Fists had easily seized. Below was another matter. A whole subterranean domain of fierce Abhumans inhabited the excavated intestines of this stark little world.

The inhabitants, of course, were Squats—members of that rotund little race which had evolved away from the human norm inside the cavernous entrails of precisely such planets as Antro during millennia when those worlds were isolated by Warp storms. Tough, technically adept, they remained outside of the Imperial writ thereafter, pursuing their own devout form of ancestor worship.

Most Squats were staunch allies of the Imperium.

Not those of Antro, so it seemed.

Quite the opposite.

From prisoners captured during the taking of the spaceport, it was plain that Fulgor Sagramoso, the upstart godling, had played upon the Squats' passionate sense of independence and upon their religion. *He* was their bastion against that distant, miscomprehended Imperium which would swallow them up and force them to adore a crippled immortal Emperor on Earth rather than their own sacred forbears. Or so Sagramoso had persuaded them.

Did not Fulgor worship his own forefathers too? Had he not shown his Squattish allies holograms of multitudinous, oft times dusty statues of the Sagramoso clan dating back for thousands of years?

Did Fulgor not sacrifice his enemies in chains to those same ancestral busts and sculptures?

Aye, he did! He was almost a Squat in his devotion. Or so the fools thought. And that was why Sagramoso had declared himself to be a god—so as to divinize his forbears too.

For this *act of reverence* the Imperium aimed to destroy him—and would root out any such brand of worship from the caves of Antro likewise, as well as slaughtering the venerable old folk whom Squats revered as Living Ancestors...

So said the perfervid prisoners, before they were executed. Nothing could persuade them otherwise.

And before the Fists descended into the endless vaults and vents and crannies of Antro, full of aberrant clever tech, Lo Chang had preached a hasty battle sermon.

"We of the Legiones Astartes shun genetic deviants, do we not?" he had declaimed. "For the mutant is the melter of Mankind into misshapenness! Whereas we are Mankind Plus, the perfected ideal, are we not? For its own wise reasons our Imperium tolerates such dwarfs because their mutation is stable, and for the mineral wealth they produce, and their cunning dexterity, and their tenacity as fighters. So do not underestimate these little men, Brothers! But do not trouble your souls about ravaging this whole world of shrunken traitor dupes in order to reach Fulgor Sagramoso. Otherwise our Crusade is in vain, and Sagramoso will return with savage Squattish war-brethren to Karkason. *Delve, and destroy...*"

Below ground, this strategy proved less easy to implement.

Sagramoso's own strategy here plainly mirrored that in

Fidelis City, where he had hoped to funnel the Fists into the reach of Titans—which had been renovated for him, without a doubt, by these tech-minded Squats of Antro.

Here inside Antro his trap, and his defence, consisted not of seven adamantium giants but of thousands of angry dwarfs, buzzing and stinging like fire-bees as their nest was invaded...

Abruptly, a section of the cave wall crumbled.

Purulent yellow light washed into their temporary sanctuary as á toothed power-saw sheared through rock like flesh. A hammer-drill erupted outward, withdrew, punched another hole. Metal-jacketed teeth tore at lumps of stone. Jutting jaws crunched and ingested, the greed-crazed mandibles gulping the shattered rock into...

...a broad, tungsten-plated head...

...from which orange eyes glared, recessed within plasteel-reinforced orbits akin to skewed spectacle frames.

Tubular nostrils inhaled dust vigorously.

Twin torches, welded to the beast's brow ridges, projected that sickly light.

It was an Ambull, of course—and the hideous creature had been radically cyborged to make it an even more potent, swift tunneller.

Since it had halted its forward motion on encountering the great pocket of vacant space—and was now chomping around to neaten the aperture it had opened—the Marines, lurking motionless, held their fire a while longer, awaiting a full view, captive to a certain fascination.

Saw and drill, slotting into grooved elbow-chucks, replaced the creature's original forearms. Control cables corded its plated body like external muscles standing proud; nor could much of its original face remain...

More significantly, as regards dwarfish expertise, it was *stealthed*—by some noise-suppression field. Its excavation work produced no deafening reverberations, only the cracketting of chewed-up stone.

And as for the debris which it gulped into its cavernous throat...

Why, that throat must conceal a secondary, artificial gullet—a mini warp portal which could transmit the pulverized material to another location, to some distant goaf or gob where waste accumulated.

Else, how could the adapted creature have proceeded through the new tunnel it had drilled and cut and devoured?

This spoke of valuable, ancient wizardry.

The transformed, slaved Ambull reeked of rancid oil, hot vulcanized rubber, bestial alien sweat, and bitter breath—a whiff, almost, of the Warp itself.

Even foreshortened by its mining implements, its reach was long; while its massive legs were short, a splay of claws...

As the creature stooped, its rider appeared to view in the penumbra behind the torches, backed by the profounder dark of the tunnel.

The Engineer was ensaddled upon the Ambull's lower back just behind a bulging spur of polished bone inset with brass control knobs—a surgically metastasized excrescence from the Ambull's spine. Pewter-beaded thongs fringed the dwarf's scuffed brown leathers, which were studded with tiny steel hammers. His greased, fiery hair swept back to a knotted short pigtail. His monkey boots rested in stirrup-pedals which flared out from his mount's ribs.

And he was well armed.

An antler-like bracket sprouted from the Ambull's right shoulder. Presumably in normal times this served as a rack for other auxiliary tools. Now a tasselled ochre banner dangled from it, displaying a hammer rune. The antler supported a gimballed heavy bolter gun...

But this Engineer was no warrior, for a warrior might have raked the cave with explosive bolts as soon as could be, prior to exposing himself.

Sleek rockfaces moved—became saffron power armour—and fire spat economically at the rider and his tunnelling beast.

The leather-clad dwarf flew backwards out of his saddle, bloodily tunnelled through with bolts even before those exploded in mid-anatomy, wrenching the Abhuman askew.

Bellowing, the cyber-Ambull lurched forwards. Its saw shrieked. Its mandibles clashed, grinding out sparks. From its gaping mouth belched a hail of pebbles which pinged off Biff's suit. However, the beast was already fatally injured, its armour and inner organs ruptured, its mech-components short-circuiting...

Its torch light a-dying, the Ambull sprawled out of the tunnel mouth.

Lex was the first to climb over its back to peer.

The new tunnel curved away into utter obscurity at the limit of his suit light. "Ample enough," he drawled by way of report; and proceeded, crouching somewhat.

Yeri thrust himself into the passage so as to stay directly behind he whom he still loathed—notwithstanding brotherly courtesy and the intimacy forged by combat. Aye, *loathed*—and therefore must safeguard; else how could he retain a target for his bile? A cynosure for his contempt?

So the case seemed to Biff, at least...

But then, Biff never had leisure for such sophistries during his own formative years. For *thunking*, yes. But squirm-feelings, no way. Nor did he nurse any desire to indulge himself in such digressions nowadays. Knowledge—and *pattern*—were what figured in the sticky spider's web of the cosmos that entrapped and consumed all of its denizens in the end. Knowing how to walk the Way of the Knight.

Blood, of course, too. The sacramentally spilled blood of enemies.

That Ambull's blood, staining the stone, was a rusty haematitic orange.

Maybe Yeri's peculiar relationship to Lex made sense to Yeri, and gave him a pattern, of sorts.

Sarge Stossen's mech-voice grated out an order to Biff to bring up the rear, behind Stossen. So far as the Sarge was concerned, Lex could stay in the lead.

The first shall be first, mused Biff, *and the last shall be last...*

His powered boot crushed one of the dead dwarf's hands.

"Sarge," said Biff into his microphone, "air ain't too foul here. Dwarf was breathing it. Should we maybe pause to... eat his brain? He's gotta have known the layout. Mebbe he savvies where Lord Sag's lair is. We erase *him*, and the Abs don't matter much."

"You really think that was uppermost in the Ab's mind when he died?"

"No," admitted Biff.

"I'm well aware of your exploit with the Titans, Tundrish. We hail you for it. Fact is, though, you three all lucked out on Karkason... You know why? Because when you killed those Moderati and their Princeps those guys were absolutely concentrating on how to use that Emperor machine. That was uppermost in their brain-pans, right?"

"I guess so."

"Our Engineer dwarf would be thinking mostly about operating his beast-machine."

"I just have a feeling I might suss the Tao of these tunnels. The Ley of the layout. If I had a little more to digest."

"Maybe our Biff should eat the *Ambull* instead?" suggested Lex from up front. "More his style, I'd have thought..."

Stossen guffawed harshly, a slurry of razor blades being sucked down a drain.

"I tell you, you three *lucked out*. And those guys you ate on Kark were true *human*. What Marine wants to pollute

161

himself with the brain of an Ab unless it's absolutely vital? So just forget about being Corporal of a Cannibal Corps..."

Biff was aware by now that Sergeant Faust Stossen regarded even friendly Squats with a passionate nausea as caricatures of the true human species. No use trying to persuade him. Maybe it wasn't such a bright *thunk*, after all. Repetition was insectoid. Flexithunk spelled *survival*.

Those animated ikons would need to race around inside Biff's own brainpan a while longer, trying to suss out the Tao of the Tunnels, to spy the Way of the Web...

Biff's spider tattoo itched, as it hadn't in a long while. The newly hewn tunnel cramped itself around the advancing recce squad as if intent on squeezing shut, encasing them in it as metal fossils. The hulking, crook-legged Ambull had created enough clearance for its rider-master as well as itself. Yet the eagle power-armour still scraped from time to time.

The route cut a lazy, descending arc for a kilometre—to the northward, according to the compass runes projected upon Biff's faceplate—then it wended eastward. Dimly they lit the way with their suit-lamps, only allowing enough leakage of radiation so that their enhanced eyes could spy the lineaments of the tunnel. Less light, and even Marines would have been whelmed in absolute darkness, for here in the bowels of Antro—in a new passage where no phosphorescent lichen yet grew—their straitened surroundings were more profoundly obscure than during the darkest moonless night, when always some faint illumination leaks upon the senses from any natural sky whatever.

This sensory deprivation was compounded by electro-magnetic isolation—it had been quite some while since the Sergeant could raise any comprehensible radio response from Lieutenant Vonreuter. Before, radio waves had at least bounced capriciously through the maze of tunnels, however much hexed by static. No longer was there any channel to higher command. Only feedback howled. A few distant audio *crumps* and crackles... even those died away.

A nagging suspicion grew in Biff as they proceeded, yet it was Yeri who voiced the doubt...

"Much of this tunnel was made beforehand," he commented. "The excavator beast couldn't have cut so much since we seized the spaceport. See, this part's more cleanly finished. Back where we started, the walls were rougher. Faster work."

"So?" asked Stossen.

"So maybe the last part was punched through fast. Maybe that Engineer intended to lure us along here at the cost of his life? Can you turn, Biff, if we're attacked from the rear?"

Biff paused.

Yes, he could turn. Though only just, and to a certain extent courtesy of the smoothness of the tunnel walls in this vicinity.

He gazed back along the pitchy tube of stone, imagining that lumps of darkness were dwarfs...

Claustrophobia had never bothered Biff particularly. He had *crawled* through tubes before, never mind *walking* through one. Biff was a child of claustrophobia, to whom open sky presented an alien threat.

Yet oh that in the vastness of the universe there could exist so many tight pockets which could so compress a man! Most of life was condensed by the narrowest of horizons. Biff's own life used to be compressed in such a fashion—though he had always sussed that more existed, vastly more to which he could aspire...

If only people could dwell everywhere throughout the cosmos—if only space itself was as habitable as land, if only vacuums were breathable, and if plants and creatures floated everywhere in the void, equally dispersed—why then, each living person could probably occupy as his own sole abode a volume equivalent to a whole large world. All to himself, to himself alone...

Here he was instead, in a cramped passage tucked inside a harsh ball of rock.

See the cosmos, and *crouch*...

The cosmos was mostly a void of empty neutral lifelessness, within which the tiny businesses of life were so often none other than the dealing of death. Death! Thus spake life to a universe which at once harboured millions of swarming worlds yet at the same time essentially comprised... nothingness, vacuity. Thus life addressed that universe in its own terms—only, more loudly so, since life engaged in the trade of active death.

Ach, philosophy...!

Leave that to Yeri.

Leave leadership to Lex?

No...

"Light up ahead," reported Lexandro.

"Douse all suit lights," Stossen ordered immediately.

The far light brightened gradually into a disc resembling an aqueous azure eye that was watching them approach: a file of flies walking towards...

A spider shape writhed in Biff's inner vision, superimposed upon that distant eye like branching carmine veins. The spider's legs danced anticipatively—Biff's guardian, yet also his nemesis.

A faint heartbeat throbbed ahead; then many contrapuntal heartbeats. Liquids gurgled faintly.

They emerged into a seemingly deserted hydroponics plant: a long low blue-lit cavern housing hundreds of shallow tanks from which vegetables burgeoned in vivid botanical eruptions. Thorny purple pumpkins, gloryberry vines, variegated gourds, velvety meatfruit trees...

Fluted pipes gargled. Rune-dappled pumps throbbed softly. A generator of arcane design hummed. There was an alien aura to all the equipment, as if it were a hybrid of long-forgotten baroque human tech and of some sinuous, elegant, eldritch crafting by another species.

Frescoes of ancient Squattish warfare decorated the broad vault and walls. Doughty bearded dwarfs, whose exo-armour was laden with chainwork and charms and pendants, and whose belts were clasped with ornate golden buckles, were attempting to annihilate alien warriors in harlequin garb. Slim, tall, and eerily hand-some, those exotics wielded glowing swords; while the Squats favoured axes. The dwarfs' breastplates were decorated with scenes from some earlier heroic victory—or defeat. Hard to tell which. Victory blurred into defeat, into victory. A frieze of incomprehensible Squattish runes perhaps was barbaric poetry.

The contrast between the buoyant, fertile garden and the Stygian tunnel had quickly aroused Biff's animosity.

When a great stone hatch swung open to disgorge the very *image* of those painted hearthguardians in identical armour and trappings—as if they were simply emerging from the flatness of the frescoes into three-dimensional solidity, though wielding now a medley of bolt guns, plasma pistols, and laspistols—Biff fired at those targets without hesitation...

Chapter Thirteen

Pumpkins splattered apart—and so did a couple of Squattish bodies, though their armoured rinds were harder.

In the immediate return fire, plasma hit Stossen repeatedly, melting his right shoulder pauldron to slag, disabling his arm. His suit, of course, would anaesthetize the area, even if the pain pleased a part of him.

Inflamed with battle and careless of their vegetable heaven, the Squat hearthguard ducked behind tanks and machinery. Chanting invective, they pumped plasma, searing light, and explosive bolts through a hundred metres of torn fronds and stems. Tanks ruptured; nutrient liquids spilled in a shallow tide.

Half a dozen more Squats appeared at the mouth of a large tunnel giving exit from the cavern. They wore ochre flak-jackets with scarlet piping. Brandishing bolters and rock-cutters, these newcomers signalled their intention of hemming the Marines within the hydroponics plant. Consequently Lexandro charged in their direction, power-leaping through a tangle of vines.

In Biff's mind's eye the spider expanded, stretching itself

like a web before suddenly clutching tightly around the pus-armoured figure of Lexandro.

"No, don't go that way, Lex!" Biff shouted. "It's too easy! Drop back to the narrow tunnel."

It was the kind of warning cry that Yeri might have uttered, and indeed Yeri did add his voice a moment later like some echolalaic Psittacus bird:

"Drop back, Lex!"

"Cowards!" Lex took a moment to mock.

The armoured hearthguard were hustling from cover to cover, spraying a swathe of fire except in the very direction of their ochre-clad kin. Vegetable ichor spattered the sanguinary frescoes, adding gangrenous hues.

"Follow d'Arquebus!" ordered Stossen just as Lex reached the other dwarfs. Now that Lex was in close, he was using his power glove to punch. The rock-cutters of the flak-jacket brigade clashed fountains of sparks against his gauntlet as of knives being sharpened on a grindstone.

How nimbly those dwarfs danced in and out of range, taunting the armoured giant like cunning hairy rats baiting a wild bull auroch. Lex seized one and crushed its neck with a squeeze of his plasteel power fingers, so that the Squat's eyes popped right out on their optic cords upon the hirsute cheeks.

Snatching another by the arm, he threw it so powerfully against a wall that for a moment the body actually hung in position as part of a fresco, held by a glue of brains and blood. A fungoid mass seemed to have erupted from the painting. Then the corpse fell.

In Biff's humble opinion Lex burst through that little gang of Squats all too easily. That gang was suspiciously underarmoured and underarmed compared with the hearthguard who were so ostentatiously kitted out. If a hearthguard's gun jammed, he could snatch two replacements from holster or bandolier. But the flak-jacket fellows? A few bolters—and rock-cutters!

Lexandro was through into the exit tunnel, with Yeri in hot pursuit. Then Stossen, right arm dangling uselessly. Then Biff.

A thunderous clatter of bolts erupted as the hearthguard pursued. Biff fired rearward in reply.

The din almost drowned an ominous crashing noise. Biff suspected, *suspected*, that the orifice by which they had entered the hydroponics garden had been blocked...

The tunnel they now hastened along was rib-roofed and lined with stout pillars. Fat cables looped along from iron hoop to iron hoop. The pillars were carved from naked rock, and each was embossed with runes or with stylized Squattish faces. These pillars seemed to be the very bones of the planet, the mystic anatomy of a world laid bare. Fierce little pursuers darted from one pillar to the next, hugging those adornments for protection.

The tunnel debouched into a fan-vaulted chamber splaying upward from around a central pillar. So the Marines halted by that pillar, from which they could cover the various approaches. Several passages snaked away—upward, downward.

Along one of of those passages lay the corpse of a man—of ordinary stature, and dressed in bloodstained silken Sagramoso livery.

Was that another lure...?

For who had killed the Kark?

Surely Marines hadn't done so. Surely no other Marines had yet penetrated so deeply into the granite nest.

In which case, had the Kark's own Squattish allies been responsible? Thus Biff reasoned.

But Biff was the rearguard, the arse-flap, busy firing the occasional bolt back along the tunnel to deter the slyly advancing hearthguard. Stossen, powersword in his left hand, was already gesturing Lex to investigate the corpse.

Biff's exploding bolts scattered splinters of stone from

Ian Watson

carved columns, causing several angry squeals. He had no
spare bolt magazines left, though. Soon he'd be an empty
arse, with only a power glove to claw and pummel with. So
yes, the only way was onward...

Though which choice of onward?

Yeri darted after Lex to cover him.

"Guy's been axed," Lex reported. "Chest stove in.
Wasn't a power axe. There's some chest left."

Were some of the Squats conceivably *fighting* Sagramoso's minions, resentful of his sway over their stronghold?
This seemed implausible to Biff.

Maybe the Squats hoped that the Imperial Fists might
imagine something of the sort. The spreading of confusion
was a tool of war, too.

Biff *thunk*.

Had the recce squad been lured here especially to find
this corpse? Would the Squats, if sufficiently hard-pressed,
sue for peace and offer up a corpse which they swore to be
that of Fulgor Sagramoso? In reality it might be that of, say,
a twin brother kept by Sagramoso in some dungeon or in a
stasis casket expressly for some such future contingency,
should a substitute some day be needed.

How many of his Kark minions did Sagramoso have here
inside Antro? Not too many could have come along with
him in the survival ship. But others could have been here
already, overseeing their Lord's economic interests.

How many others of his loyal retinue might Sagramoso
sacrifice—aye, blatantly with a Squattish axe—so as to
maintain a pretence and safeguard his own life?

Sagramoso might calculate that Battle Brothers would
not envisage such a ploy. Would a Commander Pugh
sacrifice Marines under his command so as to save his own
skin? No. No pious Chapter Commander would. Lord Pugh
had his own taste buds excised as penance, once...

To kill one's own men! Would many scumgang leaders
even contemplate treachery of this order?

Of course, Sagramoso thought he was a *god*... And gods demanded sacrifices from their most ardent and pious followers, did they not? Willing sacrifices!

Thus did the Emperor on Earth feed on the souls of shiploads of bright young psychic youths so as to sustain his own life-in-death...

The God-Emperor's feast of souls was reputed to be a bitter, agonizing one for him.

Ice crawled up Biff's spine. Here were patterns... of passages, tunnels, caves—and here were other species of patterns too, patterns of subterfuge and semblances.

Still guarding the rear, Biff was about to voice his *thunks* when, with a roar, a cyborged Ambull charged along the tunnel from the direction of the ravaged garden.

It was a giant of an Ambull, a veritable living tank. Improvised armour plates hung from hooks on its hairy, horny barrel of a body. Riding it, strapped in to the saddle, an armoured Squat War-Brother hunched over a heavy bolter. Cables linked the rider's helmet to the control hump on the beast's spine. A second heavy bolter, of antique design, had replaced one of the creature's forearms, and a shuriken catapult the other.

Shuriken stars whinnied off Biff's armour. Several bolts impacted on his plastron. A detonation half-spun him around. He felt his buckled armour crimp his flesh within, and blood flow then solidify.

Grasping a column to steady himself, Biff fired at the dwarf squatting on the thundering cyborg-beast. A bolt shattered the War-Brother's grinning hairy face—and the Ambull passed Biff by, bellowing and blundering, to crash into the central pillar.

Deprived of its command-mind now that the rider was dead, the beast was savagely confused. Biff swung back to cover the tunnel.

Click.

The click of imminent death.

The click of an empty bolt gun.

Tossing his useless weapon down, Biff rushed to the frenzied Ambull, which was still trying to push the pillar aside. His power gauntlet tore the mounted heavy bolter loose—his gauntlet, or himself? He wasn't sure. The beast bucked and kicked but since it seemed to think that its true enemy was that pillar, Biff forebore to poleaxe it. For each movement made his side ache fiercely.

He thought that his subcutaneous carapace had been quite deeply punctured. Perhaps an inner organ had been ruptured. His visor readout flickered a few red tell-tales, bloody cyphers interposed upon his field of view.

Pain lanced through him—and he welcomed the pain as an earnest that he was alive, and far from paralysed.

Swinging round, he sprayed a burst of bolts along the tunnel at the oncoming hearthguard. Percussive detonations cascaded, ricocheting. Lugging the cumbersome weapon, he backed away in the wake of his Brothers, noting dully how the gun's stock was inlaid with tooled silver and how its barrel was studded with round-topped cabochon-cut garnets. Truly, the weapon was part of a treasured war-hoard... How sweetly it would grace a trophy niche in the fortress-monastery...

His liver was lacerated, he realized, squinting at the phantom diagnostic runes that overlaid the scene.

Yet that was not especially fatal for a Marine.

And pain would only lend him strength.

Yeri shouldered Lex aside with a blocking tackle. A Squat sniper was taking aim from a high catwalk...

They had entered a cavern crowded with engines. Some of these burped and thumped vigorously; others were quiescent or moribund. Iron catwalks angled around the walls: up, down, hardly ever straight. Steaming pipes, the girth of a Squat, choked one exit tunnel as if they were hot worms infesting the bowel of some constipated leviathan.

The little Abhuman, in his dingy, red-piped flak-jacket, seemed absurdly diminished as he angled a multi-melta. Its support tripod was clamped to the catwalk. The dwarf's whole body appeared to be but a mere mottled hand wrapped around the grip of the large weapon—a fleshy appendage to its polished power cell, its ribbed accumulator, its clustered vent-grooved barrels.

A beam of effulgent heat brushed Yeri's shoulder, melting his pauldron superficially, spraying effervescing beadlets of liquid metal.

The main force of that discharge struck an antiquated, dead machine of grinning grilles, fluted coils, and counterbalanced brazen globes. Some worthy *ancestor*, perhaps, of younger engines still operating in this room, preserved by the superstitious dwarfs for the sake of machine honour...

Liquefying, the ornate device slumped in upon itself, shrinking into a bubbling, wrinkled scrotum of sintered alloys.

Swivelling, Yeri fired at the sniper and was satisfied to see the thermionic generator of that heavy weapon rupture. One of his bolts had penetrated that middle chamber. The pivoted barrels jerked upwards, slamming the grip down upon the marksman, who squirmed away howling across the catwalk, clutching for one of his several supplementary handguns.

A burst from Biff's captured heavy bolter chewed that high iron eyrie and the ambusher. Staggering at the recoil, the ex-Scumnik let his weapon sink. He pressed his damaged armoured flank with his power glove as if to infuse its strength into his wounds.

"*Apologies* for bumping you aside, Brother Lex," shouted Yeri, "Otherwise you'd have been somewhat... slagged off."

"*Gratia, Frater*," Lex replied sardonically. He used a phrase of the hieratic tongue, as though to indicate his personal detachment from those thanks—and maybe also to stress his awareness of the furtive and galling ceremonial being enacted between the two "brothers".

"Heat's so tiresome, isn't it? Melta-beams... Heat-sinks..." Lex made to slap a fraternal gauntlet upon Yeri's warped and blistered pauldron.

Yet Yeri was already ostentatiously scanning the other catwalks, training his almost empty weapon here then there to emphasize his ongoing vigilance on Lex's behalf.

How Yeri's tattooed cheek-runes itched, at long-remembered indignity. Tush, Yeri was almost as proud as Lex himself. Yet at least he wasn't manic.

An almighty din began a-booming back along the passage they'd come by. Clashing armour; the bellowing of a goaded Ambull; random boltfire.

Yeri heard Biff voice the opinion, "We're being *herded*, Sergeant."

"Imperial Fists, herded by *dwarfs*?" Tightly controlled loathing was evident in the tone of the lamed officer.

Biff was still pressing his punctured side stiffly with his plasteel gauntlet as if he had devised a new form of salute—which might propagate through his plating, poultice-like, into his torn anatomy, into the superhuman snail within the shell.

"Sir, should we fight our way back through those... scum... try to rejoin our comrades and report? And reload, 'course. This heavy bolter should help clear the way..."

"Scum" should appeal to the Sergeant's nanophobia, his antipathy to little neo-men.

"Report?" jeered Lex. "Report *what*?"

"The axed Kark we found, of course," said Biff. "That's peculiar."

"A route to the rebel Lord is what we must report, or nothing!" brayed Lex. "Are we feeling weary, Brother?

Are we feeling wounded?''

"It's nothing vital," Biff snapped.

"An injured Fist fights on," declared Stossen. "I certainly shall. But a Fist *thinks* too. Why should they 'herd' us, as you put it?" he demanded of Biff. "Do you suppose Sagramoso wishes to *capture* a squad of Fists? Why so? As hostages? That's ludicrous. To interrogate us about our battle-plan? The plan's simple: to sweep these warrens and extinguish him. Pah! Why should he wish to capture four Marines? Tell me that!''

"Dunno, Sir. *But...*''

"Battle discipline, if you please!''

"Riff-raff," Yeri heard Lex murmur. The former Lordly Phantasm loped into an inviting tunnel mouth. Uniquely, Lex seemed able to make power armour adopt such an insouciant gait.

Haughty, headstrong, and burning with a pious devotion: was it even possible to humble him? True humbling must occur in his very *heart*, like a fierce thorn taking root within to pierce him inwardly forever.

True humbling must, perhaps, issue—somehow—from Rogal Dorn himself...

Could Yeri even possibly be the agent of such humility? He must try to be.

Thirty minutes later, deeper into the bowels of Antro, and nearly bereft of all ammunition—their stings almost all drawn by a spasm of surprise attacks—the recce squad trotted into an arched corridor where the granitic wall was banded with spiked hoops of adamantium.

At the far end, an ancient gnome hobbled aside after allowing that first tantalising glimpse of himself. Bald-pated, with a snowy bush of beard, and an ornately wrought golden neck chain, the gnome had clutched around himself a robe that sported a stiff collar so high as to be almost a hood. . .

Stossen called out, ''That's one of the titches' Living Ancestors! Collar the wizened bird, and we'll squeeze him for juice—''

In fact Lex was already darting forward to try to snatch such a living trophy.

All four of the Brothers were well along the corridor when the spiked hoops sprang outward from the wall on massive pistons.

The hoops instantly divided the passage into little prisoning cells with cramping, impaling bars too puissant for a power fist to wrench aside or bend.

Once again, the Living Ancestor peered round the far lip of the passage. He grinned wrinkledly.

Concealed hatches popped open in the stonework. Hairy Engineers' arms reached through to cut open armour with spinning blades.

No matter how the Fists braced themselves or bucked in a paroxysm of resistance, they lost their suits piece by piece. . .

Yeri felt sick to his soul at his failure to forestall Lex's capture.

Biff was cursing in scum argot.

Lex giggled derisively at the busy, if cautious, dwarfs who were dismantling his armour, denuding him.

''You're *tickling* me!'' he mocked.

And Lexandro's blindfold was at last removed. . .

Disarmed, disarmoured, and denuded, the four Marines lay shackled to slabs of granite speckled pink as if meagre blood was oozing from within the stone.

After the indignity of the corridor of cages, the hoodwinked Brothers had been dragged in chains for some distance—using traction machines, by the sound of it.

Loaded on board gritty flat wagons—or so Lex judged—

they'd then been conveyed through rail tunnels for perhaps ten kilometres...

Unloaded, they were dragged again. Then they were lifted and shackled firmly before the redundant chains were unwound, and the blindfolds too...

The cave they were in was easily as spacious as the Assimularum hall of the fortress-monastery, which could hold a thousand Battle Brothers. Glowglobes lit the vault hazily.

Lexandro craned his neck. This chamber held perhaps a hundred dwarfs. Most were seated around the front tiers of an amphitheatre cut from naked rock. Many of the Squattish audience were hearthguards or guildmasters, armed to the teeth and gorgeous in finely decorated armour. Others wore plainer brown fustian. Most were loudly mumbling some incomprehensible chant, though some sat silent and grim-faced.

In the proscenium area, where the slabs were positioned, several snowy-bearded Living Ancestors occupied carved stone thrones—subordinate to a larger throne set back upon a dais.

A stout, brown-bearded man reclined in that larger throne underneath a canopy adorned with a writhing eight-pointed sunburst. But for a bulging black silken loincloth, he was nude. By contrast with his full beard, his trunk and limbs were quite hairless, sleekly so, as if lately shaved. Other people might shave their chins, but this person shaved his creamy body... whereon muscles rippled like some potent tide advancing and retreating. The pupils of his eyes were dark coals. His nose was of the snubby Sagramoso variety...

The Lord, no less. Flanked by Kark guards clad in black silk and armed with shuriken catapults.

Lexandro tested his wrist restraints. At the cost of some damage to flesh he could perhaps manage to rip the left hand shackle out of the rock. His ceramically reinforced bones would take the strain. The right-hand shackle seemed impervious.

He glanced at his companions.

Biff's side swelled, lividly bruised, studded with dried cinnabar...

From what Lex could see, Stossen's shoulder was a sorry wreck. Flesh had charred back to the bone. Lex honoured the man for his endurance. Surreptitiously, if fruitlessly, the Sergeant was straining to release himself...

Smoke arose from bronze tripods cradling smouldering cinnamon incense. Overhead, stirred by the breath of leering ventilator gargoyles, the scented haze faintly mimicked the contours of twisted phantom faces. These emerged, glaring down sombrely before dissolving, only to reform again.

That strange guttural chanting intensified—though not all of the Squats were participating. A Warlord, with heavy golden chain dangling down a carapace breastplate tooled with ancestral faces, frowned dubiously at those...

...faces in the air...

His gaze dropped towards Fulgor Sagramoso, and the Warlord shuddered.

Lex craned his neck to see why.

Faces...

Faces were forming in Sagramoso's own flesh...

The rebel lord might have been a contortionist at some dirtworld fairground, able to command the play of his muscles in unique fashion. The tissue of his chest and belly and thighs was puckering, rippling, conjuring the semblance of physiognomies. Features were moulding themselves in the substance of his body, obtruding, then sinking back again—only to give rise to new snub-nosed countenances.

On his chest.

On his belly.

On his broad thighs.

How could it be?

Was Sagramoso truly a god?

Several of the Living Ancestors regarded the performance with wonder—though one Whitebeard eyed the transformations with evident repulsion and suspicion.

Sagramoso gazed piercingly around the amphitheatre.

"My own sacred ancestors are gathering!" he proclaimed in a throaty growl. "Aye, gathering to protect us. See how they manifest themselves in my very flesh. Can *you* call back *your* dead ancestors thus, Honoured Ancients?"

Several Whitebeards looked *very* impressed.

"Now I am becoming my own ancestors, Reverend Ones! Their power is gathering. Soon I shall summon your own most distant forebears in similar fashion. They will speak to you through lips that open in my skin—" Drool oozed from Sagramoso's mouth.

He seemed hardly in control of himself. Yet he hauled himself upright. His torso and thighs quivered with those gathering mute masks of flesh struggling to be incarnated, yet he lurched towards the slabs where Lex and his Brothers lay stretched out like beasts awaiting butchery. One of the entourage handed Sagramoso a chainsword.

The plasteel teeth blurred into near-invisibility as the weapon activated.

The rebel lord loomed over Lex, his body in weird flux, undergoing seeming birthpangs. A whole family of inchoate parasitical visages jostled for priority.

Sagramoso swished the chainsword to and fro. Nightmare and death stared down upon Lexandro.

Chapter Fourteen

But Sagramoso passed Lexandro by, and surveyed Stossen who was muttering prayers to himself in horror.

A smile twisted the Lord's lips, and he nodded to himself. Holding the buzzing sword just above the Sergeant's waist, Sagramoso intoned absurd jargon as if he were being operated by some alien ventriloquist.

"Chi'khami'tzann Tsunoi," he slurred. And more, and more.

What manner of words were those?

The former lord of Karkason quivered. The faces in his flesh grew agitated. His voice altered timbre, becoming high-pitched as he prayed: "Almighty Master of Fortune, Grand Conspirator who moulds the lives of men to change the course of history, as I seek to change it, accept this... *offering.*"

Lowering the chainsword slowly, he sliced the now screaming Sergeant—who fell silent soon enough, blood bursting from his belly to harden into knots of dark rubies. Sagramoso cut until he had bisected his victim, dividing him in half upon the granite block.

Lex's own stomach muscles crawled. A hormone-spiced stink insinuated into his nostrils—for the Sergeant's bowels, deprived of any control, had evacuated themselves.

Sagramoso smeared his hand into that excrement. Holding up his besmirched palm, he licked.

An aura of smoke wreathed the Lord's head as if his dark hair were smouldering—smoke that sought to achieve an ectoplasmic, ghostly form, which quickly writhed away into shapelessness. Were twin protrusions pushing up from his shoulder girdles underneath the skin?

In the palm that was stained with the expelled contents of Stossen's intestine, an eye appeared. Oh how its gaze disconcerted that seeming skeptic among the Whitebeards! Quitting his throne, the oldster hobbled to confer with a seated hearthguardian.

"Forge our destiny!" Sagramoso shrieked.

He appeared to be in some pain. Staggering, he almost dropped the sword. Then he was jerked erect. And even so, his head looked sunken as though his corded neck had contracted. Both of his muscular pectorals assumed firm features, the nipples becoming nub-noses, jelly eyes blinking above those, and mouths opening below like two ichor-lubricated wounds.

Was Yeri whimpering with dread?

Yes...

Lexandro heard the poor ex-tech mumble some pathetic litany of the Imperial Cult taught to him at his mother's knee... while Yeri clenched his fingers tight.

Biff too seemed to be in feverish distress.

Nor were so many of the dwarfs united in their enthusiasm any longer... Some voices cried out raggedly.

When the mouths in Sagramoso's chest began to speak glutinously, Lex's own mind was assailed by tentative questing tendrils whose touch was nauseating.

Tendrils of maddening mutability cast all in doubt. His sacred vows to Rogal Dorn... the sanctity of the Emperor on Earth... the loyalty of the other Fists, who had surely abandoned Lex to this fate... As had Dorn, who was *dead*, dead forever. As had the Emperor, who was all but moribund, and whose reign was now surely drawing to its close, yielding to the reign of... *what?*

Why, of eldritch magic from some bizarre, monstrous dimension at right angles to sanity. Whither Lex's own soul would shortly be sucked—so therefore let him yield it obediently.

"The *pattern*," Biff was babbling. "Oh what a mad twisted pattern—"

The leftward mouth in Sagramoso's chest urged, "Kill the other mundane Marines quickly! Slice them in twain and eat their ordure! We shall summon a horde of cackling *Horrors* to swarm all over the invaders and rout them with sheer fear—"

So it promised.

The rightward mouth was of a different opinion. "Nay, your star is almost set, Lord Sagramoso," it called upward to his face. "Your fate is sealed. Therefore let us abandon all restraint! Forsake the corset of normality deliriously! Yield yourself utterly to Change!"

Anxiety clouded Sagramoso's face. He swayed in indecision.

"I am surely a god, am I not?" he asked himself aloud.

One mouth replied, "Yes."

But the other, "No."

"You are the tool of a god—"

"You were worshipped. You demanded worship. You accepted terror-filled adoration—"

"Your craving for worship summoned *forces*—"

"Your craving for change in the cosmic order and your cruelty summoned the violent powers of change—"

"And the name of change is none other than... Tzeentch."

"*Tzeentch. Great Tzeentch.*"

The very syllables of this strange name plucked at Lexandro's sanity. That name seemed so puissant, so eternal, and so all-dissolving. It conjured such vistas of space and time in turmoil, swept by the whirlwind which was that magic word into ingenious new geometries that no ordinary mind could ever hope to grasp; nor ever should try to, lest reality be tormented into nightmare...

"Aid me, Rogal Dorn," prayed Lex.

...Rogal?

...Dorn?

The howling, omnipotent name—*Tzzzeeeeentch!*—almost obliterated the Primarch's name as if "Rogal Dorn" was but the puny mewling of a baby cast adrift in a straw cradle in a black ocean of chaos.

Rogal...

...Dorn...

TZZZEEEEENTCH.

Somehow Lex clung to that frail talisman of his Primarch, even knowing that he would soon be sacrificed to the power behind that other mighty name, to become—if he was lucky—an enslaved, gibbering mite of digested soul within a vast, evasive embrace.

An ever-so-distant, yet steadfast voice whispered ultimate warning in his mind: *Deny the Evil. Believe in me till you die.*

Squattish faces were forming in the rebel lord's flesh now—obscene, grimacing caricatures.

Lips opened to gibber, some greeting the dwarfish audience seductively, others mocking it. The chanting in the amphitheatre had become very ragged by now. The skeptical Living Ancestor raised his arms in protest. He glared at Sagramoso as if to annul his eerie magic by force of will. From the staring bulbous eye in Sagramoso's palm a sickly violet hue shone out.

During moments which measured out eternities of continuing existence for Lexandro, the Living Ancestor and the glow of the Eye contended silently. Sagramoso, still hefting the power-sword, hardly moved.

Yet the old dwarf was faltering—while his peers shuffled about in their thrones, uncertain in this hour of need whether to side with their wise old crony or with the human godling.

Kark guards and hearthguards, allies until now, eyed each other with deepening suspicion. In these moments, pregnant with the advent of an inconceivable power, all allegiances and former certainties were protean; loyalty was but a mask, while truth assumed a series of contradictory faces.

"Oh our sacred Ancestors!" cried the ancient dwarf in anguish.

"Why, here we all *are*—within this body," called out one of the mouths in Sagramoso's chest. "Do you not know us, Venerable Rimbeldorp? Why, this man is the next thing to a god!"

"The *next* thing," echoed the other mouth ambivalently. "Soon he'll become a veritable daemon of the Lord of Change."

"What sort of Lord is that?" demanded the elder known as Rimbeldorp shrilly. "What daemonry is at work?"

One mouth laughed, slapping its lips together.

The other harangued Sagramoso. "Slay the other three Marines, you slow fool! You who worshipped yourself! We will bring you something worth worshipping. You hungered for power. Why, power is coming."

Horns were sprouting from Sagramoso's shoulders—frail, feeble horns as yet.

"Taste the products of their loosened bowels to tantalize Tzeentch! He loves the transformation of meat into manure. Such is the Cycle of Change! He will bring back the dead inside living flesh. His abominations will turn sane men into madmen, and living bodies into cadavers."

"*Tzeentch*," intoned the other mouth.

"*Tzeentch*," chanted numerous Squats, mesmerised. "Oh sacred Ancestors, return from the dead!"

Rimbeldorp gestured fiercely at the hearthguard he had conferred with. Brandishing an axe, the armoured dwarf hurried down towards the sacrificial slabs.

Since he appeared intent on carrying out the urgings of the mouth, none of Sagramoso's escort sought to interfere. The redbearded Squat leapt on to the slab which held Yeri, raised his axe high...

...and brought it down...

...severing the shackle which restrained Yeri's right hand. The blade, clanging against granite, jarred loose from the little man's grasp. He cried a loud "Ouch! and clutched at his wrist, massaging himself.

Lex's wits spun. Had the dwarf *intended* to free Yeri? Yes—he must.

Yeri, so close to the spectre of his own death, hardly realized this. Rearing, with his freed hand he seized the little man and threw him violently aside. The hearthguard's head cracked open against the corner of the slab that held the two halves of the Sergeant, a knotty girdle of cinnabar encircling his waist. Blood flowed from the crumpled Squat's cranium.

Yeri tore at his other, pinned wrist. Using it as a lever, he wrenched the shackle free. Sitting up swiftly, he reached down for one of his pinioned feet—glancing as he did so towards Lexandro, with promise in his gaze.

"I'll save you from this!" he cried. "By Dorn, I'll do it!"

A shackle sprang free.

Craning his neck as much as he could, Lexandro saw Kark guards levelling their catapults at the contorting naked body on the block, now only fastened by one ankle. They were awaiting only their Lord's order—lest by slaying Yeri themselves they might abort the ritual of the blood-offering. Once Yeri was fully free, they wouldn't wait a moment longer.

Lex imagined Yeri hurling his self-appointed bodyguard person obsessively towards the slab that bound Lex himself—while a hail of shuriken stars sliced through Yeri's skin, ruptured his carapace, scalpelled his organs—and that body collapsing in a dying heap of protection upon Lexandro stiflingly and insultingly, embracing him in his death throes.

How could Lex possibly deter his wretched *brother* from this obscene act of quixotry, which he had read in his look, and which he was *sure* was impending?

"The *axe*, drekbrain!" Biff bellowed in Trazior patois. "Hoy the axe at Lord Saggy!"

Wide-eyed, Yeri jerked away from trying to free his other ankle. Somehow his frantic gaze took in the tensing catapult wielders, and he comprehended.

He seized the fallen axe. He hurled it.

The engraved blade spun over and over. It struck Fulgor Sagramoso full in his chest between those two contentious mouths.

Both mouths cried out at once—one in an anguish of frustration, the other snarling mind-curdling curses.

A tide of nausea swept over Lex, blurring his perceptions—his grasp of the world—to such a degree that he gagged, almost vomiting with vertigo. Up was down. Left was Right. All was fluxing. Hallucinatory pink fumes gusted from Sagramoso's open mouth, like some cloud of diluted blood vented underwater, as the rebel lord rocked in agony, clutching the haft of the axe locked there in that rib-rent cleavage in his bosom. Foggy, twisted pink creatures seemed to fill the whole amphitheatre—squirming, clawing creatures of suckers and claws and grinning fangs. They packed the air—as if they had been there *all along*, and only now were rendered visible... as if those insane beings were the ultimate texture of reality itself, and behind all appearances—hidden within the very texture of the cosmos—lurked such festering daemons, coexisting with air and void itself, swimming unseen even through the spaces occupied by human bodies, eager to manifest themselves if only they could, to claw and sucker tight... and feed. And giggle and snigger. Lex could not *hear* their crazy laughter, but he could well imagine it.

And it came to Lex then that the Warp through which starships flew was the true home of such creatures; that the Warp was dense with a shifting flux of potential entities such as these—coalescing, dividing, bubbling into phantom existence, and dissolving again.

Starships might well be little fortresses of plasteel and adamantium, and devoutly shielded, yet in the light of his new vision they were but... eggshells, soap bubbles of sanity.

Knowing this—this madness—how could he ever again traverse the Warp with his Battle Brothers without experiencing constant dread? Without suffering a sickness unto death?

The destabilising flux of vexed mutability plainly affected the minds of everyone in that cavern. Karks finally fired their shuriken catapults—at the Ancient who stood opposing the conjurations of their fatally wounded lord. Blood sprayed from the entry points of the razor-sharp spinning stars. Hearthguards replied with bolter fire. Some hearthguards shot at one another.

Sagramoso rocked to and fro, barely alive, held up as though by puppet strings. One of the mouths in his chest puckered out of existence, but the other gaped wider. Its lips peeled back, curling and fattening, yawning ever wider—to *swallow* Sagramoso into themselves, incorporating his tissue into their own *immaterium*.

Lex gawped at this impossible spectacle, more appalled by such a sight than by his own predicament, shackled naked as he was while a murderous battle raged across him and above him...

Yeri had at last torn himself loose.

And he *did* cast himself upon Lexandro—as the butt for any stray bolts or stars. He hid from Lex's gaze almost all the thronging phantasmal entities... even as those were weakening, losing coherence, thinning and drifting towards Sagramoso, back to their source.

Gaps were showing in that mouth-traversed man where parts had been digested, sucked elsewhere. Organs hung dripping loosely in mid- air, strung by tubes and nerves and arteries...

"Vileness," that muscular bulk hissed into Lex's captive ear. "Madness..."

The two mobile pink lips flayed Sagramoso, enlarging, peeling him open, one of them travelling down the remains of his trunk, the other navigating the residue of his back. Cloudy ghosts of madness were sucked in to the gape of those lips to mingle with the exposed organs which themselves were becoming mouths.

And just then an explosion rocked the seething chamber. Just then a coughing thunder spoke.

Armoured dwarfs began to fly apart as if they too were vaporous, bloody ghosts.

Dwarfs died fast.

So did the remaining Karks.

On the blasted threshold of the cavern had appeared two Librarians of the Fists in lustrous armour, their storm bolters firing rapidly.

The psychic Librarians of the Chapter in their sublime, engraved Terminator armour!

The daemonic maelstrom stirred by Sagramoso had guided them here as surely as bees to pollen, or rats to an abandoned baby.

Bolts tore into those mobile, travelling lips that were consuming what still remained of Fulgor Sagramoso.

Did all of those bolts even detonate within the known universe of sanity? It seemed not...

One last time the lips screamed: *Tzzzeeeeentch* –
In vain.

With a glutinous slurp the ravaged lips swallowed themselves.

The treacherous nausea was to linger long in Lex's mind, connected intimately with the memory of the pressure of Yeri's body upon him, shielding him... though what shelter could there be from an insanity which existed only a membrane away from the ordinary world?

Chapter Fifteen

Deep beneath the Apothacarion of the fortress-monastery lay an Isolatorium.

In common with the nearby dungeons where Surgeon Interrogators plied their trade, the isolation complex was fabricated of adamantium. Furthermore, it was shielded psychically in the way that starship hulls were shielded—with a layer of psycurium alloy to resist the seductive dreams and ravenous nightmares of the Warp, and to repel entities that inhabited that zone where raw thought could become hideous substance.

In extremis the whole Isolatorium—as well as individual chambers within it—could be blasted free of the fortress-monastery and detonated.

The cells, of varying sizes, were coated internally with black rubber by way of protective padding. Diagnostic sensors and extrudable chirurgical equipment studded their ceilings like malign nipples.

It was here, to a triple cell, that the armoured Librarians had finally brought the three brothers—locked in stasis caskets—for scrutiny and therapy.

Freed from stasis, but secured in this impregnable chamber, the three brothers had been asperged and drugged and exorcised and mesmerized.

Canticles from the Codex Astartes played constantly from several speakers in the rubberized ceiling, weaving a polyphonal web of additional protection and reminder of sacred duty.

Somnified, the three brothers had been interrogated by the Chaplain attached to the Librarium. Their very dreams had been dissected.

Now at last Lex, Biff, and Yeri were declared cleansed. To mark which, silver purity seals hung round their necks and wrists and ankles.

The question which remained was how much these three young Marines should be permitted to *remember* about the dénouement to the Karkason crusade...

For they had witnessed abomination.

Abomination...!

A Librarian of the Fists could cope with such horrors to a remarkable degree. A Librarian was graced—or cursed— with a potent psychic streak. He was relatively learned in the wiles of Warp daemons. All Librarians must pore over occult texts chained within a restricted room in the Librarium—the very hasps of those locked volumes were enchased with prohibitive runes.

Such investigations were by no means the metier of an ordinary fighting Marine—who could easily be vexed to madness by exposure to manifestations of such evil, world-warping forces.

It wasn't unusual to erase the recent memories of Marines who had been thus exposed and sorely affected by the experience. Such spiritual casualities might even require really radical mind-wiping, returning them to the condition of innocent infants.

Yet Yeremi Valence had been instrumental to a large

degree in writing *finis* to Fulgor Sagramoso—with that ancient Squattish axe.

At the ultimate hour, the conjuring of a daemon of one of the unspeakable Chaos Powers—and a consequent cascade of gibbering deadly daemonic underlings—was aborted.

Admittedly, premonitory psychic tremors had led the Librarians to that arena-cavern. The Librarians had followed the scent of Chaos like some red thread through a labyrinth—to scourge it.

Yet had the axe not been hurled, the Librarians might have arrived too late. Giggling fiends might already have been boiling out through the maze of tunnels, spreading madness and death amongst the invading Marines.

Surely the survivors of the recce squad deserved to remember the details of their victory?

Yet on the other hand, the members of the recce squad had let themselves be lured to become sacrificial victims, stripped of their armour...

Dusky Librarian Franz Grenzstein, his cheeks nicked white with duelling cicatrices, stood surveying the brothers who had now been allowed gold-emboidered hassocks to kneel on.

At his side, Chaplain Geistler, in alb and chasuble of the Cult of Dorn, force sword in scabbard. That grim-eyed man's shaved brow was tattooed with a vermilion starburst resembling a lurid birthmark. In his right eye he wore a scrutinizing monocle.

"As we understand it," Grenzstein was stating in measured tones, "the Chaos Power known as Tzeentch conceives plans to alter history—schemes which are altogether too devious and farflung for any human being to hope to comprehend..."

Patterns, thought Biff. *Arcane patterns.*

Chained on that slab, he had almost been on the point of grasping a certain pattern... Yet it had eluded him in the ensuing swirl of nausea and mutability...

The Librarian went on, "We doubt that the cursed Fulgor Sagramoso understood the peril of *possession*, even towards the very end."

"Possession, Sir?" asked Yeri humbly.

"Aye... *possession*. The emergence of a daemon within a living man—whereby he will act as a conduit for its power, and will progressively assume the warping marks of Chaos. Moreover, we doubt that Lord Sagramoso even realized how his blasphemy rendered him liable to such possession..."

"His impious craving for worship...," added the Chaplain. "We found no evidence of the stain of Chaos in the ruins of Sagramoso's palace. No idols, other than of himself. He made himself vulnerable unwittingly. He believed he was a miraculous godling, and he became a puppet of Tzeentch."

Grenzstein shrugged. "Still, this is not the province of a Chapter such as ours. We of the Librarium must be *aware* of Chaos. Yet we do not ourselves aim to contend with Chaos, unless compelled to. We have signalled for an Inquisition research team to investigate Karkason and Antro too."

"Antro will soon be brought within the fold!" promised the Chaplain. He coughed to clear his throat, for the salvation of a world was an emotional matter.

Yeri looked at the Librarian. "Sir, could the presence of so much psycurium in Sagramoso's vaults possibly have acted as a kind of lens around him...?"

It was Geistler who answered. "Maybe! Though that's a mechanistic rationale. The universe is far from being a machine, Valence. Or, if so, it's an *infested* living machine which protrudes from a swamp of turbulent spirit... Cleave to that explanation of Sagramoso's corruption, if you wish, to help salve your sanity. And adore the Emperor and Dorn, so as to scour the eyesight of your mind. To scrape your eyeballs clean of phantom parasites!"

Space Marine

Biff's hands clawed at the air to try to inscribe the hex pattern he still felt he was on the point of sensing—a hex with which to banish horrors that were currently invisible and undetectable yet which might nevertheless be hiding in the very air he breathed.

The Chaplain raised an eyebrow.

"Ah, you're sketching the *crux dentatus inversus*... The toothed, upside-down cross. Would that power sign really have banished an agent of Tzeentch, had you made such a sign at the time? When you yourself aren't a psychic adeptus? Alas, No... The axe blade answered Tzeentch. And that must always be the Star Warrior's final response. *Weaponry*, wielded with ingenuity and foresight. The toothed power blade, and the bolter."

It had been Biff's *idea*, of course, to throw the axe which had shattered both Sagramoso's rib-cage and his deluded hopes as the flux of changes took full hold of him.

Perhaps the axe had been a blessing for Sagramoso. And perhaps not. Swallowed half-alive by those lips into the Warp, where and what was Sagramoso now?

Lexandro remained unsure whether the three of them, in the final analysis, were being praised or blamed. Thank Dorn they had not brought the taint of this... corrupting *Chaos*... back into their fortress-monastery! It had been such a very close call—as close as Yeri's body squashed upon his own... pressed bravely, yet in seeming parody of the true valour that was Lex's own destiny.

If only they could have erupted into that amphitheatre in full armour, fully armed! Yet how would they have found the place if they had not followed that teasing trail into a trap?

Truly, their survival and their triumph over the heretic was hedged irritatingly, *damnably*, with many ambiguous might-have-beens.

"You are clean. You are clear," concluded Chaplain Geistler. "Pray constantly that you will never again find

yourselves in the presence of such a malevolent power.
Still, you conducted yourselves adequately. We will allow
you to remember—how a blasphemer against Him-on-
Earth met his end. Yes, Valence? Your eyes are questioning
me.''

''That old gnome who told the hearthguard to unshackle
one of us with the axe—''

''Indeed, he must have sensed the truth—somewhat
late.'' The Chaplain frowned. ''He died—absolved, in a
sense. No doubt the Inquisitors will bear that fact in mind
when they purify Antro.''

The Librarian leaned forward. ''You're concerned with
the... justice of their future treatment?''

Yeri nodded.

Damn fool Yeri, thought Lex, harping on the fact that *he*
had not primarily been instrumental in freeing himself!
How much finer if he had torn himself free unaided.

Or if *Lex* had done so...

Grenzstein tapped his fists together. ''Don't confuse
gratitude for a serendipitous event with any... cloying
compassion towards the author of that event, Valence,'' he
said. ''True justice is quite simply the will of the
Emperor.''

''You *will* remember,'' promised Geistler, ''but you will
not be otherwise honoured. The manner of Sagramoso's
departure from the cosmos shall remain a black secret—
restricted. You may tell none of your Brothers other than
that Librarians rescued you. You will swear this before you
leave the Isolatorium.''

The Chaplain had brought a bulky burden with him into
the rubber-bossed cell, wrapped in black satin. He had
handled it with exquisite care. Might the satin conceal some
final psychotheological device for diagnosing any stain of
possession?

No...

For now Geistler peeled the inky fabric aside—to

disclose a stasis case with a magnilens insert.

"If you ever break this vow, your bodies will slowly be immersed alive in acid until only your bones remain. Then execrations will be carved upon every inch of those, and your skeletons will be cast adrift—for some alien to find, in awe and horror, in a million years time, or a million more. And perhaps to hang in its alien temple, as hoodoo trinkets."

Within the box was... Dorn's right hand, the surfaces of the carpus, the metacarpal bones, and the phalanges dense with scrimshandered heraldry.

Dorn's actual hand, borrowed from the Reclusiam...

Lex understood now how narrow was the ledge their lives had been poised on ever since they entered the Isolatorium—balanced between honourable euthanasia if they were tainted, return to duty as amnesiacs perhaps requiring much retraining... and return as themselves entire—which only the most solemn of oaths could permit.

Geistler held the transparent box tightly as, one by one, the three brothers placed their right palms upon the surface, barely inches above the actual bones of Rogal Dorn.

Each recited after the Chaplain: "*Per ossibus Dorni silentium atque taciturnitatem fideliter promitto...*"

Only then were they at last released from the Isolatorium... to walk up presently past a surgical interrogation cell where a Squattish Living Ancestor gibbered to himself...

And so, as ever, the fortress-monastery flew onward through measureless nothingness and endless night from year to year, the far stars only shifting their positions by a fraction.

Within, the great community went about its familiar regime of existence, a regime so long sustained that almost any activity was gilded with ritual, a rich thread in a tapestry ever a-weaving.

Weapons practice. Prayers. Pain machines. Feasts. Duels of honour. Expeditions of squad and company size...

Yeri was the first of the three brothers to fight a duel in the Hall of Steins, fixed in the Boots. He fought to defend Lex's honour, to the latter's embarrassment, and was sliced across the jaw in the contest. Thereafter Yeri tended to make his chin jut, displaying the scar that honoured his supposed devotion to a Brother...

Biff, somewhat to his own surprise, was the first of the three to feel the scrimshaw itch. Before many years had passed, he was often to be found in his cell polishing an antique jackknife on a gritty piece of lizard skin, or buffing a finger bone on a wheel of unstitched muslin to raise a fine lustre on it, or treating the osseous pores with paraffin. The primal, primaeval feel of that ancient blade appealed to him more than a sophisticated silicon carbide graving tool.

The art appealed to the atavist in Biff—just as the final delicate etching bespoke the way in which his own crude bone and brawn and brain had been refined into a gracious maturity. His flesh as fine as marbled beef massaged with milk and wine, though almost as tough as marble... A mighty delicacy of intellect and feeling, balanced upon a ruthless brainstem...

Biff's first finished scrimshaw scene, inscribed minutely on a single finger bone, depicted a Librarian in Terminator armour advancing through dwarfish armoured warriors. This was judged worthy to be placed in a small silver reliquary set in a niche along the Corridor of Comfortless Courage. Lexandro hinted sinisterly that Biff's scrimshaw image was perhaps "just a little too near the knuckle."

The three brothers flew with the whole First Company to a great space hulk which was reported by a freighter captain as drifting in the void, and approaching the vicinity of a prosperous industrial solar system. There, they destroyed a lair of Genestealers before those cunning and savage alien enigmas could infest the planets of that star, hypnotising and hybridising with the citizenry...

The three brothers helped suppress human pirates and green-skinned alien pirates...

They helped restore a deposed lord, Vendrix—just as they had overthrown the Lord of Karka's Sun...

And in the Librarium the Astropaths maintained devout contact with far Earth, which likely none of the Fists would ever see, even if they lived to the age of four hundred years.

Earth! Hub of humanity—ever struggling to sustain the grievous burden of overseeing, however sketchily, the affairs of a million scattered worlds. Some far planets might only win scrutiny once in a decade, or once in a century. Swathes of stars could shine unnoted for a generation. These were only those where the human race festered. Millions of other star systems were still mere celestial coordinates, if they were accurately charted at all.

Ten years passed by.

What was ten years to the Imperium—or to the galaxy? It was but an eyeblink.

To Lex and Yeri and Biff it signified a steel stud drilled into their foreheads... so modest, so discreet... yet so dense with each of the five and a quarter million minutes that had passed for them in the interim.

Minutes of purity and prayer and pain, of devotion and of the dealing of death.

Necromunda? "The deathworld"... their far-off, one-time home? Why, the entire galaxy was a realm of living death. Only through death could the Imperium, and humanity, survive; and they were death's angels...

PART THREE

Tyranid Terror

Chapter Sixteen

"We're going in through its anus," Biff whooped
boisterously.

Indeed. Indeed.

What else could that puckered sphincter be, in the white
bony hull of the vast, gastropoidal alien vessel?

The leviathan that loomed ahead seemed a cross between
a nautilus and an omnivorous, space-faring snail. It was the
length of a four-K asteroid, and almost as high where its
shell spiralled upward in a circuit of increasingly small
osseous chambers. The shell was bleached chalky by aeons
of radiation.

Even as the armoured Fists, tightly packed into a
stretched boarding torpedo, stared at the forward viewscreen in its mount of bronze bones, that sphincter pulsed.

It expelled a quick milky cloud, which the torpedo's
sensors assayed as consisting of bitter liquid dregs, foul
gas, and ashy debris—the fart of a leviathan...

Far away, a shadow had darkened the Warp...

At first, and for many years, Astropaths and starship

Navigators had hardly heeded that enroaching smudge within the phantasmal realm through which ships skipped from star to star in weeks or months instead of thousands of years; and through which the psychic communicators forged their mind links...

For the umbra seemed small, being far away—no more than a minor maculation, an inky blemish in a distant corner of the eye of the galaxy.

It appeared from beyond the reach of the Astronomicon, the Emperor's psychic beacon projecting from Earth as a lantern in the darkness.

It lay far to the celestial south-east, originating beyond the imperial frontier where the cone of space and stars known as Segmentum Tempestus abutted on Ultima Segmentum—though ''frontier'' was only a euphemism for a total evaporation of known human presence into a void of unknown suns; and similar vacant gulfs aplenty existed within the supposed frontiers...

That shadow was distant. Being distant, it seemed a trivial puzzle, a mere mole on the face of the heavens.

However, the galaxy is to a star cluster far larger than a whale is to a microbe; and a miniscule macula could be vaster than the sphere of a hundred suns.

That shadow must be a psychic force—for all was ultimately raw *thought* in the Warp. The shadow must be the echo of a vast mentality—slumberous, now awakening... to what purpose?

If that mentality were of the ordinary universe of reality, it must be mountainous to cast such a thought-shadow.

Mountainous—or else multifold as a swarm of locusts...

Or somehow... both of these at once.

Presently, astropathic signals from outrider worlds in that easterly spiral arm of stars were quenched... though years might pass until their absence was noted.

Some Astropaths who served the Inquisition tried to penetrate the nature of the shadow, and died insane. They raved of cold, empty gulfs of timeless void that stretched out between galaxies, vacancies too vast for sanity. Nothing human could cross such immensity. Yet something had crossed. And had crossed the gulfs between other galaxies, previously. Inexorably.

Those Astropaths died—yet not before exonerating *Chaos* of responsibility.

The departments of several High Lords of Terra were notified: the Adeptus Astra Telepathica, the Navis Nobilite and the Chartist Captains, the office of the Astronomicon, the Adeptus Terra.

Reports, illuminated by scribes, were sometimes pigeonholed.

Gradually, awareness of a threat was gathering—though still whelmed in ignorance.

The fortress-monastery of the Imperial Fists was, and long had been, traversing Ultima Segmentum, describing a slow arc through those easterly marches which would take almost forever to complete...

Many more worlds had fallen silent. Ponderously, the Imperium had awoken to a creeping nightmare.

Some understanding of the *alien* cause of this was retrieved by an otherwise disastrous expedition launched by the Blood Drinker Marine chapter into that now mute, umbral zone of the fringe. Other Marine companies had failed to return from forays; and one entire Chapter, the Lamenters, seemed to have vanished utterly.

After years of planning, imperial battleships were now gathering in Ultima Segmentum.

Marine Chapters, whose names were almost legendary, were about to collaborate on a thrust into that shadow zone. The Space Wolves, the Blood Angels, the Ultramarines, the Blood Drinkers... and the Imperial Fists.

During the coming crusade the Fists might meet the same fate as the Lamenters—so that their fortress-monastery might fly onward eventually, empty of Battle Brothers, bereft of command guidance, a castrated abode of servitors and cyborgs who would continue the rituals of maintenance in the lost monastery for millennia more, robotically, senselessly, alone in their corridored world of deserted firing ranges, forbidden chapels, taboo laboratories where dust would gather throughout aimless millennia... if the Fists failed.

In a speech from the balcony of the departure bay, Lord Commander Pugh had impressed on his Fists that Space Wolves, Ultramarines, Blood Angels were all valiant, dedicated chapters—but that Fists were pre-eminently *planners* as well as fighters; *thinkers*, wise warriors.

What the Imperium, itself awakening to an impending new calamity, needed now above all was knowledge of the nature of this creeping threat—of the substance that cast the terrifying shadow... a substance which seemed intent on devouring the entire south-east spiral arm—in a few centuries or millennia– and then perhaps *all* of the human galaxy, within a few tens or hundreds of aeons...

"We're ramming in through its arse!"
Indeed.
As were other Fist-packed torpedos, aimed at other orifices where the alien hull might prove vulnerable...
A sun shone distantly, biliously illuminating the outermost methane gas-giant of this solar system. The planet, of churning poisonous cyclones hundreds of miles deep segueing into the pressurised liquid manure within, was a verdigris crescent cupping gaseous darkness. Pallid sickle moons attended it.
Known to the Guild of Navigators as Lacrima Dolorosa, the sun seemed from certain perspectives to be a teardrop dangling from an eye-shaped constellation. Beyond Lacrima Dolorosa the starfield thinned, its diamantine

lactic veils torn into rifts revealing the ultimate night of the extragalactic void—from where the blot in the Warp had issued: the shadow of whole fleets of these molluscoid alien ships, arriving in the sprawling, half-charted galaxy of Man—and of Abhumans and unhumans, and of an inhuman, unspeakable *Chaos*—after a voyage which must have measured millennia.

Those ships...

They suggested fossilised ancient creatures which might once have grazed the submarine abysses of giant worlds, sucking up whales as if whales were minnows; creatures which had petrified a hundred million years previously yet nevertheless were still virulently *alive*. Still ravenous...

A thousand such ships, many of them even more gargantuan than the torpedo's own chosen target, were now drifting in to the Lacrima Dolorosa system.

Yet this thousand was perhaps only one per cent of the swarm that summed up to the substance that cast the Shadow...

What manner of creatures dwelt inside such convoluted, organic-seeming ships? Creatures which might still perhaps be slumbering, for the most part...

Hopefully, still slumbering... whilst the eerie fleet drifted past that outermost gas-giant on a course inward towards Lacrima Dolorosa III, a world of feral human beings who had relapsed into barbarism at least ten thousand years previously, according to some ancient Administratum archives.

Now the legendary "gods" of those barbarians would wage war with monsters in their skies... unnoticed and distantly to begin with... until in the end alien fiends might gorge themselves on that lush and savage world.

Unless the Fists and Ultras and Angels and imperial battleships repelled this rolling invasion.

Which seemed unlikely.

The natives of Lacrima Dolorosa III were almost

certainly doomed—an event which in itself was of no account, a fate that was inherently trivial. Except, of course, to the victims...

The prize, here, wasn't a dispensible world of savages but rather *knowledge*—of those intruders from the Dark Deep, to the nature and purpose of which only scattered, dire hints as yet existed...

A coccyx of bleached bone jutted into space, bearing the sphincter at its tip like a quartet of triangular haemorrhoids clutched within bands of livid muscle. Where the heads of these scarlet protuberances touched, a tiny hole still puffed acidic discharge.

The nose of the torpedo impacted rupturingly in that meatus, wrenching its tissue open, burrowing deeper convulsively with thrusts of its jets as the Fists clung to stanchions.

The torpedo rocked as a shaped charge on the nose-cone erupted, blasting a passageway ahead. Swiftly the spring-loaded cone itself petalled open, becoming a fourfold hatch pressing fiercely against the inner anal walls in the manner of a surgical dilator.

"Out, out, out!"

This rectum of the alien ship curved rightward, aslosh with steaming cloacal fluids, banded with slowly pulsing purple peristaltic sinew. The high shriek of escaping atmosphere had already diminished to a whistle as the injured anus cramped tighter, reflexively, around the girth of the plasteel troop-carrier which had penetrated it.

The colon itself soon branched into multiple oozing tubes too small to enter. But the side wall had been lacerated into thick gristly ribbons. Captain Helstrom and Lieutenant Vonreuter sliced at a mass of blast-dissected cartilage with their power swords, carving a crude wide doorway that bled gluey snottish threads.

Beyond: a hooped oval chamber leprously aglow with a

skin of white algae, and ankle-deep in glutinous dank sludge. A trio of tall deltoid doors stood open upon ribbed corridors. Tubes looped along one corridor like glossy intestines strung on crutches of varnished bone. Swollen varicose veins webbed areas of tissue between the ribs. The curved jambs of those doorways trembled, holding back a pulsing curtain of puckered flesh.

Each door was some kind of mindless slave-creature, anchored by tentacles, whose only role was to open and shut.

As more Marines crowded into the chamber, Yeri was thrust towards a door and poked one of several softly glowing green nodules on its muscular rim with the barrel of his bolt gun, prying experimentally—as an ex-tech well might. The stiff fleshy curtain relaxed with a sigh, shutting itself tight but for a long dimpled crack.

"We're being shut in!" exclaimed someone.

"No—" Yeri probed again. The door dilated open once more. "Pressure of the blast must have activated the doors..."

"It got all those buttons to push at different heights," Biff observed. "Must be critters of lots of different sizes on board—"

And the tallest must be at least twice a man's height...

Lex rubbed condensation from the outside of his visor. The air was so humid. However, a silver ikon of nostrils winked upon his field of vision. So the atmosphere was breathable enough.

Captain Helstrom was calling for the two Marine Scout squads to vacate the torpedo and join their armoured seniors, further packing the chamber.

They, of course, wore no helmets, and swore at the full impact of the foetid odours, of which the Marines' suits merely brought a diagnostic whiff to the wearers' olfactory lobes.

The alien ship wheezed and rumbled, droned and

gurgled—from afar off, nearby, who could tell? Vibrations propagated through the flesh and bone. Echoes haunted the corridors.

Algae on the walls of the chamber was sliding—clumping into bizarre blotches. Were those recording the nature of the damage to the orifice by which the Fists had entered?

"Dumb design, those doors," sneered Biff. "If your arse craps out, you don't want half your guts flying outa the hole. You want your inner bulkheads shut!"

"They *would* have closed," said Yeri. "But then the shaped blast ripped through and pushed with just the right pressure to open them—"

A whirring of wings...

From along one corridor flapped a cloud of scaly, violet, batlike creatures. Claws serrated their wings. The rushing cloud thickened rapidly, purpling then blackening the corridor. Biff hit at a control nodule on the door jamb—but that door must be heeding some ultrasonic signal broadcast by the cloud. It stayed open.

Hand flamers brought down dozens, hundreds of the creatures. Blazing clusters, fused together by the ignited jellified oil, sizzled in the sludge. The door also blazed, its muscles and rooted tentacles writhing as if agonised.

Still more bats thronged, squealing, into the chamber, clotting the air. Marines clawed down fistfuls, crushing the flying vermin. A Scout shrieked...

"Stand still! Do nothing!" bellowed Helstrom.

He was right. He was right.

The bat-things weren't intent on the Marines at all. Mindlessly they were attaching themselves to that opening which power swords had carved in the tattered wall of the colon. Reaching out, they hooked together. Thus they created a protective patching membrane made of themselves.

More bats dived upon this, thickening it. Claws pierced

neighbouring bodies. Hot sulphurous juices squirted, vulcanizing the rubbery anatomies, stiffening and fixing them in place.

Presently the gaping hole was sealed.

Most of the rest of the horde quenched the burning door with their bodies. At last the flow of bat-things ceased. Late comers settled upon the colour-coded blotches of algae and began to feed, digesting whatever information those contained, or perhaps erasing it as obsolete.

In three separate groups, Marines and Scouts began to move out cautiously along the trio of diverging corridors. Whenever they returned—if ever they returned—they would cut or blast their way through that stiff membrane of a thousand dead beasts to reach the torpedo...

A curdled light suffused the broad bone-braced passageway that Yeri trod along, dogging Lex's heels. Biff trailed a little way behind. He was keeping an eye on the half dozen raw Scouts. So was Sergeant Juron.

Juron and he weren't worried that those mighty rumbustious striplings might rampage away impulsively down some side branch. They were conscious of what full Marines sometimes murmured of as the "can-airy factor".

Legend had it that long ago in the foul toxic depths of Necromunda scavvy gangs used to carry a twittering yellow birdie in a box on expeditions into unknown chambers. That birdie was sensitive to levels of pollution. The melodies it tweeted were a litmus of the air quality. If it shut up, or keeled over, better slap on a respirator quickly or else die in spasms.

'Course, any such morsels of captive live protein had long since vanished down guys' and gals' gobs on Necro—'cept up in the high towers maybe. Nowadays you had reactive patches to show up poisons, 'suming you could find or trade or steal some; and most Scavvies couldn't...

Yet the saying lingered on. "Can you breath the airy?

Send in a can-airy!''

Sure, the Scouts had respirators in their kit, but they didn't have full armour because their carapaces weren't meshed in to their nerves yet. Thus they were a kind of litmus, a kind of can-airy. And by now the full Marines had their visors open so as to conserve their air tanks. So Biff kept a wary eye on the can-airy Scouts.

Normally, he guessed that Lord Pugh wouldn't have sent Scouts on a first foray into such an environment. However, the whole chapter was in on this mission to penetrate a trio of the alien vessels. The other cousinly Chapters were targeting similar groups of ships—while imperial battle-ships stood by to blast as many more as possible apart. If possible.

Willy-nilly, it was can-airy time for Scouts, who couldn't seal themselves up tight.

If Lord Pugh lost too many of his Scouts, would he find some other part of his own sensory system or his anatomy that was disposable, as a penance? After taste buds, what else? Perhaps his eyes? Perhaps he would have those replaced with harsh schematic cyberlenses which would eradicate any softness from his perceptions?

Pushy Lex paced ahead with Vonreuter as though he was the Lieutenant's special aide. Vonreuter was an almost albino blond, with washed-out limpid eyes and duelling scars that seemed like little teeth set in his cheeks. The party numbered thirty—their stretched boarding torpedo had been capacity-packed with ninety men.

So far, so good.

Or bad.

Walls in this region were a mass of mauve jelly-blobs oozing thin strings of blue exudate on to a disconcertingly glowing spongy floor. Each bootstep printed a temporary luminous puddle in that sponge. Iridescent beetles dropped into these from the ceiling where they had seemed like glittery scales. They spun in a frenzy of drinking—and died, floating belly up.

As the spongy material resumed its former contours, arachnids darted from fleshy puce vents low down the walls to chew the beetles and vomit the cud into those same vents. These arachnids were little more than oversized jaws and a digestive sac mounted on six flexible spidery legs.

Jointed arches, which ribbed the walls, flexed occasionally. Sometimes a questing tentacle wavered out from a hole in the bone. Vents sighed gases, adding an ammoniacal reek to the hot wet cocktail of sweaty vapours, tart pheromones, sour xenohormones, mildew, spice of attar, and a pervasive odour of not-quite-nutmeg. Oh for Lord Vladimir Pugh's inability to savour.

"This whole ship seems biological," Vonreuter was saying, as he cut down one such tentacle. The appendage flopped about and grew hexagonal ruby eyes on stalks. Snakelike, it tried to slither away into a purulent yellow depression. The Lieutenant sliced it up with his sword. "So I'd say we'll find controlling organs somewhere deep in it. Like a heart, and kidneys..."

Organs.

Deep.

The passageway branched. The saturated sponge continued for only a few metres along the leftward fork before withering into a scrofulous mat where carmine slugs were grazing. Clusters of polyps were melted glutinously down the walls, releasing larvae which wriggled into vents. The tunnel was shedding its lining, revealing ridgy cartilage, plates of grey gristle.

Across the base of the rightward passage there swelled a large pink cyst. It was suggestive of some giant mutant female ape's bum presented for fertilisation. A low labial crater wall surrounded a semblance of a mouth with floppy lips pressed shut. The cyst was two metres across.

Marine Dolf Harlan was the first to try to cross the obstacle. He shut his visor before treading tentatively upon the side of the cyst prior to leaping. The surface was slimy. This would not have mattered, except that just then a larger relative of the patching bats came flapping at Harlan. It wrapped hooked wings around his helmet.

As Harlan tore it loose, he took an inadvertent step forward.

He began to slip.

The cyst pulsed, dilated.

Harlan fell through its open lips.

Fell? He almost seemed pulled, so swiftly did he disappear through the floor.

The lips clamped shut again.

Vonreuter radioed to Harlan in vain. In vain he consulted the disposition readout on his faceplate. Dolf Harlan had vanished utterly from anywhere in the vicinity.

"Either he was disintegrated immediately," said Sergeant Juron, "or else he travelled elsewhere double-quick. In which case—"

"Lower a sensor down," the Lieutenant ordered.

The rune-painted sensor dangled on a fine strong chain like a thurible for burning incense to Rogal Dorn.

Chain ran through Juron's gauntlet as sensor then tether were sucked down through the inner labia of the cyst—fiercely, till almost all of the chain had paid out. When Juron clenched his power fist and pulled, he drew up only a metre's length of tether. The rest, and the sensor, had disappeared, severed.

Juron and the Lieutenant consulted the small veneered telemetry screen clipped to the Sergeant's arm.

"Warp echo here, Sir. This thing's a teleporter—"

"There's no sign of reality-reentry—"

"Sensor must still be in the warp..."

"Harlan too?"

"Where's the sense in a teleporter that doesn't take you to any real destination?"

"Garbage disposal?"

"This thing's bigger than human size. Got to be for transport."

"No controls for co-ordinates."

"Maybe depends where you stand on the rim. Maybe you *stamp* out a signal. Harlan could be right at the heart of the vessel by now."

Yes, the cyst was an organic teleporter through warpspace—but to where?

Lex spoke up, brandishing his bolt gun. "Permission to follow Brother Harlan, Sirs!"

Yeri clamped tight on Lex's arm. "No you figging well don't. You're only saying that to get out of my sight, away from me."

Lex's reply was brief and withering. "Away from *you*?"

Before either officer could respond to Lex's offer, the cyst in the floor convulsed...

Chapter Seventeen

Marines and Scouts drew back just as the great cyst ejected an armoured form.

No, it wasn't Harlan's. Nor was it any Marine's!

Before anyone could even dream of firing at this possible attacker, the suit slumped on to the floor—a dead weight.

The armour was tarnished, mottled, and blotched as if its very molecules were diseased. The figure possessed two arms and two legs—yet crooked, crab-like ones. The suit was made all of ring segments, a flexible carapace of narrow jointed hoops unlike any style that Biff remembered studying in the scriptory... The helmet was a flattened domelet, featureless but for discolourations.

While one Battle Brother held the strange suit's annulate shoulders, another strove to unfasten that helmet smoothly.

It wouldn't budge.

With a twist of power the Brother wrenched that helmet free......releasing a dusty memory of long-bygone decay—and exposing a broad low knobby head resembling that of a turtle, parchmented with withered brown leathery skin. Quite mummified, in the sarcophagus of the suit. The eyes had dried to tiny buttons on threads.

Long since.

The Lieutenant tested a skin sample with the antiquari-ometer from his tool pouch.

"The Carbon XIV reading gives an estimate of fourteen thousand years, plus or minus two thousand."

Aeons since...

In another galaxy, way back before the molluscoid vessel must have even commenced its crossing of the deeps...

A sense of awe stole over the Fists.

The alien's banded gauntlet still clutched, clawlike, a handgun of convoluted design made of some ceramic material.

As in this galaxy, so in others far away... *death* was the currency, so it seemed.

Vonreuter retrieved the defunct gun for future study.

"This thing must have boarded the ship just as we're boarding it now," he surmised to Stossen. "I guess it stepped into this transporter cyst..." He scrutinised the acidic blemishes upon the armour. "And the transporter dumped it in... a solution of acid. Not a powerful acid. Its suit wasn't eaten away... More like a..." His voice wavered into disgust. "A stomach acid. And there our alien intruder stayed for the next fourteen thousand years..."

"Until we gave the transporter critter hiccups by sliding a chain down its gullet," murmured Biff. "Can we get Harlan back by making this figging thing puke? How 'bout dropping some choke grenades down its gob?"

Juron nodded slowly.

"If this teleporter beast's instinct is to throw intruders into some digestive bit of it, we can't use it ourselves... How does it tell intruders... from residents? How do those residents tell it where they'd like to go—whoever they are?"

"Use choke," said Vonreuter. "But give the grenades some ballast. They're too light as they are. Use the alien's body.''

Two Scouts held the turtle-creature up in its suit, over the
lips of the cyst. Biff tore the skull loose and tossed it away.
In rapid succession he thumbed three of the self-priming,
coin-size grenades from the dispenser on his plasteel
sleeve, and dropped these hastily down the vacated neck of
the banded suit. The Scouts hurled the suit down through
the cyst whence it had come. It vanished.

They waited.

Down in the unseen guts of the teleporter creature, where
a gagging gas spewed from a headless suit, the dead alien
soldier would be enacting a minor, long-delayed revenge
against the creature which had choked it inside its own
armour, stifling it on its own foul alien breath...

The surface of the cyst vibrated.

A groaning throb issued from the pursed lips.

Presently a bilious miasma drifted out—but no Harlan.
No Battle Brother.

The Lieutenant was receiving a crackly signal on the
command band; after which, he addressed his men.

"Terminator Librarian Captain Steinmuller advises all
squads to thrust blast grenades into any floor cysts they
come across. The Captain's Warp-sensitive. He says this
creature is a worm-tangle. Most of its body exists in the
Warp—he senses dozens of these feeler openings. The
worm's tuned to every native of this ship—because they're
all keyed in to some strange composite mind. That mind's
vaster than this ship, he says. It makes him sick to think
how big. *All* the ships are part of it. The transporter worm's
been bio-engineered...

"By Dorn, we've simply been wasting time, trying to
recover Harlan! I shall scourge myself in a pain machine
for the sentimentality that masks timorousness—a reluc-
tance to advance, an excuse to linger!"

The Lieutenant crooked his power glove so as to eject
the tiny disc of a grenade directly at the lips of the cyst. The

Ian Watson

shielding armour though it was of no other consequence to
him.

The cyst erupted.

Its pink lips tore apart, shredded, revealing a hairy grey
well—misty and indefinite. Its throat dissolved into a
grainy nothingness, smearing out of ordinary existence.

Darting to the rim, Vonreuter fired another grenade.

But the worm's throat was already crimping tight
reflexively, folding in upon itself, amputating the ravaged
mouth. The grenade travelled hardly any distance down
before seeming to implode rather than explode. From the
rim of the cyst flesh was flowing, bunching to seal the hole
with bulging tumorous tissue—as the Lieutenant leapt
back.

Wrong way to do that, reckoned Biff. *Stickin' the
grennies in a suit was subtler. That way, the worm gulped
the bait right down its gob into its guts...*

His totem spider was haunting his vision again, waving
innumerable long sinuous legs. Legs that faded in and out
of existence, leading to locales far and near...

There were *invisible* tunnels in this ship, living tunnels
through the Warp, which no Marine could use.

And the denizens of this vessel were all linked by spidery
mental legs...

The Lieutenant sucked in his breath as he harkened to the
com-band.

"Squads are under attack," he relayed to his men.
"*Genestealers*—and something worse... a claw and spike
creature that bounces along... Genestealers! Can this be
where they come from?"

Juron shuddered. "Do you reckon they've been *bred*—
like that worm, and the patch-bats?"

"Genestealers don't have any tech of their own, do they?
We find them adrift in hulks, but they don't seem to
comprend machines."

218

"Not our sort of machines. Maybe that's because they're only used to a living machine."

"I swear this ship's been created by something. It didn't create itself."

"Whatever sort of critter could create Genestealers?"

The humid atmosphere was tetchy, oppressive. Vonreuter swore. "Why haven't *we* been attacked yet?" He seemed to take this as a personal affront.

Or as though an attack might relieve the tension.

Plainly the Lieutenant's feelings communicated themselves to Lexandro, who power-leapt over the tumouring cyst, to range ahead on point. Of course, Yeri followed him, alert to peril.

"Wait," called Vonreuter. "Beware the brash boldness that masks lack of foresight!"

Though how could there be foresight, where all was whelmed in mystery?

Has to be a body that co-ordinates, reasoned Biff. *Something that houses the overmind. Something physical in this ship. An organ. And it'll commune with similar bodies in all the other ships—telepathically through the Warp— like so many different brain cells, to add up to the Shadow Mind...*

The lootenant said as much regarding a heart and kidneys. Find that mind-organ, and skrag it, and the local denizens might experience a spot of difficulty...

Vonreuter decided to divide his men into two sub-units. The taciturn Sergeant Ruhr would accompany one group along the leftward, cartilaginous passageway. Sergeant Juron and he would lead thirteen others in a quest along the passage of the cyst.

Thus the three brothers of Trazior, together with seven Battle Brothers and three of the canary Scouts, were soon proceeding in the company of that same Sergeant who had led them so tellingly and boldly when they seized Sagramoso's Emperor Titan.

219

Subdivided deployment made sense in such passageways where at most three Marines could fight side by side. Dividing, and spreading, the Fists were like lethal bacteria invading the body of a behemoth.

Lex grinned at the Sergeant, plainly exhilarated by the opportunities this new disposition of forces might offer. Juron was no slouch. And Vonreuter could probably be encouraged to wild deeds.

Yeri noted Lex's grin—and Biff registered Yeri's trepidation.

Very much on the alert on behalf of his loathed brother, Yeri was feeling ominous qualms as to Lex's degree of self-control...

How thin is the line, mused Biff, *between loathing and love...*

Between animosity and admiration! Or even... adulation, adoration. Ardour!

Ach, Yeri pursued some grand abstract dream of "justice"—but he didn't savvy the spider-patterns in his very own soul. He failed to comprend his own inner tangle.

The focus of Yeri's faith, at his tech mother's knee, had been the Emp.

Add to that later, the blessed Rogal Dorn.

But then Yeri developed this twisted fixation upon Lex... as a way of expressing Marine valour and piety.

Which meant that his piety was in fact some way from being as pure as he imagined.

It dawned on Biff that paradoxically Lex must, for Yeri, be *standing in* for the remote Emperor in some strange dreamlike regard. Lex had become a substitute personage close at hand who represented aristocratic supremacy and ruthless disdain. Disdain—and therefore apparent injustice—was what the Emperor must needs exercise towards all mere individual human beings—for the sake of the whole human race and its future. Injustice, within a vaster tapestry of eventual triumphant virtue...

In no way could Yeri rebel against the harsh God on Earth. Nor could he even allow himself to contemplate the slightest doubt or anger. Indeed, resentment would be as futile as for a flea to feel offended at the conduct of a cudbear in whose pelt it dwelled.

Yeri surely did feel a streak of bitter antipathy towards Him-on-Earth whom he must serve and adore. *Lex* was the repository for this dark, unadmitted rancour which must coexist with worship deep in Yeri's soul.

Which meant that, should Lex be killed, Yeri might start to question his whole faith. It would seem as though his own focus of fervour had betrayed fatal frailty. He might lapse into heresy.

Huh, thought Biff, convinced nonetheless of the truth of his analysis.

He patted his bolt gun with his power glove.

Megabossgod's namenz is Death..., he reminded himself. No need to confide his suspicions as to this kink in Yeri's faith to a chaplain. None whatever.

He ought to. But he wouldn't.

Thus Biff would in turn act as protector to Yeri. This twist amused Biff richly. Only he, the ex-scumnik, had the sophistication to understand Yeri's heart. And oh no, he wouldn't pull the rug out from under Brother Valence. Biff's would be a secret sort of protection, knowable only to Rogal Dorn in a private prayer. How much more honourable this was than Yeri's vulgar bodyguardianship of pretty Lexandro; than the ex-tech's ambivalent, hate-streaked fawning.

Biff realized, then, the extent to which he himself was also meshed in this sticky web of brotherhood...

Suppose one brother died. All three were so intimately bound up in one another's destiny. Therefore perhaps all three would be doomed to die. Maybe there was a sickening inevitability about this.

The namenz is Death, spake the Spider, clearly, inside

Biff's head. *Death is the namenz.*

Biff heard those very words. They weren't voiced by Rogal Dorn, but by something deep and atavistic. Maybe that was the very voice of Necromunda, world of death, from which he thought he had escaped, now reaching out across the years and across the light years to reclaim him.

A terrifying wave of superstition swept over Biff, rocking the superstructure of rational *thunks* which he had painstakingly erected within himself. He sketched a hex sign with his power glove, and whispered a confused, hopeless prayer.

"Spider spirit, don't betray me. Rogal Dorn, array me in your light."

He had sinned in thought. He had thunked too far. His nimble mind had performed a deconstruction job upon Yeri's motives. In so doing, Biff had almost cast impertinent doubt on the supremacy of the Emperor and the Primarch, had he not?

At one remove... using Yeri Valence as his mental model...

Biff's facial tattoo itched fiercely, as though its outlines were being renewed, re-etched with knife-point and caustic acid and dye.

Deconstruct, he thought giddily. *Destruct. Destroy.*

Seek and learn, by all means—but most of all, *destroy*, to appease the hungry Spider... which no longer seemed to be an avatar of wisdom guiding Biff to intuitions of hidden patterns, but an instinctual power ravenous to survive through the spilling of alien blood and ichor.

Fists must be clever.

Yet cleverness was finally a self-deceit.

Biff slapped Yeri's shoulder pauldron.

"Have faith, Brother," he urged.

Yeri, who could not see Biff's crazy grin, misunderstood.

Of course he would misunderstand.

"Lex won't get away from us into the embrace of

death,'' replied Yeri. He spoke as though he had actually seduced Biff into his own endeavour, as a secondary bodyguard for lordly Lexandro d'Arquebus.

Yet perhaps it was an appropriate reply, after all. Perhaps Yeri did now have a true partner in the preservation of that impetuous, disdainful brother.

''We'll embrace death together, all three,'' muttered Biff, as if cursed.

Three bodies, bound together.

Three corpses-to-be—and keeping invisible company with them, the powerful courtesan of the cosmos who was neither male nor that other sex either, but who was neuter— as exactly befitted... *Extinction.*

Many of the Marines must have been suffering similar soul-riving pangs inside that eerie living ship. Many Battle Brothers might well have been praying that their faith would supercharge them...

The passageway was now hooped with traceries of cartilage dripping ichor. Clumps of sickly luminous cyanotic fungi protruded like bunches of hernias, nibbled by iridescent insects with gauzy wings. Stagnant sludge coated the chitin plates of the floor. Long tapeworms of silvery hue slithered in this shallow, sticky morass, sucking the slimy bilge in and shedding body segments resembling soft flat ingots. Crabby creatures with coppery carapaces carried these off in their pincers. The air reeked of a heady tart vinegar and fruity rot.

A bloated beaked belly on crooked bony legs was gorging blindly upon a pulsing fibrous tumour that thrust out from one wall. As they came upon it, the surgeon-creature reached capacity and ruptured. It released shredded, dissolving cancerous tissue into the sludge.

A replacement scavenger-belly, initially as slim as a collapsed lung, reared up on its stick limbs in turn and began compulsively plumping out. Several other flat bellies stood waiting in line to feast on this distortion of the passageway until they burst...

Hitherto burpings of gas, gurglings of juices, swishings, throbbings, and rumblings had serenaded the Fists' advance. Now these noises hushed ominously—in time for those Marines with heavy weapons to unsling missile launcher and plasma gun.

From a floor-cyst some way ahead, erupted a creature of greenish hue—composed entirely of huge hooked claws and spikes, or so it seemed at first glance.

It bound across the sludgy floor towards the Fists, propelling itself with flicks of a spike-tipped tail. And already a second such creature had emerged from the cyst...

The tail was a fat spring of banded muscles. A powerful thruster-leg with twin claws resembling sharpened hooves aided its rapid forward motion. From its horny loins a long fierce knife-like organ protruded, quivering. Overhead the creature brandished a single leathery hand of huge grasp, ridged with vertebrae. Two knotty fingers ended in curved talons; one in a scimitar-claw; and the thumb in a cruel gouging hook.

Midway down the body—that spring-loaded body of massive hooked blades—a distorted face bulged. The fanged mouth snarled, agape. Crazed eyes staring fixedly, close set above a tiny nose.

An almost *humanoid* face...

Bolts tore into that body, shattering the leering face. Yet tail and foot still propelled the clutch of claws and thrust of knife with remorselessly mighty hops.

Plasma gushed, melting and fusing the giant reaching hand. Nevertheless, the loin-organ jerked forward, impacting with a Brother's groin-guard. The spike actually penetrated a weld in the armoured pouch before snapping off, twanging.

The Brother cried out and staggered.

The twisted, melting residue of the hand descended around his helmet. His visor was still open. The burning remainder of the hook-thumb ripped out an eye before the grabber's death throes entirely disabled it; before its wrecked, ripped, charred corpse collapsed.

Its headlong assault had shielded the rush by its partner. Even as bolts ripped into that second creature, it reached a Scout. His head vanished entirely within its leathern palm. Its claws sunk into his back and chest. As it dragged him up against it, its disembowelling spike slashed upward.

The second creature soon died too.

The Scout would take longer about dying—maybe even long enough to be evacuated...

His Brothers dragged him against a wall, tethering him to spurs in the cartilage so that he wouldn't slip down into the sludge.

The now-one-eyed Brother, power fist clamped across his groin, protested at being assigned to guard the Scout.

"I *can* carry on, Sir."

Juron shook his head.

Lex had loped to lob grenades into the transporter cyst, dogged by Yeri. Biff watched Juron turn the homicidal assassin-creature over with his boot. With growing revulsion the Sergeant scrutinised that brutish viridian humanoid face, its toothy mouth locked open in a rictus of death. So vastly disproportionate was that overhead grabbing arm that the face had seemed to be located in the creature's chest.

"Its face looks like... images of *Orks* I've seen," murmured Biff. "Though as for the *rest* of it..."

Vonreuter swore to himself in anguish of soul. "By Him on Earth, the blasphemy of it! I swear this thing *is* made from Ork seed—"

"Didn't know as we much liked Orks, Sir," said Juron.

Nor did they. Nor did they. Orks were an anarchic, quarrelsome, piratical race.

Ian Watson

It was Orks who had seized those three hives out in the ash wastes of Necromunda, compelling the long march culminating in much slaughter and destruction. The Imperial Fists felt a *prejudice* against Orks—though equally, without the provocation offered by those green-skinned brutes, would the Fists have been moved to establish a base on Necromunda which was to prove so fertile a source of future recruits?

Thus many Fists also felt a kind of twisted bond with Orks—who were only noisy homicidal trash, and posed no ultimate radical threat to the Imperium. Such as this vast fleet of gastropoidal living ships seemed increasingly to pose...

"Don't you see, Zed?" asked the Lieutenant, lapsing into intimacy. "This... assassin creature... has been *made* from Ork seed. Look at its green face! Ork genes have been perverted into this foul, lethal shape..."

"Pretty good weapon," grunted Biff.

"Yes, pretty good." Vonreuter's tone was bitter. "These... beings... on board this ship—these *things* from another galaxy!—must have gathered Orks from some frontier star on their way into our galaxy, and done *this* with them."

He was incensed. "Oh I reserve the right to kill all Orks I come across. Oh yes I do indeed. But they remain our *own* galaxy's Orks—the human galaxy's, our Emperor's galaxy. How dare extragalactic creatures come here to harvest and pervert our natives!"

The Lieutenant kicked the corpse. His voice hushed. "I don't believe *we* could accomplish this trick... No, I don't. Or else we would have..."

"Seems as how they made Genestealers," said Juron. "Made 'em from something else, I guess. Now this... And what else besides? What other species might they have their eyes set on?"

"Could it be... any species whatever they come across?

226

Including... us? We *mustn't* leave any dead Fists behind! I must communicate this thought to the Terminator Librarians. Imagine if the creatures that can transform an Ork into this self-propelled weapon could lay their claws on our Progenoid glands! If they could capture the code of our blessed Primarch!'' Vonreuter almost gagged.

"So where are the alien filth?" asked Juron.

Lex had ranged quite some way beyond the destroyed teleporter cyst, accompanied by Yeri. Now he shouted out from beside a muscular door he had teased open:

"*Pay-dirt, Sir!*"

Chapter Eighteen

In a ribbed vault huger than the Fists' Assimularum Hall, hundreds of vile creatures thrust from nooks in the walls— an array of angular gargoyles.

Coated in an integument of translucent resin, these motionless creatures seemed hewn of porous coral of amber, russet, and golden hue. Long fang-jawed heads reared upon vertebral wind-pipes from a humpbacked thorax—heads whose greatly elongated occipital region suggested that a substantial brain greater than human size was contained within the elliptical skull.

The creatures all possessed six armoured limbs. The two upper arms were dextrous, with clever-looking hands. The two lower arms had claw-tipped spades as secondary hands. The legs were jointed, and horny-hoofed. Between rump and thorax was a wasp-waisted girdle. The upper body perched flexibly upon the lower armoured haunches. These erect hexapeds were twice the stature of a man.

Slime from orifices that honeycombed the walls oozed slowly over the embalmed creatures, lending them a lustrous glaze in the light cast by...

...by several slab-footed stumpy humanoids with foetally large bald heads. Their arms had been abolished, becoming mere vestigial nubs poking back from the shoulders, as though otherwise they might attempt to tear off the parasitical organic machines that infested their faces. Tubes plunged into their mouths, their nostrils, and their eye sockets. A clawed foot held tight to the dome of their skulls. A single large eyeball, cinctured within a bony cup, rose above that foot-fixture... and beamed out leprous light... now bathing the intruding Marines.

"*Blasphemy!*" lamented Vonreuter, as those silent humanoid searchlights shuffled through the slime which drained across the pitted floor.

One of the Scouts vomited; and Lex rounded on him.

"Moron! You're putting your juices into this ship—to taste."

The Scout apologized as if Lex was an officer.

Yeri stared at the armless searchlight dwarfs in a fascination of disgust—and of rage at the limited destiny so tyrannically engineered for these purpose-bred cripples.

"Human stock," he muttered. "They come from *human* stock..."

"*We* breed cyborgs," Biff reminded him quietly.

"Ah, but in the Emperor's service," Yeri retorted tightly. "That's very different, isn't it? That's sacramental labour. Isn't it? *Isn't it?*" he demanded, his voice giddily trembling on an edge of hysteria.

"Of course it's different," Biff agreed. He hated the impious thunk which had prompted him to compare two such very different situations. He must stop thunking. In this terrible alien ship the subtleties and equivocations of thunking might prove both damnable and lethal.

Yet another thunk did promptly intrude—a more Fist-like thunk, which he might be wise to voice quickly...

Before Biff could utter his thunk, Yeri jerked a power thumb at the giant gargoyles.

"We could take a *trophy*," he snarled at Lex. "We could cut one of these loose while it's still hibernating. Take it back for experiment. To squeeze info."

"Yesss," said Lex softly. "A trophy..."

A trophy of fame... After surgical interrogation, one of those great dire skulls might excellently well be mounted in a chapel...

Whatever was in Yeri's mind? wondered Biff.

Ah... Biff comprended. Furnished with the most impeccable of excuses, namely a paralysed prisoner, their team would be obliged to withdraw. Precious Lexandro would be honourably removed from a location which seemed all too likely to kill all of them, and him, before too long...

How Yeremi's obsessive fixation was twisting his reason, and almost perverting the call of duty—oh so justifiably and piously!

"Sarge," Biff said to Juron, voicing his thunk, "these gargoyle beasts mightn't have been roosting too long. They mightn't be too deep in their Sus-an state."

"Mightn't they? Why?"

"Well, if this ship has already raided some solar systems in our galaxy so as to take Orks and humans and... manipulate their genes... to create living weapons and torches... these beasts must have been up and active within recent years. They haven't been sleeping for aeons. We should kill 'em all quickly. They're just... snoozing... in between stars."

"*Unless*—" Lex threw this word solitary and naked into the debate.

"Unless what?" demanded Juron.

"Unless," continued Lex, "other parts of the ship *have* been active—but not this one. Maybe this lot haven't batted an eyelid since they left Andromeda before Rogal Dorn was born! Scared to touch them, aren't you, Biffy? That's the truth of it."

Oh, Lex was most seduced by the notion of carrying back such an important souvenir. Yeri looked pleased at his own guile.

Lexandro smiled unpleasantly at Biff. "Easier to *skrag 'em* all where they're hanging—that's what you think, eh? 'Skrag' *is* the correct scumnik parlance, isn't it?"

One of the searchlight dwarfs focused upon Lex, but the creature seemed otherwise mindless so he paid it no heed.

Lex sneered. "*I'm* not scared of touching horrors, Biffy-boy... Permission to cut one loose with a laser, Sir?" he requested of the Lieutenant.

"You're right, d'Arquebus," agreed Vonreuter. "We're here for knowledge as much as to exterminate. Knowledge precedes extermination. Knowledge *perfects* extermination."

The Lieutenant snapped a lasgun loose from a thigh-holster on his plasteel cuisse. Silver runes embossed the barrel. After adjusting setting and focus deftly with his power glove, he handed the weapon to Lex to do the honours.

Lex stepped up to the petrified monster looming from the oozing wall.

"Yes," whispered Yeri.

A searing needle of coherent light lanced from the gun.

Resin cracked.

Resin burst.

Slime sprayed.

Steam billowed, assaulting nostrils with a sour vinegary whiff.

A long golden eye clicked open.

A spade-claw jerked.

The dragon-creature which loomed over Lex twitched. Lubricants began filtering from its pores.

The periscopic eyeballs of the searchlight dwarfs swivelled. They beamed that ashen radiance more brightly at the ranks of gargoyle-dragons poised in their slime-coated brittle sheaths.

A crackling as of a frozen lake being trampled by mastodons propagated around that foul organic cathedral den.

Everywhere, resin was cracking.

Great dragon bodies were shifting fractionally—or, to the alarmed eye, seeming to shift—as though fossils were softening back into flesh inwardly.

"Blast 'em all!" howled Vonreuter, swiftly changing his mind as to the merits of transporting a supposedly paralytic monster.

"Back off, d'Arquebus! All fire at will!" bellowed Juron, entirely in accord.

Yeri shot the searchlight dwarfs first, blowing away their periscope eyes, blasting their blasphemed humanoid tissue apart.

Lex, who had leapt back cursing in frustration, fumbled with the setting on the lasgun to restore its pristine lance of deathlight.

The chamber dinned cacophonously like some giant drum being beaten from within by frantic percussionists as the Fists sprayed exploding bolts around the walls into every slimy niche occupied by those towering six-limbed alien nightmare-knights...

As those segmented, horny, hunchbacked bodies jerked...

As slime and sluggish purple blood suppurated...

Biff fired *skraggingly*, sensing a great Spidergob of Death suffusing his limbs, a god who was *this* galaxy's totem.

This god eyed as anathema such creatures from another island-universe who would devour his children. His myriad festering offspring—human beings and feral humans, Abhumans and unhumans the like of Orks—were rightly the Spidergobs to devour!

The human galaxy—its starry spiral arms winding

around a blazing core which concealed a black eater of stars, a pit of ultimate night—was web and spider at once... spinning slowly, greedily feasting on the life that it bred so fecundly...

These creatures from beyond the Dark Deep were of a foreignness so utter that the Spider-God awoke, and, beholding them through Biff's eyes, twitched with a flux of nauseated antipathy...

Or so it seemed to Biff. And Biff knew that the Spider would very likely also consume him too, as a bloody gobbet to soothe its dyspepsia.

At last the Fists ceased fire. Did any of the aliens, savaged in their embalment, remain alive? The ribbed, spattered walls were hung with hundreds of wrecked cadavers which might still twitch, but which surely posed no further threat...

Yeri's gaze darted all about the chamber, alert for any wounded dragon which might nevertheless launch itself, stumbling, at Lexandro.

Thus Yeri was the first to see a sphincter door pulse open and three fully alert kin of the slaughtered rush through, hissing enragedly.

Two carried long devices resembling great golden drumsticks of tissue and cartilage torn loose from the shoulders of some flightless alien bird. Spurred contoured bone, with a menacing hole in the end, protruded.

The third waved two shimmering swords of yellow horn, one in each upper hand. A spike jutted from the pommels, the sting-tail of some mutated armoured worm which formed the hand-guard, stubby parodies of mouth-fingers clinging tight to the base of the blade.

Blazing gobbets erupted from the holes in the fronts of the drumstick-guns, streaking like conflagrating phosphorus, screaming through the air.

One gobbet ploughed into a corpse hanging from the

wall, bursting, spattering sizzling acids.

The second struck Vonreuter on his thigh-armour, and began corroding, *eating through plasteel*, as the Lieutenant swiped at the clinging volatile smear.

A hideous crackling noise issued from the swollen butts of those guns as the wielders, hands plunged deep within, cranked some trigger.

Already Yeri was returning fire.

Biff too.

And Juron, and the others.

Those eerie drumstick-guns did not fire again immediately. They crunched, within, and shuddered—in which short span of time bolts tore into the snarling nightmare-knights... so that when the guns did emit new flaming projectiles, the guns were already tumbling from the dying creatures' grasp.

No bolts reached the sword-wielder, though.

Those razor-sharp horns swished through the air, aglow, in frenzied circuits, as the warrior advanced. Bolts were simply batted aside by the scintillating aura of force conjured in mid-air.

Juron and a limping Vonreuter both converged, waving their power-swords.

Each attacked one horn-blade.

As the humming monomolecular edges of their swords met those force-field-spinning razor-horns in shuddering collision, rainbow energy cascaded.

One horn split, its worm-handle shrieking.

The other locked with Vonreuter's blade, bearing down upon him from his alien assailant's greater height. The creature lashed out with a hoof. This impacted on the acid-weakened zone of his thigh, buckling the fast-corroding armour. From between the towering alien's legs its spiked tail jerked upward into the crumpled cuisse, piercing through into the Lieutenant's muscle and carapace.

But its blades no longer wove that cordon of energy.

Lex had circled at speed. Firing upward, Lex shattered that great-brained head.

The creature collapsed over Vonreuter, bearing him staggering backward to the ground, impaling his thigh even further.

Juron and Lex wrestled the monster off the Lieutenant, wrenching out the dripping tail-spike.

Vonreuter moaned, then smiled as the pain caught up with him... before his suit's opiates quenched the distracting pangs.

Juron hauled the officer upright. Vonreuter tottered, then stood firm, though momentarily grey-faced. Some poison had perhaps entered his blood, and his blood was neutralising it, manufacturing anti-toxins at speed.

Yeri was trampling upon one of the bone-guns, breaking it open. Cautiously he peered at the organic, steaming innards... discovering a brood chamber of tiny chitinous ammunition-creatures... a large curled-up beastie with tough mandibles... for stripping that casing of chitin?... a vomitory firing chamber...

Giddy with the death he had brought to the sword-wielder, Lex made to stamp his boot down upon the guts of that gun which Yeri had just exposed. Lex would show him how to erase it from existence.

Yeri thrust against him—"Don't!"—but Lex's boot crushed one of the spilled ammunition-creatures.

Immediately that its shell was cracked, the vile green softness within gushed acrid fire, wreathing Lex's boot... which he plunged into a pool of ooze to extinguish.

"The gun's made of different creatures joined together, using each other," Yeri said to Juron, who nodded but seemed indifferent.

"Well killed," the Sergeant said to Lex.

Then they all headed through the open door, along a great passageway that dripped turquoise mucous.

Cocoons bulged from niches. Lex broke one open with

his power-fist.

Within, draped in slime, hunched a paralysed tattooed human woman with braided ropes of brown hair, her breasts and belly alike swollen with a slow pulsing commotion of what might well have been larvae...

"No time for this right now," gasped Vonreuter.

When they entered the next chamber—a gloomy glaucous cave with long feelers questing from the walls—a voice addressed them in Imperial Gothic.

A throaty, sibilant, hissing voice, it framed the syllables of human language with some care, but correctly.

"Kindly do not use your weapons upon me—"

So they did not fire immediately.

The figure that spoke was enmeshed in those medusa fronds, and it was only the height of a Marine...

"You a prisoner?" asked one of the Fists.

The figure that emerged was six-limbed—a centaur-dragon. Four of its limbs were powerful, hoofed legs. Only its two thick potent upper limbs were arms... Consequently it was no juvenile form of the alien nightmare-knights, although its weasely face was similar. Its skin was thick and horny.

"I am *Zoat*," the centaur said. "Please cease your confused intrusion into this home. You should honour the Masters from beyond the Deep. They shall find a suitable use for you as part of the multi-body that supports the Great Mind—the Mind that shall spread through all the universe."

Its voice was lulling, hypnotic—so they listened.

"Your... engenderings... will partake in a Great Work," it announced. "The Masters tell us that the Great Mind senses that there are... savage entities... within the Warp which this galaxy floats upon, as glittering scum on a black lake—"

"*Tzeentch...*," muttered Biff. Yeri darted a look of utter

warning at his brother. With power-glove, Yeri mimicked the scribing of anathema upon bones...

"*Chaos*..." Biff made a hex sign. Yeri looked on the point of leaping to muzzle Biff, lest Lex's bones be put in peril.

"Yes, *Chaos*," sang the centaur. "Thanks be to the Great Mind that Guides, the Masters are immune to corruption!

"Your galaxy is crumbling under this corruption," it hissed. "Our ships shall take your flesh, extract your genes, and forge instruments that will wash your worlds clean of..." It stared at Biff, eyes glittering, "...of the taint of *Tzeentch*. And... of other taints," it added. "Do you fear the torments of this Tzeentch?" Oh, it had picked up on the name Biff murmured.

"And... of the other kindred torments of Chaos?" it asked. "Under the wise guidance of your new Tyranid lords all flesh shall finally be remoulded into pure tools, serving the Tyranid Overmind, which shall expel and quench all this tarnish utterly. You can never achieve that. For the traits of chaotic tarnish are written within you. We can unwrite what was written. We shall delve for your daemons and expunge them! This is our message to you: withdraw, relinquish, yield, and serve. Your stars shall be saved by the Masters!"

Vonreuter's voice shook. "Don't listen to this talk of daemons, lads. Of Chaos... it's *verboten*. There are nouns and *verbs* that *oughtn't* ever to be uttered—"

"But is this not *true*?" asked the centaur. "How foolishly your pretend otherwise—when our Great Mind can intuit in its dream the features of the Chaos that haunts you all. Your puny Empire is a mere cobweb."

"Heresy," snarled a Marine.

"Yet it is so! It is so! Your rulers know this very well. Are you not concerned with truth?"

Biff itched to kill this suave freak who sprech ed

ImpGoth so slickly. Yet he forced himself to listen.

"Your Imperium is a tattered cobweb," the centaur repeated sympathetically. "You cannot bind the dire Gods of Chaos. Nor can you resist our fleet. Haa, but we shall give you a useful place within our homes—and we shall purge all taint. For we can extinguish those daemons by altering all the flesh and minds they feed on."

"We've seen the use you made of Orks and people!" shouted Juron. "Mincing machines and searchlights!"

"Yet those are happy beings—united within our purpose. Are you happy? No, you are clouded with dreads, and transfixed with terrors."

"Woz it talking about?" cried a Scout.

"Don't listen," said Juron.

"Some of your other comrades have *already* listened to us Zoats—and we shall not need to destroy them. They have laid down their weapons—to serve our Masters in... in the crusade... against Chaos."

"That's a lie." A suave lie.

"Why should we lie, when we could kill you?"

"Because your figging ship isn't fully awake yet!" retorted Biff.

"Why should we trouble to learn your language?"

"Yeah, how did you manage that trick?"

"Because Marines have assisted us. The Chapter of the Lambs..."

"The *Lamenters*?"

"Yes, indeed."

"So where are the Lamenters? Show us one!"

"We Zoats are ambassadors," the alien beast said, quite failing to answer Biff's enquiry. "We are well-bred negotiators. Kindly escort me to your fortress-ministry. Monastery."

Biff jerked a thumb at Lex. "Try negotiating with *him*— he's well-bred."

Yeri panicked at this seeming incitement of the alien

towards his own warped focus of adoration. Quickly, he stepped in front of Lexandro, who responded with an affronted shove.

"A *living* trophy, Brother Tech!" snapped Lex. "Don't try to grab him for yourself."

"We can't take an unknown alien spy into our base," protested Brother Kurtz.

"That's another name for ambassador: *spy*," agreed Brother Volkman.

"Brothers!" Lex appealed, silkily. "Lieutenant, shall we avail ourselves of this offer? We have excellent accommodation beneath our Apothacarion, do we not?"

Vonreuter's wound was obviously troubling him. He seemed confused, unable to assess. Tentacles wafted from the walls, questing softly. The Lieutenant's head nodded.

"Take over command, Juron," he murmured. "I have some toxins in me that my body doesn't recognize..."

"Sarge," said Lex, "you led us when we seized the Titan together. Now we can seize... *this*."

"I shall come with you willingly," promised the Zoat. "I shall come quickly. Kindly let us go now—in case some warriors of our ship surprise us. They are not... diplomats, as I am."

Juron frowned.

"I shall warn you about the Chaos Powers our Overmind senses in this galaxy," the Zoat vowed.

This was a mistake.

Juron groaned, "*No...*"

Chaos was pollution of the innocent. A Marine, to be a knight of the Emperor, must be purely innocent.

"Sir," said Yeri, "shouldn't we advise our Librarians? Shouldn't they accept the surrender of this... ambassador?"

The Spider writhed in Biff's mind. "According to this Zoat," he said slowly, "some of our Brothers already surrendered, overwhelmed by the opportunity of serving these Tyranids. Now *it* wishes to surrender... quickly. How come?''

He thunked. ''Isn't it simply saying *anything*... so as to waste time until some warriors arrive? Because it's figging desperate to stop us heading any further in this direction, and finding something vital? Doesn't fancy its chances against a whole bunch of us, though! So it's lying.''

Within an instant, the fluent alien diplomat became a ravening beast. It leapt at Biff so swiftly that it was upon him before he could fire a single bolt...

Chapter Nineteen

The Zoat tore Biff's helmet off.

His helmet, and head too.

The sheer strength of the alien beast!

Wrenching upwards, it lifted his cranium and his brain and his neck tissues—stretching, then snapping—in one fluid hoist. Stripped bare, Biff's cervical vertebrae stood upright from the collar of his suit. They seemed to be the nozzle for a fountain of blood. This fountain swiftly died. Even as his body still stood there headless, his blood had set to cinnabar.

As the Zoat rushed Biff's detached head aloft, Lex was appalled to glimpse Biff Tundrish still living for some seconds. His astonished eyes goggled from their orbits through his open visor. The shock had not quite yet thundered upon his consciousness to quench it utterly.

To see a living head torn loose... and that head being able to know, for hideous instants, that it was deprived of a body...

For a moment Lex could hardly comprehend. Here was some daemonic conjuring trick, such as the possessed Lord

Sagramoso had perpetrated, or had endured! This alien monster boasted of making bodies mutable. It had talked of Tzeentch, the Lord of Change. Tzeentch the forbidden, Tzeentch the expurgated...

But no. No daemonic trick. Sheer brute strength.

The Zoat hurled helmet and head at Lex. Lex dropped his bolt gun so as to raise both power gloves to catch the head.

"No!" howled Yeri—whether at the decapitation, or at Lex's rash folly in dropping his weapon, who could say?

Lex clutched the helmeted head before him. It was like some absurd limbless crab-creature with a metal shell. The spider tattoo leered its venomous Scumnik heraldry. Life *still* flickered distantly within those bulging bloodshot eyes, life that was fast ebbing away within the embrace of the spider—shrinking, receding, sucked down a horrid infinite dark well.

Lex snarled at that face, thrust so suddenly up against his. He bared his teeth in fury at its impertinence in shocking him thus—as well as in disgust at its fate.

And he smiled madly too. For Biff's lips seemed with tormented effort to be trying to form a last, breathless word... of damnation, or of desperate life-desire...

Jarring his own helmet against Biff's, jerking his own face forward, Lex either bit or kissed those purpled, near-corpse lips. Which, he knew not, though he tasted blood. All meaning eluded Lex right then. He anointed Biff's lips with his own spittle as one might kiss a hand-bomb...

Lex registered that the Zoat had leapt upon Brother Kurtz. It was rending him apart even in his armour. It was using him as a shield even while it tore that massive shield asunder.

So Lex hurled the head at the Zoat.

Nor did Lex miss.

Biff's helmeted head struck the Zoat's skull with all the force of a power-toss—and bounced away, to roll against the wall, where glossy jelly-tentacles hastened to invade it.

No doubt it was fully dead by now. But how appropriate that Tundrish should *biff* to the last. His brain—and braincase—may well have been reduced to their original simple destiny as a nutting, head-butting instrument... Yet he was honoured, too; for even in his death throw he had butted for Rogal Dorn.

Even in its berserker fury, the Zoat staggered briefly, before discarding broken Kurtz. It leaped at limpy Vonreuter, who was confused by toxins, to maul him.

"Shoot! Shoot!" screamed Juron.

Guns racketed.

Bolts exploded.

The Zoat was deconstructed.

The Lieutenant had lost an arm. Vonreuter slumped—as Biff's armoured trunk had already slumped.

Brother Kurtz lay dying.

Yeri hastened to Lex's side, and stared him in the face—accusingly, so it seemed.

"Did that head *bruise* you?" he demanded. His tone oscillated between recrimination and warped concern.

"Bruise me...," muttered Lex, hardly comprehending Yeri's question. The shock that Lex had experienced almost transcended that which Biff himself must have endured during his last moments. The ex-scumnik "brother's" demise had been absolutely thrust in Lex's face.

"Bruise me...?"

His whole soul was bruised. He felt such an inexplicable emptiness—the like of which, perhaps, Biff had also experienced at the sudden absence of a body. Lex sensed a parasitical presence—for a ghost seemed to hover by his side. Fading, diminishing, like a distant echoing cry.

"So," the Sergeant said tightly. He kicked the destroyed Zoat by way of punctuation. "Must indeed have been desperate. Prevent us from proceeding, yes indeed. Tundrish has proved his point—fatally. Saved us from making a serious error. Saved us. Dorn be with him always." He happened to eye Lex as he said this, and Yeri frowned.

"Saved you? Saved you for what?" Yeri hissed at Lex, offended. "Set you up for a worse death, more like." This prospect of death appealed strongly to Lex. The contemptible ex-scumnik was now honoured above his other two "brothers". The proper balance of hierarchy should be restored.

Why, Biff had even disarmed Lex... in a sense. How instinctive it had seemed to catch the head of a Brother. *Clever* Zoat.

Lex swiftly recovered his bolt gun from where it had fallen.

"If you're so concerned, you could have given me *this*," he snapped at Yeri. "Sir," he said, "we must be very near a major organ. An undefended one."

"I'm going to report about the *ambassador* first, and what it said." The Sergeant closed his visor, to do so. He mustn't want his men to hear any more distracting mention of Chaos Powers—which had only been a ploy of the cunning Zoat, after all.

Lex paced, furious with impatience.

Juron opened his visor again, looking grim.

"We *need* to knock out a major organ. Librarian Grenzstein is dead. Let's go for it, lads."

A great cloacal passageway led towards a door that pulsed tightly, purple muscles contracting in spasm as if to hold itself shut against any intruder.

Corpses of some dead Marines and slaughtered Tyranids lay in slimy blue ooze. Scavenger creatures were dissecting humans and aliens alike. There were leathery pouches with gaping razor-jaws on a dozen short scuttling legs. There were writhing suction-tube snakes and there were bat-winged transporters with hook-feet.

The pouches were biting through Tyranid hide, butchering the aliens into joints. These, they gulped whole.

Then they waddled, swollen, to lips in the moaning, capillary-webbed walls, which swallowed the bloated pouches. A hiss of gases suggested some pneumatic channel behind those orifices. Serpents were invading the suits of the Fists, apparently liquifying the contents of flesh and bone to slurp out as slurry. Transporters fluttered, gobbets hanging from their hooks.

A snake leapt up at Scout Dietrich's hellfire bolter. The scavenger serpent latched tight. It spewed steaming caustic juices that dribbled over the Scout's glove as he tried to shake the snake free.

A slash from Juron's power sword bisected the snake—once, then twice. Its mouth still gripped the gun, nevertheless. The barrel was corroding, warping out of true.

"Drop the gun, Dietrich!"

None too soon. The Scout's gauntlet was dissolving.

Running past mobile pouches and snakes, trampling some, knocking other winged scavengers from the air, they arrived at that reluctant, puckered door—and Juron lasered it apart.

Biff's dead. Biff's dead. This truth gonged in Lex's mind, provoking stupid hilarity at the scumnik's demise—head torn off, indeed! That barbaric, presumptuous head... Forever *thunking*... That hideously ugly tattoo... And provoking resentment too, at being upstaged by such an underling—all be it a *Battle Brother*. Yet the event also triggered a wild weird pang of soul-pain. A searing sensation of amputation... A sense of void within... of the abortion of a parasite which proved, by its absence, to have been of some perverse value and significance, after all. Biff had been an ever-niggling subtext to the pious litany of Lex's life. He had lent significance by contrast.

Yes, damn it, significance!

A glossy blue chamber yawned beyond the lasered

ribbons of the dying door.

Across the floor sprawled a giant green... gland? Some body- organ of the ship, to be sure...

It was some cancerous arching slug. Great splayed suckers attached both ends of it to a floor that was composed of quivering larvae-like tubes. These linked a perimeter of thick cables to nodules in the pulsing gland-mass. Red and purple excrescences blobbed from the organ, oozing hormones. The air stank of musk and hydrogen sulphide, of rotten eggs and perfume.

As the Marines blasted the green slug with bolts, the organ spasmed. Bubbly ichor sprayed. Springy bundles of tendrils lashed out from the rips in its exploding surface. Nerve-tentacles, deep rooted in the floor, tore loose.

And Lex felt the ache of amputation—of a dimming of connexions with other parts of himself—intensify abominably. At that moment it was as if Biff had previously been joined to him, fused flesh to flesh, and mind to mind—and now was being torn away all over again even more cruelly... to be extinguished in gibbering, insane darkness.

Yeri clutched at Lex.

"We're losing touch with each other, Lex... We mustn't! We mustn't—!"

So Yeri was feeling this bizarre spasm too... this amputation, this abortion of a part of oneself...

"I can feel Biff *gone*! Don't you sense it, Lex? It'll be like this if *you* die! Such utter desolation. You mustn't die! Not here, where death is magnified... You must survive. Get out of here. I challenge you to a duel, Lexandro d'Arquebus. Do you all hear?" he cried to their companions. "I am challenging d'Arquebus to the duelling boots because... because..." What cause could there be? What adequate formal insult? "Because he caused Tundrish to *die* by believing the Zoat's lies himself! The Zoat lied, and Biff died—to prove it otherwise!"

Lex laughed at Yeri, to hide his pain. "You're being

hectic, Brother.''

''Brother... Yes, Biff *was* your secret brother—and mine! Now that he's gone, we're closer, aren't we, Lexy? The two of us. And I'll see you *damned*,'' he cried passionately. ''Is my challenge witnessed?''

No time for witnessing challenges...

As the tattered leaking green slug slumped, a cyst erupted through the floor with a shriek of tearing tissue. A flesh volcano burst open, unfolding its lips.

Aye, summoned by the dying slug-organ...

Tyranid warriors, wielding those deathspitter guns and whirling boneswords, stumbled hissing into the chamber.

Five... six looming Tyranids.

For a moment they paused; and that ghastly cracking reverberated as the component creatures within the guns chewed the husks from the living, poisonous ammunition.

Those boneswords weren't glowing with an aura, as the other ones had glowed... Two of the Tyranids collided, snarling, with one another. The aliens seemed disorganised and confused, uncoordinated... as if suffering from shock, from rupture, alienation from their fellows. These ruthless puissant dragons were almost *vulnerable*... now that the green slug-organ had perished.

Lex tensed.

And what went through Yeri's mind at that precise moment?

That Lex was about to rush into their midst, bolt gun blazing? That Lex would seize the chance of great honour, of slaying those vicious extragalactic dragonoids single-handedly—and recklessly?

That Lex was about to kill himself in defence of his Brothers, so as to win some greater measure of repute than scumnik Tundrish?

That Lex, though not in a literal sense, was also about to lose his head?

Lex must not thrust himself forward fatally, and so steal

himself away into nothingness—or into the embrace of Dorn—as Biff had done...

Before the other Brothers could even begin to open fire, Yeri pre-empted any such lethal move by Lex.

With a bark of apology, Yeri snatched Juron's power sword from him.

"Pull out, Sir!" he cried. "Report about the Zoat's lies! I'll hold the beasts off!"

Yeri leapt towards the Tyranids, bolt-gun spitting fire, sword humming—preventing his Brothers from shooting, else they would kill him.

Briefly Juron stood non-plussed.

For Yeri *had* seized that power sword away from his officer in combat. Yeremi Valence would deserve... disgraceful reprimand, the pain glove, maybe even execution... if he lived.

Therefore he must die honourably...

Six towering Tyranids could surely ensure this, no matter how malcoordinated they might be. He who had helped Juron seize that Titan deserved no less—such thoughts must have raced through the Sergeant's mind. For Juron decided to back Yeri up.

"Do it, Valence!" he cried, even as Yeri fired into the thorax of his first target, and swung his power sword to connect with a bonesword of his next opponent. "Pull out, lads! Back to the torp!"

A blazing, acid gobbet erupted screaming from a deathspitter, impacting on Yeri's plastron.

A bonesword descended upon his helmet, its serrated edge snapping.

Spade-claws reached for him.

"*Pull out, d'Arquebus!*" bellowed Juron. "*Withdraw!*"

Premature! Premature. The climax of their intrusion into this grotesque, gastropoidal starcraft should have been *Lex's own* glorious death.

His glory... his death. His death; his glory...

By withdrawing, Juron was saving Yeri from dishonour for his fevered deed... which had prevented Lex from carrying out almost the same impulsive action...

And *that* was why Yeri had really seized the Sergeant's sword. So as to force Juron's hand.

Lex felt tempted to disobey the Sergeant; to wade in with Yeri, side by side. To stand shoulder to shoulder with that... despicable embarrassment. With that leeching spurious brother...

Wouldn't other Brothers reproach Lex for leaving Yeri here? Wouldn't Yeri thus have won at long last? Wouldn't he have succeeded in humiliating Lex?

Assaulted by Yeri's bolts, a Tyranid snapped apart midway, its horny wasp-waist demolished. The hooves of its mighty legs drummed. Its sting-tail jerked in orgiastic convulsion—while its upper body fell, head roaring, claws and digits raking the floor.

Yeri was firing blindly now, swinging the power sword blindly. A Tyranid's claws were inside his helmet, raking his face, scooping jelly, and he was screaming... rapturously.

"*Out! Battle order! Back to the torp!*"

Lex obeyed Juron.

It proved to be a timely order. As the surviving Brothers pounded through the reeking passageways, Juron let them hear the clipped reports on the com-channel. Other parties were returning from deep penetration, too.

Alien resistance had slackened off, become chaotic, as though the ship was stunned. Yet wisdom counselled withdrawal, for this was primarily an info-raid. Info must be digested. *Seizing* the ship as such had never been a prime concern. Indeed, that would have been a vain endeavour, given the organic character of the vessel.

Now the Fists were setting powerful delayed-action demolition charges in that oozing, many-chambered womb of monsters as they withdrew. Soon, scavengers might begin to try to eat those charges, to digest them with caustic juices.

Lexandro expected that the pang of amputation, the aborting spasm, would come once more to him on account of Yeri.

It did not come in quite the same way. It built slowly, parasitical upon the pain he couldn't help feeling at Biff's passing.

Lex did not intuit the exact moment of his other brother's death. Yet Yeremi Valence was dead by now. Lexandro knew that full well.

The disoriented Lieutenant Vonreuter, whom they had hoped to collect en route, lay half-chewed by scavenger macrobes. Fortunately, his chest was still intact, so Brother Mahler, who kenned the art, paused to harvest his progenoid glands.

In a sense, the Lieutenant would live on.

Unlike Yeremi...

Unlike Biff, whose decapitated body had become a feast for iridescent beetles breeding fast in the shell of his suit in that chamber where he had challenged the Zoat. After flushing out his husk with flames, Sergeant Juron shoved a charge down the neck of Biff's armour into a chest a-rattle with bare ribs, shreds of black carapace, and crisped beetle.

And so they withdrew, withdrew.

Of the ninety men who had erupted into the Tyranid starship, sixty-one returned to pack into the boarding torpedo...

...which blasted hindward out of the anal sphincter, carrying them into the clean stark emptiness of space.

Other torpedos were departing from other vents in that great blanched nautiloid vessel—and from other vessels.

The particular extragalactic craft they had been inside

began to shudder silently, on screen, as charges exploded within.

It did not rupture. However, Imperial battleships began launching plasma and barrage bombs at other invading coiled leviathans.

How elegantly those human battleships drifted, pulsing out their seething balls of plasma. Those were vertical cities, spiry and crenellated, ghostly in the light from distant Lacrima Dolorosa—cities bonded to spear-blade decks that jutted out for a full four kilometres with underslung warp-keels far to the forrard. Quite as much bulk hung below the poop as soared above so that each vessel seemed afloat upon its own reflection in a lake of quicksilvered glass.

Long-range guided barrage bombs erupted against the towering alien hulls, cracking chambers open.

Throbs of incandescent ionised gas, compressed in containment fields, burst, bringing inferno where atmosphere gushed, a furnace blaze that imploded inward.

Yet there were a thousand invaders; and from the gaping mouths of the most gargantuan snail-ships there now began to spew a stream of ominous beaked white baby vessels, each the size of a small corvette. These sped in swift, if lazy-seeming, arcs towards their tormenters. They swam through space like so many blanched fossil foetuses.

Laser batteries on the decks and towers of the cathedra-line battleships opened fire, stitching the void.

Ivory foetuses erupted.

Yet there were so many of those.

Others dived upon decks, upon spires. Silent explosions shattered the serenity of those battle-cities, tearing their elegant plasteel tracery, blasting cavities which gushed a mist of shattered weaponry and personnel...

Spread over cubic megaklicks, the battle drifted past the jaundiced gas-giant and its pallid moons, inward.

As yet, in the zenith at night, those feral barbarians on Lacrima Dolorosa III wouldn't even be able to glimpse the very brightest of the carnage, still so many hundreds of millions of klicks away was their jungle world still.

Chapter Twenty

In the gallery of the Solitorium which jutted below the fortress-monastery, Lexandro knelt alone, searching his heart.

He ignored the vistas of bilious nebulae and of ten thousand stars—those tiny cyanotic lanterns and angry carbuncles frozen in their fevered burning in the void. He scorned the pastel dapple of stained starlight dimly washing upon the plasteel flagstones through the mullioned oriel windows.

Lieutenant Kroff Tezla, the total amputee, was long gone, back to his Blood Drinker Brothers. A frigate from that Chapter had taken Tezla home at the end of the Gathering of Commanders preceding the Lacrima Dolorosa crusade.

Lexandro was alone.

The memory of the mutilated Kroff Tezla remained, lolling in his cup-shaped cart, attended by simian servitors.

That staunch man!

And on one lonely day three "brothers" had visited him, out of almost impertinent curiosity...

Yeri had wondered whether Tezla regretted his survival. Lex had quibbled, in order to score a point over Yeri. Then he had asked whether Brothers of that exotic, sanguino-philiac Chapter supped each other's blood—an intrusion upon Tezla's privacy which had irked the man, an intrusion upon grief.

And upon his terrible separation—from his Brothers, and from his own limbs.

Now Lexandro was also separated, spiritually amputated, in a way he had never been able to envision; in a manner that he never could have foreguessed. All of his prayers to Rogal Dorn were as dust or wormwood. Futility haunted him—a gulf deeper and more annihilating than any heat-sink.

He recalled his confession to Chaplain Lo Chang of the cratered moon-face, in a chapel where a Tyranid skull now hung, its jaw snarling, its swollen occipital braincase jutting back into a niche draped with purple velvet in the manner of some vertical jewel box.

Lo Chang had sat behind a filigree screen, upon a pain-stool—not so much that he should experience due anguish at a Brother's admission of shortcomings... Nay, the constipative pangs induced in the nerves of his buttocks may have been subtly pleasurable... but so that thus he might sympathetically take into himself some of the confessee's misery, then defecate this discomfiture out of his own body, metamorphosed into crass waste matter, fit to be jettisoned.

"When I pray now to our Primarch, to dedicate myself afresh," Lex had whispered, "cold void yawns within me... where previously the spirit of Dorn filled me with his presence, his heat, his glow... It's as though Rogal Dorn has withdrawn his aura of blessing, his grace..."

Thanks to the Lacrima Dolorosa crusade, somewhat more was now known about the workings of the Tyranid hive fleet.

A fifth of the gastropoidal vessels invading that solar system had been destroyed or disabled—either by Marine boarders or by battleship bombardment—before the depleted Imperial forces had withdrawn from the area, leaving the incoming snail-ships to gorge on the jungle world and its ignorant inhabitants.

A fifth of the invaders was perhaps one five-thousandth of the estimated mass of vessels in the entire hive fleet. Unless this was an underestimate. Perhaps it was. Much was still whelmed in darkness; hidden by the Shadow in the Warp.

A fraction. Yet still... a measurable fraction.

And the hive fleet moved slowly, in historic terms.

Though swiftly, in cosmic terms.

And it would replenish itself. And make slave-monsters of more men, by harvesting their gonads and the genes in their cells with which to breed living tools.

But still, the crusade as such had succeeded, had it not? More was known.

More about the vast Genesplicer-Queens that spewed out their ruling Tyranid offspring and also the whole gamut of biological constructs conceived by these Queens... Genestealers, Zoats... and the cloned living weapons and living tools genetically crafted from captured slave-species. More was known about the Energy Cortexes that pumped fluids around the living ships. More about the Sensory Clusters that transmitted neuro-chemical signals.

More about the Hive Mind Synapses, which united each individual ship with the mass of ships, sustaining in total the Overmind, and sharpening the perceptions of Tyranids and constructs...

"You destroyed the hive mind synapse," Lo Chang had explained patiently to Lex. "That organ is what links a Tyranid ship into the hive fleet Overmind. It bonds the damned creatures and their bio-constructs within the vessel, attuning all the brood-kin almost telepathically. The closer they come to it, the more powerful its influence. Your own psychic profile was only point zero one, I believe... Yet the proximity of that slug-organ could have magnified aspects of this a hundredfold. Our Terminator Librarians sensed the power of that organ; but Librarians are trained to resist such... disruptions.

"And then your Brother Tundrish died horribly, very close to you. Very close.

"Hence your anguish—and your astonishment at such anguish.

"You're now blocking off the aura of Dorn from your traumatised mind, to protect yourself from... being overwhelmed. The death of Tundrish still afflicts you.

"Of Valence too. That pang has flowed through the channel of infinite loss cut by the slug-organ as it perished.

"Open your mind to Dorn, d'Arquebus. Let Dorn's light flush away the deathly darkness."

But it was useless.

How galling it was to know that Biff and Yeri had traumatised his mind by dying...

Lex must purge that invidious taste of gall, for it shamed him.

He was shamed in the knowledge that Biff had died heroically—saving them from folly, from the deceit of that Zoat. He was shamed that Yeri had also died, officially at least, a hero... though actually a victim of obsession, bent on safeguarding Lex from lethal heroics.

He was chagrined at being ashamed.

Astonishedly, he grieved—at being deprived of a part of himself by Yeri's death, and Biff's.

Was Lo Chang simply guessing at that hundredfold effect? Was Lex's grief, and guilt, simply mediated by a great arching green alien neural slug?

Or was his grief, his sense of amputation from his two brothers, genuine?

Did it matter which?

Aye, it did. For he knew that now he was brotherless, amongst Brothers.

Ten years earlier, how he would have welcomed this freedom from the demeaning shadows of that pair from Trazior...

Yet now... He who had forsaken his own bloodkin—his two silly sisters—was forced to admit that, unrecognized by himself until now, acknowledged at last only by virtue of *absence*—of terminal, irremediable absence—he had gained twin brothers, twin shadows of himself... who had now vanished, so that, rendered shadowless by their deaths, Lex's own puissant flesh and blood had become curiously insubstantial to him.

At Lo Chang's urging, he prayed again, in vain.

Dust.

Ashes.

"You must chasten your soul in the Solitorium," said the Chaplain, "till you can find a *modus salvationis* for yourself."

The Chaplain had waddled from behind the screen towards the consecrated Ablutorium cubicle to relieve himself of the freight of Lexandro's confession.

But no weight had lifted from Lex's spirit.

So Lex knelt alone with the universe, which could swallow any soul, or world, or species.

Out there amongst the stars were rebel lords and insurrectionists... Those could be neutralised. There were eerie aliens such as Slanns and Eldar, brutish aliens such as Orks... Those could be stalemated.

Now the cunning ruthless Tyranids were invading remorselessly to incorporate human and alien flesh as twisted tools into their own enigmatic imperium of the Overmind...

Whilst, occultly hidden yet ever liable to erupt,

unspeakable Powers of Chaos corrupted the cosmos like plagues...

Amidst those silent stars, deafened by void, death-rattles chattered amidst screams of madness.

Fists must clench firm. Superhuman bodies, crafted from fierce devout archangelic Primarchs by the God-Emperor, must resist all heresy.

As yet, Lex's body remained unflawed.

Mighty, but comely.

He thought of Yeri's azure eyes—ripped out by claws; of his blond locks, the runes on his cheek, his fawning insolent jealous smile.

He thought of Biff's sharpened teeth and green eyes and grotesque tattoo, and his greasy black hair—all torn off in a bundle.

How could Lex adequately honour his dead brothers so that Dorn's grace would return to him once more?

Gradually, he realized how.

First he went to Biff's deserted cell.

A skeletal hand lay half-engraved upon the small work-table, beside the buffing wheel and a pitcher of paraffin. During the time-dilated absence of the Fists, dust had settled on these—dust which no Servitor had dared to suck or lick up, though the floor and sleeping pallet were kept impeccably clean. An ikon of Dorn hung on the wall.

Lex picked up that ancient jackknife of Biff's from amongst some patches of lizard skin. He let his finger test the blade and the point. He drew a line of carnelian blood, then shrugged. Biff's big fists might have been able to scrimshander with such a primitive tool, yet Lex doubted his own skill.

His attention shifted to a silicon carbide engraver lying long neglected on a shelf, coated in more dust than knife or wheel; and he took this elegant little stylus with him.

En route to the nearest scriptory, nodding to passing

Brothers, he encountered a cyborged cleaner and thought to have the graving tool cleaned and polished by that gastropodic semi-automaton.

Then he thought better. Growling at the mute servant, he himself licked the tool and buffed it on his pus-yellow tunic till the rune-etchings on the silver shaft shone.

Some candidate-acoltyes were studying in the scriptory. New muscles for the Fists. Aye, muscles and muscular minds. On screens Lex noticed pages of the *Codex Astartes* displayed. One acolyte had opted for fully illuminated calligraphic presentation. Each sentence of the sacred manual of Marine organisation commenced with an uncial capital letter set in a gold and silver cartouche of decoration. Lex smiled briefly at this acolyte, who shivered, awed by such fleeting notice from a mature Battle Brother with a long-service stud in his brow.

Seating himself at a vacant console ornamented with ormolu, Lex tapped in data till the screen found what he sought and displayed a tabula topographica of the Apothacarion sector of the fortress-monastery...

The little chamber was, as he had expected, empty of any surgeon interrogators or techpriests. Scientific attention was elsewhere, focused upon the samples and data which Fists had brought back from the Tyranid nautilus-ships. Perhaps this room had been out of use, in any case, for a decade.

Here was the selfsame laboratorium which Sergeant Huzzi Rork had shown to the three brothers in that holo long ago, on Necromunda.

Here was the identical steel framework and the mechanical hand-gibbet. Here was the clear vitrodur hand-bath; and above it the reservoir of fluid.

On one wall, wrought in brass, there hung the snake-wreathed sceptre of surgery gripped in a gauntlet with spiked knuckles. The top of the serpent-rod opened out into sharp forceps.

Turning a spigot, Lex let colourless liquid stream into the glassy basin, half filling it.

He spat, and momentarily the fluid sizzled, fumed.

Yes, the same acid. Caustic *aqua imperialis*.

Lex laid the silicon carbide stylus on the plasteel bench supporting the glassy bath.

He stripped to his waist.

Flawless, his body; flawless.

Impeccable, except for the contour lines of bygone surgical implantations.

Unscarred by wounds, at least.

But how blemished, his soul...

Disdaining the gibbet, he slid his left hand into the vitriolic solvent.

The corrosive liquid sizzled as it began to ravage and gnaw his flesh—and a hiss escaped from Lexandro's own lips too. Only a hiss.

There he stood, his feet locked firmly in place not by bondage but by his own dominating muscles, while he endured utter torment, *relishing* that torment, forcing his fingers to remain flat on the bottom of the basin as the bubbling acid grew milky with dissolving tissue...

Long enough.

Despite the conflicting message-traffic of agony along his shorn nerves, the muscles in Lex's left arm still responded as he lifted his now-skeletal hand from the bowl and placed its bones—linked by some residue of withered ligature—on the bench alongside.

His arm, of flesh and muscle.

His hand, of bare bones.

Oh, it would be possible for the Chirurgeons to graft new nervewires and synthmusclefibre and pseudoflesh over that armature so as to rebuild his hand. He wasn't crippling himself in the long term. He wasn't denying his fist to his

Chapter. That would have been blasphemous... and blasphemy was far from his intention.

With his right hand Lexandro picked up the engraver. He powered its tip alive, and began slowly to scrimshander upon his own metacarpal and phalange bones.

Scribing in cursive script as elegantly and minutely as he could contrive, Lexandro painstakingly wrote the names Yeremi Valence and Biff Tundrish again and again upon his bones, and also the name of their original homeplace: *Trazior Hive, Necromunda.*

He sought perfection in every letter.

After two hours, when all the back of his hand was full, he turned it over and continued scribing those words across the palm side of his bones.

Now and then, tears from his eyes dropped to cool the little graving tip of the stylus.

Eventually he stopped.

Holding up his carved hand to rotate and scrutinize, he murmured, "Forgive me."

To whom did he pray? To Yeri and Biff? To Rogal Dorn? To the God-Emperor?

Though the muscles of Lexandro's left hand were all eaten away, and though his nerves had been utterly consumed as high as his wrist, yet as he sat there his engraved finger bones began slowly to cramp inward.

The miraculous constriction shaped the bones of his hand into a... fist.

A skeleton—of an imperial fist.

Overwhelmed, he contemplated that fist of wrought bones.

And he saw, in a delirium of insight, what his own personal heraldry might one day be as an officer– though he no longer craved ambitiously for any such heraldic honour...

No.

The situation was too dire.

Just when it seemed that the ever-faltering *cobweb* of the Imperium was holding the thin red line of faith against rebels and heretics, against Orks and Slanns and Genestealers, what viler menace could have appeared than the very begetters of those 'stealers—the huge Tyranid hive fleets?

What worse threat indeed? Unless, perhaps, the Powers of Chaos themselves...?

Those could never be Lex's province. He must not even think of *Tzeentch*, lest the thought corrupt him...

Oh to be on Necromunda, in a hive, viciously innocent again, scared only of demotion, pollution, gang warfare, predatory nomads, occult covens, mutants, starvation, and other petty worries.

But Lex was no longer innocent.

He was *responsible*.

He offered up the cage of his clenched bones to the Primarch...

And in his heart a different cage seemed to open up...

...to admit a shaft of Rogal Dorn's radiant light.

That familiar light transfixed him blessedly like a lance tipped with burning balm.

WARHAMMER®

40,000

INQUISITOR
by Ian Watson

In the war-torn universe of the 41st millennium, all is whelmed in darkness, and the Emperor is the only light.

Behold the *Liber Secretorum* of the so-called renegade Inquisitor Jaq Draco of the Ordo Malleus.

Is this the only hard evidence of an awesome plot to overthrow the Emperor and hold humankind in thrall? Or is it an amazing plan for the mental salvation/enslavement of the human race? A plan guided by the Emperor's own wisdom which He himself will not acknowledge lest even loyal believers rebel against it? This is the story of Inquisitor Draco, and his loyal servants Grimm the Squat and the exotic Meh'Lindi, an assassin as deadly as she is beautiful.

WARHAMMER®
40,000

INQUISITOR
BY
IAN WATSON

WARHAMMER®

The KONRAD Trilogy
BY
DAVID FERRING

DRACHENFELS
BY
JACK YEOVIL